Ethel Carnie

Miss Nobody

The Ethel Carnie Holdsworth Series
General Editor: Nicola Wilson

Belinda Webb's debut novel, *A Clockwork Apple* (Burning House), was published in 2008. She has written on social, literary, and current affairs for publications including *Tribune*, the *Guardian's* CiF and Books Blog, *Review31*, and the *New Humanist*. Belinda came across Ethel Carnie through doctoral research at Kingston University.

Nicola Wilson is a lecturer in English literature at the University of Reading. She is writing a book on *Home in British Working-Class Fiction* (Ashgate, 2014), and has published research on working-class writing in *Key Words* and *The Oxford History of the Novel in English, vol. 7* (forthcoming). In 2011 she introduced and edited Ethel Carnie Holdsworth's 1925 novel, *This Slavery* (Trent).

Ethel Carnie

Miss Nobody

WITH AN INTRODUCTION BY BELINDA WEBB

Edited by Nicola Wilson

Kennedy & Boyd

2013

Kennedy & Boyd
an imprint of
Zeticula Ltd
The Roan
Kilkerran
KA19 8LS
Scotland

http://www.kennedyandboyd.co.uk
admin@kennedyandboyd.co.uk

First published in 1913 by Methuen.

This edition Copyright © Zeticula Ltd 2013
First published in this edition 2013

Front cover image: Ethel Carnie Holdsworth. Reproduced
with kind permission from Helen Brown.

ISBN 978-1-84921-127-7

Acknowledgements

The production of this centenary edition of *Miss Nobody* is a testament to the unflagging interest of a small but vibrant community interested in the life and works of Ethel Carnie.

Nicola would like to thank Helen Brown, Roger Smalley, Chris Lynch and Nick Wilding for their enthusiasm and support, and Jean Armstrong who kindly lent out her copy of the first edition of *Miss Nobody*, from which this edition has been produced. She would also like to thank John Goodridge of Trent Editions for his work on the 2011 reprint of Ethel Carnie Holdsworth's 1925 novel *This Slavery*.

Belinda would like to thank the Newspaper Library at Colindale who hold copies of the *Woman Worker*, and Dr Norma Clarke at Kingston University, who pushed her to ask questions on Carnie that she wouldn't have automatically asked. She would also like to thank Dr Bruce Lloyd of Kennington Oval, for being both lion and feminist.

All profits from this edition will be donated to a good cause.

Contents

Ethel Carnie holding her first novel, *Miss Nobody* (1913)

Introduction

by Belinda Webb

Ethel Carnie was born in 1886 in the small Lancashire mill town of Oswaldtwistle. She died in 1963. She accomplished much - not just as a woman in an era when women were fighting for the basic right to vote, but as a working-class woman, a group that has remained too often absent, and particularly in literature.

Ethel Carnie (or Ethel Carnie Holdsworth; she sometimes wrote under her married name) wrote ten novels, several collections of poetry, children's stories, and journalism. Politically active, she also founded the National Union for Combating Fascism, and edited its journal, the *Clear Light* from 1920-25 alongside her husband, Alfred Holdsworth.

Miss Nobody (1913) her debut novel, was written between serving customers at the draper's shop her mother had taken on in Little Harwood, and between lectures at Owens College, Manchester, where she registered as a non-degree student from 1911-13.[1] This was followed by *Helen of Four Gates* (1917), *The Taming of Nan* (1920), *The Marriage of Elizabeth* (1920), *The House That Jill Built* (1920), *General Belinda* (1924), *This Slavery* (1925), *The Quest of the Golden Garter* (1927), *Barbara Dennison* (1929), *All On Her Own* (1929), and *Eagles' Crag* (1931).

Yet Ethel appears to have written her last novel whilst still in her prime, thirty-two years before she died. She had complained of being 'worn out', a characteristically northern idiom that conjures up much effort and struggle.[2] One reason for her being worn out could be to do with the form of the novel itself. It is not easy for a working-class woman to express herself, or to write from her own experience for other working-class women (her guiding principle), using a form that comes burdened with a weight of patriarchal and middle-class norms. This is in addition to the middle-class individualist perspective that is not, or certainly was not, characteristic of the working classes. Raymond Williams's insight into the issue of class and its relation to form should be invite enough for more research into the matter, instead of the dearth that many of us who have researched the topic have encountered:

> The novel with its quite different narrative forms was virtually impenetrable to working-class writers for three or four generations, and there are still many problems in using the received forms for what is, in the end, very different material . . . the forms of working-class consciousness are bound to be different from the literary forms of another class, and it is a long struggle to find new and adequate forms.[3]

Ethel's oeuvre demonstrates clearly her inability, or perhaps unwillingness, to be bound to one particular genre or form. What we would today call Ethel's 'mash-up' approach or effect (effect used to mean that she may not have consciously set out to do this), Pamela Fox claims could be one of the reasons why her work has been ignored by critics; it simply defies traditional expectations.[4]

It was through poetry that Ethel began her literary career. Time was precious, and the poetic form provided a medium of creative expression; an emotional outlet, whose imagery and the very act of writing it, contrasted starkly with the bleak, industrial and utilitarian environs in which she lived and worked. Poetry was also popular. Both as a cultural and political vehicle, poetry had gained a strong foothold amongst the working classes throughout the nineteenth century and into the twentieth. *The Northern Star*, the Chartist newspaper, was regularly inundated with poems penned by its readers. As a form for both reading and writing, it was more manageable for the time-starved, weary workers, and could rouse strong political feelings more readily than the longer and more expensive form of the novel. Byron and Shelley were particular favourites. But it would take Ethel some time to develop into a poet with a strong, radical voice in contrast to the younger self who dabbled in abstract notions of beauty and virtue. As Robert Blatchford describes in his 1908 interview with Ethel in the *Woman Worker*: 'she tunes her harp to themes which have stirred many singers: Friendship, Youth, Beauty, Night, Love, Hope and Time.'[5]

It was following the publication of her first book of poetry, marketed as written by a 'factory girl', that she came to the attention of Blatchford, one of the founders of the Independent Labour Party and founder-owner of the weekly socialist newspaper, the *Clarion*. Blatchford offered Ethel a journalist position at his London-based newspaper, the *Woman Worker*, which she accepted. She was given free rein to write what she liked and this she did, writing political pieces for working-class women, urging them to 'go out and play'.[6] Throughout 1909 Ethel moved from a regular place in 'Poetry Corner', to becoming a weekly columnist. Yet Blatchford seems to have been increasingly uncomfortable with Ethel's overtly political articles. One of her articles, for instance, seems to have invited criticism that she was painting factory workers' lives blacker than they actually were. She used a later column to respond to this criticism, telling the reader:

> I must check this romantic attitude of mind; . . . If I have given a false impression I am as willing as anyone else to be convinced of my mistake.
> I have carefully read over every word that that article contained, and would not retract one word of it.
> The factory worker is practically a beggar and a slave. [7]

By the end of 1909, Blatchford's daughter, Winifred, who had hitherto written the 'Letter from London' column, was given the prize of editorship. With it the title was renamed 'Women Folk', and a more genteel outlook ensued.

Politicised working-class women in the earlier Chartist movement, who were on an equal footing with their male counterparts in terms of voting in motions and going out protesting, were mocked on the pages of influential publications like *Punch* for being 'harridans' and 'harpies'. In the case of *Punch*, this frequent vilifying of protesting working-class women was all the more galling, given that they often bore the brunt of inequalities even within their own demographic; factory bosses regularly employed them over their male counterparts because they could be paid much less. Even when they had children, they did not have the luxury of being able to stay at home with them, having instead to farm them out or take them to work, because a family could not survive on one wage. And then the working mother was expected to keep house upon returning from long, gruelling days at the mill. The particular issues faced by working-class women remain as obstacles in our own time, with leading think-tank the Institute for Public Policy Research suggesting that feminism has failed working-class women and their needs. One can only hope that this long overdue acknowledgement can herald in an essential fourth-wave feminism.

Yet Ethel had not simply found this political voice whilst in the employ of Robert Blatchford. She, like many other working-class women in politically active families, was encouraged from a young age to absorb and engage in politics. Ethel's father was a member of the Social Democratic Federation (SDF), which was established in 1881, more than three decades after the end of the Chartist movement. Ethel's father would take his daughter to political meetings and, as the Frows comment, 'helped to clothe her instinctive socialist attitudes with scientific understanding'.[8] There was much to kick back against during Ethel's early life. The years from the collapse of Chartism to the emergence of the SDF were 'the golden age of British capitalism, with free trade and individualism the dominant ideologies'.[9] Whereas earlier generations in the north of England had grown up under the collective memory of the 1819 Peterloo Massacre, Carnie grew up under the memory of the original 'Bloody Sunday', which occurred in November 1887. Testing a ban on all public meetings in London's Trafalgar Square, the SDF and other radical groups, like their Chartist predecessors, formed a demonstration against the coercion in Ireland.

Between 1801 and 1922 over one hundred Coercion Acts were passed by the UK government in an attempt to establish law and order in Ireland. The Act introduced in 1881, for instance, allowed persons to be imprisoned without trial, and was also used to threaten newspaper owners and editors who dared to criticise the legislation. The laws even enabled the British government in Ireland to arrest those whom they 'reasonably suspected' of crime and conspiracy. Working-class activists in the UK followed these developments closely, not least because the working classes were swelled by those Irish forced to the UK to find work, and also because most could see that the coercion legislation used in Ireland could soon become the axe that was swung at themselves.

On 13 November 1887, thousands of police and hundreds of troops, including volunteer constables, formed to quell the proceedings. The demonstration, intercepted before reaching Trafalgar Square, resulted in hundreds of injuries.[10] While these mass demonstrations did not result in revolution, the sense of injustice that the police and military exacerbated through their heavy-handedness, and the heroic mythologizing of the protestors, fuelled awareness of the causes that were of particular importance to the working classes. For many women like Ethel, women's rights outside of their own political movements were also paramount, although Ethel was always concerned as to what feminism meant - or should mean - for working-class women. All of these issues, at the forefront of Ethel's concerns, can be found in her first published novel, *Miss Nobody*.

1913, the year in which *Miss Nobody* was published, was notable for suffragette struggle, with two particular suffragettes making the headlines. On 4 June, Emily Wilding Davison threw herself under the King's horse at the Derby, and on 3 April of the same year Emmeline Pankhurst was sentenced to three years in prison. The composer and suffragette, Ethel Smyth (1858-1944), set two of Ethel's poems – 'Possession', and 'On the Road: a Marching Tune' – in the song cycle 'Three Songs' (1913), dedicated to Emmeline and Christabel Pankhurst respectively. These are the names that are readily cited when it comes to women's rights. Yet most of these calls for equality were from middle-class women, and our history books today overwhelmingly present this struggle from the middle-class perspective. This is one reason why Ethel's works and, indeed, her life, are of vital importance in helping to bring yesterday's working-class women out of the shadows.

There are however exceptions to this. Jill Liddington and Jill Norris's work, for instance, has shown how active working-class suffragettes were, particularly in the cotton towns that Ethel knew so well.[11] The Pankhursts' camp, the Women's Social and Political Union (founded in 1903), has been viewed by many historians as elitist in its campaign only for a limited franchise, and the Pankhursts have been criticised for being only marginally in touch with the working-class grass-roots fight for women's suffrage. The headstrong protagonist of *Miss Nobody* is likened to an unruly Suffragette by a disgruntled train guard in the opening pages of the novel.

In reading *Miss Nobody*, it is important to understand why Ethel Carnie and her work have been neglected. This has much to do with a general disdain for working-class literature, or 'writings', as they are commonly referred to. This demarcation between literature and writings invokes the high/low culture debate, accounting for the noticeable absence of working-class texts from 'literary' canons. Predisposed to melodrama, and predominantly concerned with the collective, working-class literature loses out to the bourgeois psychological journeys of the individual. Valentine Cunningham represents the view of the academy when he observed that working-class writers fail to avoid:

[T]he faults of their sort: triteness and melodrama of plot, sentimental class chauvinism about workers, urgent dogmatisms, as well as a tendency to make the workers, especially members of the Communist

Party, into men and women of excessive heroism and unbelievably steely militancy.[12]

Both the tendentious nature of Ethel's works and the prominence of one of the key elements of her novels – the romance – are partly to blame for her neglect. Another reason could be that her most active period was one in which the dominant women's literary tradition was the 'mediocre middlebrow', which continued in full force until the 1950s. Efforts have been made to recover those middlebrow novels considered to have been unjustly forgotten, with their subsequent introduction to a contemporary readership via both feminist and mainstream publishing houses.

There are however some quarters keen on collating and excavating working-class literature. The Archive of Working-Class Writing Online, hosted by Liverpool John Moores University, is one such publicly accessible resource, and features rare material and out-of-print publications. There is also the exemplary Burnett Archive of Working-Class Autobiographies at London's Brunel University Library. Time will tell if there are more working-class women's 'writings' to be excavated and added to these resources.

While there have been too few efforts to uncover neglected voices such as Carnie's, there are those who have worked hard to sound the klaxon. Since the 1970s there has been an increased call by feminist academics such as Elaine Showalter, Sheila Rowbotham, Angela Ingram, Daphne Patai, and others, to 'rescue' women writers who have not just been 'forgotten', but overlooked and 'abandoned'; to bring them from the margins of history and introduce them to a wider audience; to give them, the shop girl and the factory worker, a 'voice'.[13] Of course, there are far fewer of these to bring to light, which should not be a cause for dismissal, but a greater motivation to study Ethel's being 'worn out'. Working-class women writers may not have maintained personal papers such as diaries and correspondence for future generations to mine, but this should only mean that those working-class women who did succeed in writing, should not have been allowed to fall off the radar. It is not as if Ethel was not popular in her own time - few writers achieve the publication of ten novels, particularly through publishers such as Methuen and Herbert Jenkins, through whom most of Ethel's works were published. Herbert Jenkins, a renowned library house, published works aimed at a mass readership, particularly those who patronised the circulating libraries, such as W.H. Smith's and Boots Booklovers'. Their titles could also often be found stocked in the more popular Twopenny libraries.

Reading *Miss Nobody*

Miss Nobody portrays elements of the three literary traditions that most of Carnie's work contains: the New Woman novel, the Chartist novel, and of course, the romance. Although the term 'New Woman' was not popularised until coined by the writer and speaker Sarah Grand in 1894, it quickly caught on to describe the woman who had shifted away from the archetypal representation of the Victorian 'clinging ivy' to the male 'strong oak', and who often wanted more than just marriage and children. The New Woman novel, whose period is largely agreed to cover 1880-1920, captures the shift in gender relations to portray some of the actual, or simply wished for increase in women's independence, away from patriarchal constraints. The term encompasses both the expanding numbers of educated women, like H.G. Wells's infamous *Ann Veronica* (1909), as well as the increasing numbers of 'office girls'. Yet the term as it has been used by literary historians and critics, has traditionally ignored the many independent working-class women of the cotton towns. *Miss Nobody* helps to redress this.

The Chartist novel, as written by high-profile Chartists such as Ernest Jones, was keen to tap into the popularity of the romance novel, and so borrowed much from that genre, such as the many un-credible plot structures and two-dimensional characters who lacked psychological depth. The tension between art and overt political statements is clear, and can also be seen in much of Ethel's work. This again brings us back to the issue of working-class writers producing working-class stories without a coherent form.

This is why it is difficult to categorise Ethel's writing into any one genre, and also demonstrates her 'grappling' or struggling with the novel form, so much so that it wore her out. It is however the romance aspect of her work that throws up the most contradictions.

The main character of this book, the 'Miss Nobody' of the title, is Carrie, or 'Car', as she is known to those who are closest to her. Carrie is an independent, hard-working young woman running an oyster shop in Ardwick, a short walk from the heart of Manchester and its various mill districts. Carrie finds escapism through Tulip novelettes, cheap romances that whisk her away from the reality of grimy Manchester and its hand-to-mouth struggles. Instead they envelop her in heady fairytales of 'love', where aristocratic men 'rescue' damsels in distress, and they all live happily ever after. These romances, supped greedily by women whose reality demanded, even necessitated, some form of escape, have rarely been treated with the same respect as other types of literature (the use of 'novelette' suggests they fail to reach the standard of the 'novel', although they were cheaper and shorter because aimed at the time-strained working-class woman). In her seminal work, *Reading the Romance* (1984), Janice Radway used reader response criticism to analyse contemporary versions of the genre and looked at the archetypes populating them, as well as those favoured by readers. [14] The readers questioned relayed the response by friends and family members to their reading 'habit', which is (still) seen as 'unliterary', frivolous and escapist. It may well be, but looking into just why these romances were so popular reveals much about the social constraints that women experience(d). Ethel knew this and used it as the sugar that helps the medicine to go down.

The popularity of romance with working-class women has long been ridiculed as little more than a pacifier. Ethel's male contemporaries added to this chorus of disapproval, including those in the Lancashire School, a group of working-class writers comprised of Arthur Laycock, Fred Plant, Allen Clarke, James Haslam, Peter Lee and John Tamlyn. In 1906, Haslam wrote an article in the *Manchester City News* bemoaning the genre:

'Romance, romance, romance', is their monotonous cry. Romance served up in penny batches; romance that depends upon nonsensical scenes, shallow thoughts, spurious philosophy, and unreal life, for its popularity.[15]

However, unlike Ethel, Haslam and his group enjoyed a common outlet and writerly solidarity in which to foster their work and ideas, all without needing to encounter the vagaries of the commercial publishing house. Instead, the Lancashire School published through Clarke's own publication, the *Northern Weekly*. Paul Salveson observes that 'without this it seems unlikely that the Lancashire School would ever have appeared at all, given its highly political content, and the strong regional thrust, through its use of dialect and depiction of local customs and culture'.[16]

Ethel's novels are not just romances. Reality takes the star turn, as Carnie portrays the situation for jobbing workers, which had changed little from the picture drawn for us in the same city by Friedrich Engels over half a century earlier. Carrie is just a short step up from the factories, and whilst she is her own boss in the little oyster shop in Ardwick, she works long hours and has little of the 'play time' that Ethel called for in her *Woman Worker* articles.

Pamela Fox, one of those critics who has focussed on Ethel, claims that far from writing romances to merely pacify, Ethel used romance as a political tool. The writer's questioning of romance features strongly in *Miss Nobody*. When Carrie marries Robert Gibson and goes to live in the marital home, the Tulip novelette romances she reads provide not only solace, but also bring her marriage into question. As she begins to compare married life to the fairytales of heady love in her paperbacks, she finds her life wanting. However, as Carrie's life changes and she is forced to make tough changes, the romances fall out of the picture. She stops reading them.

Fox argues that, being a linchpin of the patriarchal system, romance has always been ripe for critique from writers such as Mary Wollstonecraft onwards. For working-class women, however, 'beginning in a different place in relation to the convention of romance . . . it can never be fully available as an "intimate" register of cultural practices'.[17] Desiring the romance script itself, she claims, can be seen as a transgressive act. Working-class women had to be much more pragmatic. The reader of *Miss Nobody* should understand this from the first couple of chapters, and yet this practicality can be seen as a more solid and mature type of love; not the heady romance, but the long-lasting one based on mutual respect, and practical needs. Fox continues this long-running meme of necessity that runs through the history of working-class women's lives, with mothers traditionally telling daughters that 'romance was purely a fantasy with little relevance to their lives and that marriage was primarily an economic relation, rather than a fulfillment of love, to be performed as a perfunctory ritual (if at all)'.[18] It is Robert's sister, Sarah, with whom the newly married couple live, who plays the anti-romance role in *Miss Nobody*:

> Romance was a constant dread of Sarah's, being a thing to be fought against tooth and nail in herself and others. If you listened to Romance there was no telling what you might do, for you left the common sense track of everyday life, where butter is so much a pound.

It is not just the Tulip novelettes that suddenly disappear in *Miss Nobody*. One of the characteristics of the 'traditional' novel is the notion that the novelist does not introduce characters for no reason. Ethel on the other hand flits about, making her work much more realistic, in a way that Marxist theorist Georg Lukacs may have approved of, and giving regular 'walk-on' space to many characters. This includes a laundry delivery driver with whom she cadges a lift and who proceeds to tell her that he is a union man and then an atheist, as if the two belong together. What many readers may find somewhat shocking, too, is just how grounded in realism Carrie and her husband Robert Gibson are. Ethel spared the gloss when it comes to their physical attributes. Carrie, we are told, is missing a tooth, and Robert has false teeth.

Even the similes remain class-grounded so that Ethel's readers can instantly conjure up the necessary familiarities. One character, Elsie 'has a voice like a rusty kettle kicked round the lanes by brass-nosed clogs, and skin like a nutmeg grater'.

There is also the dislike of the passive-aggression that features in many of the celebrated middle-class novels of manners, where feelings simmer beneath the surface, denied any outlet. It is clear that Carrie's main problem with her sister-in-law is the latter's inability to talk out her irritations with her brother's new wife. Carrie struggles with keeping her feelings to herself, especially when she detects them repressed in others. In this, she is similar to Brontë heroines when Ethel writes 'yet there was something in the wild moor made still more desolate by the storm that gave her a savage joy'. The metaphor reflects the natural instincts unfettered by mannered middle-class norms; it was the freedom to be a woman and to be angry, for working-class women had much to be angry about. Some of Ethel's later novels, and particularly the 1917 *Helen of Four Gates*, is more Brontë-like in its Gothic darkness, situated as it is in the same land. There is not much distance between Oswaldtwistle and Howarth. *Helen of Four Gates* achieved the fame of the big-screen, filmed as a silent 'melodrama' in 1922, and directed by cinematic pioneer, Cecil Hepworth.

Ethel's honest depictions of the issues faced by working-class women may have been quite shocking in its day, although Anne Brontë featured the scourge of domestic abuse in the earlier *The Tenant of Wildfell Hall* (1848). The author does not shy away from the matter-of-fact brutality that marks the lives of some of the women around Carrie, which only contrasts so vividly with Carrie's relationship with the kind, progressive Robert Gibson. Introduced to one of the residents of a lodging house, we are told 'that he had kicked his wife to death . . . his daughter was on the streets and his son in the penitentiary, because sand-hawking did not pay so well as stealing'. Ethel links the violent devastation right back to the door of capitalism, and the deep-seated, bubbling anger caused by unlived lives, and unexplored potential, through poverty - generation after generation - that could rage through and destroy families. Liza, another minor character to whom we are introduced when Carrie moves to Greenmeads to begin married life, and who is suffering domestic abuse, casually holds up a bread knife, threatening to 'put it clean through thy heart' of her husband, who is about to belt his son for fear of his wife making him soft.

When one realises how much Ethel Carnie achieved through the unique role she inhabited in writing for working-class women and as an anti-fascist campaigner sounding a determined clarion call, one can only deduce a silencing. Ethel Carnie was silenced. Not by any one person, but by our learned literary and political institutions. That is a strong statement but how else can it be described when the first known English working-class woman novelist has barely been heard of amongst feminist and literary theorists - let alone by anyone else? It is even more puzzling, however innocent you are of our canons and structures and how they are formed, when one evaluates not just her novels, but also her journalism, her poetry, and her political activism. This, a long overdue reissue of her debut novel, *Miss Nobody*, can therefore be seen as being presciently titled. The working-class woman was, and arguably still is, Miss Nobody.

Once fighting against the patriarchal canonisation of overwhelmingly male writers, many academic feminists now seem concerned only with the middle-class middlebrow, apparently unaware of their own practice of cultural and class-based imperialism. The potential for such misreading and neglect was sensed in Ethel's own era by critics close to her. The *Woman Worker* columnist and critic, Keighley Snowden, wrote, 'Schooled critics can point out many a fault in Ethel Carnie's verse. Most likely they will refuse for a long time to notice her'.[19] The tide is however turning. In 2011 Trent Editions took an important step when it re-issued another of Ethel's works, the 1925 political novel, *This Slavery*. With the publication of this centenary re-issue of *Miss Nobody* (the first of a projected series of the works of Ethel Carnie Holdsworth), Kennedy & Boyd demonstrate the commitment needed to educate and inform many more of Ethel's importance, in addition to the long-neglected issue of working-class women writers in general (then and now), as well as their impressive record of political activism. We are fortunate in having a small band of Carnie champions, not least Nicola Wilson and Kathleen Bell, as well as a forthcoming biography of Ethel, by Roger Smalley.

If the answer to the question of why the dancer Fred Astaire is more often praised than his dancing partner, Ginger Rogers, when she did everything he did, but in heels and backwards, then Ethel Carnie did far more than even this when compared to the middlebrow women novelists who many have championed because they once failed to make a place on the male-dominated canons. Ethel was an activist on the front lines of class and gender, and worked hard to eke out precious time to write, from the business and pressures of working in shops and factories to sustain herself in order to do so. One can only hope that this re-issue will serve to bring her more firmly out of the shadows so that one day Ethel Carnie will be considered as she rightly was - a Miss Somebody.

Works cited

1. Roger Smalley, *The Life and Work of Ethel Carnie Holdsworth, with particular reference to the period 1907 to 1931* (PhD thesis, University of Central Lancashire, 2006), p. 58 (Forthcoming biography *'Out of the House of Bondage': The Political Vision of a Lancashire mill girl, Ethel Carnie Holdsworth 1886-1962* (Lancaster UP, 2013/4)).
2. Margaret Quinn (Ethel's daughter) to Ruth Frow (N.D., mid-1980s?), transcript of telephone conversation and notes in Ruth and Eddie Frow research materials, Ethel Carnie Collection, Working Class Movement Library, Salford.
3. Raymond Williams, 'The Writer: Commitment and Alignment', *Marxism Today* (June 1980), p. 25.
4. Pamela Fox, *Class Fictions: Shame and Resistance in the British Working-Class Novel 1890-1945* (Durham: Duke UP, 1994), p. 153.
5. Robert Blatchford, 'A Lancashire Fairy. An Interview with Miss Ethel Carnie', *Woman Worker*, 10 July 1908, p. 155.
6. Ethel Carnie, 'Our Right to Play', *Woman Worker*, 14 April 1909, p. 342.
7. Ethel Carnie, 'The Factory and Content', *Woman Worker*, 31 March 1909, p. 312.
8. Ruth and Eddie Frow, 'Ethel Carnie: writer, feminist and socialist', in H. Gustav Klaus (ed.), *The Rise of Socialist Fiction 1880-1914* (Brighton: Harvester, 1987), pp. 251-66 (p. 252).
9. Martin Crick, *The History of the Social Democratic Federation* (Keele: Ryburn, 1994), p. 13.
10. Crick, p. 47.
11. See Jill Liddington and Jill Norris, *One Hand Tied Behind Us: The Rise of the Women's Suffrage Movement* (London: Virago, 1978); and Jill Liddington, *Rebel Girls: Their fight for the vote* (London: Virago, 2006).
12. Valentine Cunningham, *British Writers of the Thirties* (Oxford: Oxford UP, 1988), p. 309.
13. Elaine Showalter, *A Literature of Their Own: British women novelists from Brontë to Lessing* (Princeton:

Princeton UP, 1977); Sheila Rowbotham, *Hidden from History: 300 Years of Women's Oppression and the Fight against it* (London: Pluto, 1973); Angela Ingram and Daphne Patai (eds), *Rediscovering Forgotten Radicals: British Women Writers 1889-1939* (Chapel Hill: University of North Carolina Press, 1993).

14. Janice Radway, *Reading the Romance: Women, Patriarchy and Popular Literature* (Chapel Hill: University of North Carolina Press, 1984).
15. Pamela Fox, 'Ethel Carnie Holdsworth's "Revolt of the Gentle": Romance and the Politics of Resistance in Working-class Women's Writing', in Angela Ingram and Daphni Patai (eds), *Rediscovering Forgotten Radicals: British Women Writers 1889-1939* (Chapel Hill: University of North Carolina Press, 1993), pp. 57-74 (p. 57).
16. Paul Salveson, 'Allen Clarke and the Lancashire school of working-class novelists', in H. Gustav Klaus (ed.), *The Rise of Socialist Fiction 1880-1914* (Brighton: Harvester, 1987), pp. 172-202 (p. 198).
17. Fox, 'Ethel Carnie Holdsworth's "Revolt of the Gentle"', p.59.
18. *ibid.*
19. Keighley Snowden, 'A Book of the Hour: Factory Lass and Poetess', *Woman Worker*, 3 July 1908, p. 135.

A selection of passages by Ethel Carnie from the *Woman Worker*

'The Factory Slave', *Woman Worker*, 3 March 1909, p. 214.

'Factory life has crushed the childhood, youth, maturity of millions of men and women. It has ruined the health of those who would have been comparatively strong but for the long hours of unremitted toil and the evil atmosphere'.

'Factory Intelligence', *Woman Worker*, 10 March 1909, p. 219.

Keen to dispel the misconception that still abounds, that the working class were uneducated, Ethel writes:
'If you took a stroll through a cotton mill . . . [and looked in] tin boxes that are for the purpose of holding weft, you would find a varied assortment of literature. You might find . . . Conan Doyle, Rider Haggard, Silas Hocking, Dickens'.
She then asks, 'Have you ever tried to read in the working hours of a cotton factory? It is a weird experience . . .

[B]etween the breaking of the threads and the threading of the shuttle we thieve back a little of the time that they [masters] are thieving from us . . .

I know one factory worker who can interpret the Cassius and Brutus of "Julius Cesar" in such a manner that the great bard of Avon would not blush to see it— and who reads a French newspaper every week . . .

Taken from the ugly schoolroom and plunged into the factory we waste our youth, our health, our beauty in weaving cotton'.

'The Home Life of Factory Workers', *Woman Worker*, 24 March 1909, p. 270.

'No beautiful recollections cluster about these jerry-built homes of ours: strangers lived here a few years ago—and will again.'

And yet, she says, 'factory workers, on the whole, are fond of their homes . . .

Aristocrats . . . will never know the delight with which the toiler looks around his home on Sunday afternoon . . . and feels himself the "monarch of all he surveys." You take all the shine and cleanliness for granted— servants have done it—and labour of others has made you rich enough to obtain this lovely thing and that— but we know the price of our belongings, and scarcely get time to behold them . . .

Sunday is the only day we have to live our lives. Out of the House of Bondage into the field of liberty . . .

Once I saw a picture of the crucified Christ.

That wan brow, and anguished look—you need not go into a picture gallery to see it. Stand at the gates of a cotton factory at the end of a summer's day, and see the operatives trail out . . .'

Woman Worker, 19 May 1909, p.406.

'Let me stand in the thickest throng,
And cheer the fighter with my song:'

'Respectable Poverty', *Woman Worker*, 23 June 1909.

'As in Dante's vision of Hades there appeared different circles, with their varying torments, so in the hell of poverty are ranged various stages, and in our humble opinion not the least of anguish is found in that abode where the soul of the housewife must be eternally engaged in making ends meet . . .

[I]n the back streets, with vistas of unlovely walls, there is practised an economy that is degrading and soul-killing; the counting of every miserable copper . . . The spotless step and shining door-handle tell nothing of this to the passers-by . . . they have made the ends meet, but they have pieced them with a bit of their own souls . . . A life of grinding poverty would take the grit out of a woman though she were as brave as a lion'

Suggestions for further reading

Alves, Susan, '"Whilst Working at My Frame": The Poetic Production of Ethel Carnie Holdsworth', *Victorian Poetry*, 38.1 (2000), 77-93.

Ardis, Ann, *New Women, New Novels: Feminism and Early Modernism* (New Brunswick: Rutgers UP, 1990).

Ashraf, Phyllis Mary, *Introduction to Working-Class Literature in Great Britain: Part II, Prose* (Berlin: Ministerium fur Volksbildung, 1979).

Boos, Florence S., *Working-Class Women Poets in Victorian Britain: An Anthology* (Peterborough, Ontario: Broadview, 2008).

Bourke, Joanna, *Working-Class Cultures in Britain 1880-1960: Gender, Class, Ethnicity* (London: Routledge, 1994).

Crick, Martin, *The History of the Social Democratic Federation* (Keele: Ryburn, 1994).

Fox, Pamela, 'Ethel Carnie Holdsworth's "Revolt of the Gentle": Romance and the Politics of Resistance in Working-class Women's Writing', in Angela Ingram and Daphni Patai (eds), *Rediscovering Forgotten Radicals: British Women Writers 1889-1939* (Chapel Hill: University of North Carolina Press, 1993), pp. 57-74.

----- *Class Fictions: Shame and Resistance in the British Working-Class Novel, 1890-1945* (Durham: Duke University Press, 1994).

Frow, Edmund, and Ruth Frow, 'Ethel Carnie Holdsworth: writer, feminist and socialist', in H. Gustav Klaus (ed.), *The Rise of Socialist Fiction 1880-1914* (Brighton: Harvester, 1987), pp. 251-56.

Hannan, June, and Karen Hunt, *Socialist Women: Britain, 1880s to 1920s* (London: Routledge, 2002).

Haywood, Ian, *Working-Class Fiction: from Chartism to Trainspotting* (Plymouth: Northcote House, 1997).

Heilmann, Ann, *New Woman Fiction: Women Writing First-Wave Feminism* (Basingstoke: Macmillan, 2000).

Johnson, Patricia E., 'Finding Her Voice(s): The Development of a Working-Class Feminist Vision in Ethel Carnie Holdsworth's Poetry', *Victorian Poetry*, 43.3 (2005), 297-315.

Kirk, John, *Twentieth Century Writing and the British Working Class* (Cardiff: University of Wales Press, 2003).

Klaus, H. Gustav, 'Silhouettes of Revolution: Some Neglected Novels of the Early 1920s', in H. Gustav Klaus (ed.), *The Socialist Novel in Britain: Towards the Recovery of a Tradition* (Brighton: Harvester, 1982), pp. 89-109.

Liddington, Jill, and Jill Norris, *One Hand Tied Behind Us: The Rise of the Women's Suffrage Movement* (London: Virago, 1978).

Liddington, Jill, *Rebel Girls: Their fight for the vote* (London: Virago, 2006).

Miller, Jane Eldridge, *Rebel Women: Feminism, Modernism and the Edwardian Novel* (London: Virago, 1994).

Radway, Janice, *Reading the Romance: Women, Patriarchy and Popular Literature* (Chapel Hill: University of North Carolina Press, 1984).

Richardson, Angelique and Chris Willis (eds), *The New Woman in Fiction and Fact: Fin de Siècle Feminisms* (Basingstoke: Palgrave, 2002).

Roberts, Elizabeth, *A Woman's Place: An Oral History of Working-Class Women 1890-1940* (Oxford: Blackwell, 1984).

Rose, Jonathan, *The Intellectual Life of the British Working Classes* (New Haven: Yale Nota Bene, 2002).

Salveson, Paul, 'Allen Clarke and the Lancashire school of working-class novelists', in H. Gustav Klaus (ed.), *The Rise of Socialist Fiction 1880-1914* (Brighton: Harvester, 1987), pp. 172-202.

Smalley, Roger, 'The Life and Work of Ethel Carnie Holdsworth, with particular reference to the period 1907 to 1931' (PhD thesis, University of Central Lancashire, 2006).

Swindells, Julia, and Lisa Jardine, *What's Left? Women in Culture and the Labour Movement* (London: Routledge, 1990).

Todd, Selina, *Young Women, Work, and Family in England, 1918-1950* (Oxford: Oxford University Press, 2005).

Webb, Belinda, "Romance" in 'Mary Burns' (PhD thesis, Kingston University, 2012).

Wilson, Nicola, 'Politicising the Home in Ethel Carnie Holdsworth's *This Slavery* (1925) and Ellen Wilkinson's *Clash* (1929)', *Key Words: A Journal of Cultural Materialism*, 5 (2007-8), 26-42.

Note on the text

Ethel published under her maiden name, Ethel Carnie, and later used two variations of her married name, Ethel Carnie Holdsworth and Ethel Holdsworth. Each work in this series will retain the author's name according to how it was originally published.

The copy-text for this edition of *Miss Nobody* is the 1913 first edition, published by Methuen. The text of the current edition follows the original text as closely as possible, retaining older forms of English usage and grammar, as well as the odd misspelling or inconsistency in naming.

The only typographical change I have introduced into this edition is the loss of the space commonly used before exclamation marks, question marks or semi-colons, e.g.

"What's the row ?" she inquired

is in this edition "What's the row?" she inquired

Nicola Wilson

METHUEN'S POPULAR NOVELS

Crown 8vo, 6s. each

MISS NOBODY

By ETHEL CARNIE, Author of 'Songs of a Factory Girl.'

A story of modern working class life, laid partly in Manchester city and partly in a green country place skirting its greyness. The heroine, with no heritage but that of grit, grace, and gumption, marries to escape a life of drudgery She finds that struggle and pain dwell also in the country. The scorn of the country-people drives her back, alone, to her own place. Passing through many phases, meeting many people, she learns all the sweetness and bitterness of playing a lone hand.

The advertisement for *Miss Nobody* in the catalogue of Methuen's Popular Novels, Autumn 1913, published in Crown 8vo, 6s. each (included in the end pages of the original edition).

Other well-known books in the series included Arnold Bennett's *The Regent* and Joseph Conrad's *Chance*, as well as works by Marjorie Bowen, G.K. Chesterton, Sir Arthur T. Quiller-Couch, and P.G. Wodehouse.

Ethel Carnie

Miss Nobody

TO JULIA

Chapters

Chapter I

GREENMEADS

THE nine-thirty morning train panted into the city station, pulled up, and set down and picked up cargo—humans, quadrupeds, and inanimate objects.

A young woman in a large hat and flying imitation ostrich-feather, with a hat-box in one hand and a leather bag in the other, paused inquisitively beside a little group of men standing by a cattle-van, where something appeared to be taking place.

"What's the row?" she inquired in her somewhat shrill tones, and with the bold courage of an original mind.

"Silly old cow—won't lie down—whacking it," answered one of the men between his pipe and teeth.

Carrie insinuated herself between him and his companion, a little greasy man with a gleam of lazy enjoyment in his pale eyes. From her position she caught a confused picture of cattle packed together on the floor of the van, with one animal, one alone, standing stubbornly upright. A porter was bringing a knotted thong down on the satiny hide with all the force of his arm. Once or twice he paused to mop his brow with a grimy red handkerchief.

"You ought t' be ashamed of yourselves!" cried Carrie, wincing as another thwack fell on the back of the stupidly patient animal. "Men, aren't you?" with a world of sarcasm in the inquiry.

The little group laughed, but rather uneasily. Carrie was young and pretty, and her scorn counted for something.

"Why doesn't it lie down, then?" inquired one.

"What harm does it do standing?" chirped Carrie.

The porter drew a quick breath and mopped his brow once more.

"None," he said ironically, "only it might kick the others' brains out. I never saw anything like women for talking about what they don't under—"

"Are you going on in this train, miss?" inquired the guard. "Well, hurry up, hurry up; we can't wait all day," as she moved forward in search of a compartment.

"Hurry up yourself!" she retorted, with the irritability coming from too much sympathy. She was tired, too, with the struggle of carrying luggage along crowded subways, where every other individual was a fat man with a large gold watch-chain, or a comfortable-looking dowager with her umbrella placed in a convenient position for breaking ribs.

The guard merely smiled, pushed her into the hot, packed compartment, and waved his flag, murmuring something about Suffragettes.

As the train moved slowly forwards she inspected the rack, as if calculating what amount of weight it would hold without burying the dwellers below. A pilgrim's basket full to overflowing, and which had assuredly been sat upon to contain so much, a heavy portmanteau belonging to the commercial traveller in the corner, and divers parcels, already occupied it.

She accomplished her design of finding room for her things, but in stowing them safely trod upon the corn of the woman with the purple veil, through which her face glowed like a rising sun.

"Don't mention it," she said in a pained voice as Carrie apologized; but her eyes said other things.

"Why didn't she keep her feet out of the way?" thought Carrie. "Good Lord, I'm having a bad start. This comes o' seeing the new moon through glass."

A working man in the opposite corner awkwardly offered Carrie his seat, and when she had got seated and was in better temper she looked out of the window for a few minutes. The train was passing along by a reservoir, and the many sheets of water, intersected by green banks, shimmered in the sunshine. A number of children waving their hands from their post on a fence filled Carrie's heart with a benignant influence, and some wall that had hemmed her in spiritually fell down.

"I 'ope I didn't hurt you bad," she said, turning suddenly to the purple-veiled woman.

The woman, in turn became affable, informing Carrie that she was going to stay with her daughter in Preston, who was married, and had three children, but wanted to go to the mill, so had asked her to come and be housekeeper, as she had not been well lately. The doctor said it was her heart. She had sold her household gods the day before, and felt it very much. She had always wanted to die on her own hearthstone; but the Lord knew best, she finished in a troubled way, as if she weren't quite sure of it.

Carrie returned the confidence by saying that she was going to stay for a week with her sister Clara, married to a gardener in Greenmeads. Clara wasn't a bad sort, she admitted, and it was a pity that she was troubled with sick headaches, as she had been from girlhood. Then the stout lady gave her verbal recipes for sick headaches of all kinds, and got out in a hustle as the guard shouted that she must change trains.

"Good mornin'! I 'ope you'll be better," said Carrie.

"Same to you," answered she, and went off plaintively, as if still regretting her household gods.

Carrie felt a trifle lonely when she had gone.

There were only men in the carriage, all deeply engaged in discussing the Insurance Bill, with the exception of one man who was asleep with his mouth open. He reminded Carrie of a far-back magic-lantern show her mother took them to see, where a mouse ran down a man's throat for a piece of cheese and then back again.

His hair was thin and grey, his trousers stained to almost the colour of the earth. A threadbare scarf worked at his throttle with his heavy breathing. Suddenly he started wide awake, terror in his glance as he asked in a frantic voice, "We haven't passed Colborough, have we?"

Carrie reassured him.

He sank back with a look of exhausted relief.

"N'er got no sleep last night," he avowed apologetically. "Up poulticing the kid. It takes it out o' you. If I'd missed that station now it might ha' been my place."

Half a minute later he swung out of the carriage, his pick and shovel over his shoulder.

Carrie listened a short time to the discussion, amused by the way in which each man ignored each other's argument, thinking only of his own. Then, yawning, she drew from her coat-pocket a yellow-backed "Tulip Novelette" entitled "The Duchess of Digglemore's Diamonds." It was written by a poor pot-boiler who had once cherished dreams of rising to the heights of the immortal ones, joining the choir invisible, but who had found the road too hard, and writing for posterity a thankless task.

When he received the cheque for that impossible story he had broken his fast with a mutton chop, sighing a little, too, and telling the children not to make so much noise, as the flat wasn't all theirs.

Carrie thought that the author must have been a personal friend of the Duchess to know the exact shade of her eyes. Perhaps he had been a former lover, and had sat in that exquisite room to be able to describe it so minutely.

Instead of the gritty floor of the oyster-shop she trod soft Persian carpets upon which lovers knelt to propose in long-winded poetical sentences as sweet as barley-sugar, and not half as wholesome, besides allowing the loved one little opportunity of saying Yes or No for a quarter of an hour, though telling her all the time they were dying for the answer.

Carrie herself was the Duchess for the time being.

"Oh, the villain!" she exclaimed excitedly at the crisis, and the little man in the glasses, thinking that she referred to Lloyd George, remarked fervently, "Yes, young woman, you're right."

Very soon she was alone and utterly absorbed in the story.

"Thought he'd get 'er," she commented mentally, with a feeling of pleasure. "Well, they were made for each other. I wonder how far away Greenmeads is."

Looking through the window, splashed with the rain of the previous day, she saw fields of waving meadow grass, infinite spaces of tender, blue sky bending down to them. The sky fascinated Carrie. It looked so different here in the country from the narrow, hand's-breadth between the grey houses as she viewed it in slack moments from the door of the oyster-shop.

She stared at it long, as if she could drink all that blue, soothing colour into her tired soul. She did not weep, only sighed, and then remembered that she had once heard you lost a drop of blood every time you did so. Carrie had none too much blood.

"To think of all that space being here, and none of us knowing of it," she said aloud, then, being a practical person, looked into her shabby purse of the uncertain clasp to see if her ticket was quite safe.

As the train jerked up at a small station she put her head out at the window, looking about. A tall porter whistling "Love me, and the World is Mine" sauntered near her carriage.

"Is this Greenmeads?"

"No; next station, and all the way without stopping," he answered drolly, with an admiring smile and a slow wink, at which she withdrew her hat with difficulty, on account of its size. She was not shy. She would have preferred to say something hot and biting, as she did in the oyster-shop when men got too familiar, but the train was moving off and a tunnel was approaching.

"Greenmeads," sang a fat little man as if he had been saying it ever since he was born. As she stepped down upon the wooden platform Carrie saw black hills in the distance, beds of flowers near the waiting-room, with one green bank which had the name of the hamlet shaped upon it in oyster-shells. She saw a lane with hedgerows full of bright flowers just over the threshold of the station, as she gave her ticket up to the collector, who directed her to Cherry Tree Terrace.

Halfway down the lane a shambling figure came out from the shelter of the hedge, and offered to carry her bag.

A queer-built figure of a man he was, with large head that seemed to almost overbalance a weak body. His eyes were wide, blue, and wondering as a child's whose reason is just waking.

"Carry your bag," commanded the voice rather than asked. "I know all the ways to Owd England. You're a foreigner, I can see. What part is't you want?"

He had taken the bag from her hand as he spoke.

"Cherry Tree Terrace," said Carrie faintly. Men with all their senses she could manage; she was afraid of idiots.

"Cherry Tree," he repeated, jogging on by her side. "Oh, aye, I know it. North part of Owd England wi' three trees in front, ant' moon allus risin' behind 'em. D'ye know that there's a new milkin'-machine up at Gibson's farm? No? Aye, I'd forgotten yo've nobbut just come fro' abroad an' know nowt, as it were. Yigh, t' farmer's getten a new milkin'-machine, for I yeard it myself this mornin', an' he said it could milk nine million ten thousand hundred keaws. I'm rare an' fond o' milkin'-machines."

Carrie was silent, and wondered if he was going the right way, for two paths met at this juncture.

"What country is it yo' come fro'?" went on the voice, and the big, blue eyes fastened there on her face.

"It's in England," answered Carrie. "An' they call it Manchester."

"'Ow many stations off?" waving his limp, free hand to the Greenmeads station-house.

"A good many," answered Carrie.

"Not in Owd England if it's more nor two away," he said decisively. "An' if onybody's a judge o' where Owd England starts an' ends, it's Peter Moss."

This condensed patriot now pointed to a row of chimneys in the near distance, saying, "Yon's Cherry Tree."

Holding out his hand for the coppers he left her to carry the bag the remainder of the way, and Carrie was glad to be rid of him. His eyes with that wild light in them frightened her, and the last she saw of him he was laid once more under the hedge, looking at a green leaf as if trying to pierce to the secret of its existence.

Clara was at the open door. They met without kissing, though they had not seen each other for nearly five years.

"'Ot, I calls it to-day," said Clara. "I've got a splittin' headache, so you must 'scuse the 'ouse if it isn't quite as shiny as you expected."

She would have had a look of Carrie, if Carrie had got the colour and courage washed out of her. Five years before, as she left Ardwick and Carrie for a home of her own, she had mentioned her headache. Carrie would not have felt at home without some reference to it; but after a while, as they got talking over a pot of tea and greens from the garden, it seemed to disappear by magic.

"'Ow's that Jane Libby going on?" asked Clara. "No good, I'll warrant—the hussy!"

"Married," answered Carrie, munching.

"Married! Who on earth was daft enough—" began her sister.

"Well, there were two or three, and nobody could tell how it would go, but at last she decided on James Clements; you know, 'im as 'is father put into that grocer's shop."

"She's a varmint!" cried Clara. "They allus get good husbands."

"She could put her hair up," commended Carrie. "Is your husband a good 'un?"

"Just fair," sighed Clara; "if he gets all 'is own way, an' I don't ever tell 'im 'is faults, an' keep the frying-pan goin'. He gives me the headache till I can't bear, sometimes."

"'Course," said her sister sympathetically, putting another piece of the watercress to her mouth.

"An' 'ow's Martha?" further inquired Clara, passing from the prosaic subject of her husband, and by and by had gleaned all the news of her native Ardwick.

"Where are the kids?" asked Carrie, putting her hat on the blue vase on the dresser, which she herself had given as a wedding present to her sister.

Just then they came in, two of the merriest rogues, with eyes suddenly shy as they saw a stranger.

Billy was four and three-quarters, and had caused Clara more than common anxiety before his birth, for she did not know if Joe would be good enough to marry her.

Carrie, however, had cheered her up by saying, "Never mind, Sis. A home you shall have with me, whatever happens." They never spoke of those days, but once or twice Clara remembered them and pressed her sister to have more bread with sudden warmth. Joey was two, and carried a doll, which no teasing could compel him to relinquish.

"They are ducks," cried Carrie. "Here, don't you run away from me. I'm your Auntie Carrie, I am."

"You aren't," said Billy stubbornly. "Auntie Carrie lives long way off, where there's lots of hosses."

But Carrie soon had him on her knee.

"Loverly eyes they've got," she said. "They make you feel like—like the sky does," vaguely. "I expect Joe an' you never regret him trying for that job, now? They wouldn't ha' faces like those in Manchester."

"It makes my head ache when I think there aren't no shops—decent shops, where there are sales—any nearer than Bringford, Carrie."

"Bother the sales!" said Carrie, taking another look in the child's eyes. "Ain't they *blue!* Now, Billy."

"My name's William," piped an imperial voice.

"Gives 'issel' airs, don't he?" laughed his aunt. "A regular Brown. Same old dog, Clara. 'E'll make a shine, or it won't be 'is fault. 'E's a look o' the old man, ain't 'e?"

"Carrie!"

"Well?" encouraged Carrie.

"Sometimes I shuts my eyes and thinks father has maybe made his fortune, and we'll come into it some day. He was a sharp 'un."

"He was a selfish 'un," corrected Carrie, and with a frown clouding her soft, dimpled, if rather pale face. "He was a—a—cat!" She got the word at length from her unlimited vocabulary. "As for 'is leaving a fortune—trust me he'd spend all he ever got hold of on 'is dear little self."

"'E never said a dirty word in his life," said Clara.

"No; but his life was meaner than dirt. It's surprising 'ow you can 'old up with other folk's husbands, Clara, when they were your own mother's."

From which heated sentence the reader must not infer that Mrs. Brown had had more than one husband. One was enough for her, of the kind.

Clara sighed at the accusation, and they agreed to differ.

Next day Carrie took the children out for a walk. They told her of a lovely green hill where they could pick buttercups and daisies, and roll down in the bargain, leading her docilely along. It was a lovely hill!

It was clad in long, soft grass, kindly and humorous, which tickled their faces as they rolled over and over, and lay blinking at the sky when they reached the foot with a delirious drunken feeling born of perfect happiness.

"Aunt Carrie roll!" pleaded Billy.

Carrie looked around. There was nothing in sight but a mild-eyed cow, a lonely tree, and far below the murmur of a little stream sounded drowsily on the summer air.

The shrill laughter of the children as she complied with their request rippled upwards, and the mild-eyed cow ceased grazing a moment, as if wondering at the meaning of it all.

"Ain't it *nice?*" said Billy, sitting beside her as she lay at the foot of the hill with tumbled hair and face upturned to the sky.

She never answered that comradely query.

"Nice example to set the childer," shouted a man's gruff voice. "You a grown woman, too, by the looks o' yo'." She sat up suddenly, wondering where her hat was. "Nice doings," cried the voice, coming nearer, and at last she rose to face the owner of it, a somewhat short, ruddy man, with dark eyes, fair hair, and a red rose in his buttonhole. "There's a limit to everything an' I calls this rolling business disgraceful in a woman o' your age. Your name, occupation, and address, please, or whether or not."

The children were clinging to Carrie's shabby black grenadine skirt, with the bits of grass sprinkled over it which had been flung at her in handfuls by the little imps as she rolled.

"Carolina Evelyn Brown, 190, Ardwick Road, Manchester. Oysters!" she said rapidly, with telegraphic order. Then she burst out laughing.

The sun was in her blue eyes, on her yellow, much-frizzed hair that even the curling-tongs plunged weekly into the fire for the religious "frizzing" ceremony could not rob of all its soft brightness, the shining beauty of youth.

Farmer Gibson eyed the shabby figure from top to toe, noting the strong, firm look of the rough hands, the cheap boots on the little feet, and he saw that a tooth was gone from her top set in front, giving her a sweetly comical appearance.

"What are you laughin' at?" he growled; but his growl sounded a little like a dog's when his master is teasing him.

"I ain't got any money—anything, in fact. If you summons me you'll ha' to sell my clothes."

"Those rags!" he said contemptuously. Carrie's eyes flashed this time, and she looked affectionately at the old skirt.

Under the name Caroline Brown the farmer wrote the mystic and strangely irrelevant words, *"blew eyes."*

"Married or single?" he asked next, phlegmatically, tapping his pencil on the hard, red-backed book in his hand.

"Ask your grandmother!" flashed Carrie angrily. Then woman-like she answered, "Single, so you needn't think to get anything out o' *him*. 'E ain't born yet! But look here, Mister—whatever your name is—since you've got my name down to summons me, I'll just relieve myself with givin' you a bit o' my mind. *If I'd a hill*, anybody could roll down it. You are meaner than a bloomin' policeman who looks after the parks! Come along, Billy—Joe," and she swept away, rather like a queen, for all her shabby dress, missing tooth, rough hands, and cheap boots.

"Parents living or dead?" shouted the farmer, as they climbed the hill to go down on the other side.

"Find it out," echoed angrily on the sweet, fresh wind.

As she finally disappeared from sight, Farmer Gibson lay in the grass, plucking blades meditatively. There was a light in his eyes that was too humorous and soft to be caused by anger.

Sarah had informed him of trespassers on the hillside, and he had gone out reluctantly to do his duty, and was dazzled by a bit of scoffing woman flesh.

By and by an angular figure came to the top of the hill.

"Dinner's ready, Robert," called a deep slow-accented country voice. "Don't let it go cold."

"Right!" he shouted, and sprang to his feet with alacrity.

For the first time in his life he was glad to have been sent out to chide trespassers. He hated to have to shout after the children, as a rule, making them drop their flowers as if he was a bogey, and often appealed to their generosity rather than fear, then would bid them creep low through the grass lest the bogey see and catch them, meaning Sarah.

Clara listened dolefully to her sister's story.

"Property is property," she chorused, from time to time, until Carrie lost her patience.

"Don't tell me that God made that green hill for a mean, old thing like that," she said fiercely.

"His name's Gibson, and he's neither mean nor old," said Clara, pausing in her dusting of a china dog. "When Joe lost his place through a drinkin' bout, 'e got it 'im back."

"Sympathized with him, I'll lay," said Carrie.

"That he did," responded Clara, not suspecting sarcasm. "What are you doing, Carrie?"

She had taken her huge hat and was pushing the pins through ready to put it on.

"There's a train soon," she said. "I'm going back. I'll open the shop so that I can pay that summons. Joshua! And I bought a new hat only last week; a new one, never been on! It's upstairs in the box I brought."

There were tears in her eyes as she spoke, and a smile hovering round her lips at her folly. She found it dreadfully hard to let it go, that hat, with those white and golden flowers, the green buckle and smart, high bows. What a fight she had for it at the sale! What an eager, jostling crowd outside the shop, from the sweated girl in her worn shawl, covetous of an embroidered gown at one shilling, to the wife of the small tradesman who had to keep up appearances at a cheap rate, and elbowing her one with the light of business in her eyes—a wardrobe dealer, buying to sell again. Men going past to work had hazarded a guess that it was a soup-kitchen, with droll winks, and a stout policeman had warned them several times not to go through the window or they might spoil their faces. When they got within, what a scramble! Wild cries of "That is mine! I was first!" and heartburnings and despairs to see the things they yearned for snatched by some luckier rival. Carrie had been several times warned that she would be brought up for assault and battery by some who had no sport in their compositions.

Clara was watching her out of the corner of her eye.

She knew that it was an ill wind that would blow her good, at any rate.

"I don't know," she said, with well-simulated hesitation. "I got one in the autumn. Do you think it would suit me? I wouldn't mind obliging you, Carrie. Bring it down."

Carrie ran upstairs and came down. She lifted the tissue-paper from it reverently, and handed it to Clara. Clara moved this way and that way before the glass.

"Rather young," commented the married sister, a little wistfully.

"It's just your ticket," announced Carrie. "You can have it cheap."

"Don't you think it too gay?" inquired Clara, with a smile dawning in her eyes. She stroked a ribbon, and Carrie winced, seeing it pass out of her life.

"It isn't a bit too gay," she said, and stated her price.

"Why, there's a little hole in this loop," cried Clara, adding magnanimously, "But it's nothing."

"You can have it sixpence cheaper," said Carrie, her face flushing, "and it will never be seen."

They went upstairs to settle the bargain, fearing Joe might come in. From a little bag hung up the bedroom chimney Clara took some silver. "If you get a good husband, Carrie," she advised, putting the remainder of the money back in the bag, "blind him in one eye; but if you get a bad 'un, blind him in both."

Carrie caught the one-thirty train just as the owner of the green hill pushed his plate away vowing he could eat no more.

Billy met him in the lane the next day.

"Is your aunt busy this morning?" he inquired pleasantly, holding out a penny.

"She's gone 'ome," said Billy, his eye on the coin.

"The devil she has!" exclaimed the farmer, scraping a little of the mud from his heavy boots with a knotted stick. "Well, tell your mother to tell her when she writes that she will hear from me again."

19

Billy nodded over the penny, but forgot to give the message.

Lucky-bags in Billy Lever's window drove it completely out of his head.

Chapter II

ROBERT GIBSON BECOMES ROMANTIC

THE Gibsons were highly respected in Greenmeads. They had never done anything to outrage the unwritten laws of the country village, which lagged considerably behind Bringford, the nearest town, in economics, and consequently in ethical outlook. There was neither a Trades' Union nor a dancing-room in Greenmeads, but both found a place in the town. Will Gibson, Robert's younger brother, lost a little prestige from being overheard to say that his native village was as dull as the water in its own ditches. The inhabitants were very glad when he announced his intention of going out to Canada. He had already disgraced them by going to Bringford to learn the steps of a new waltz, and after that they had felt a terrible responsibility. Robert found a few little debts Will left behind him as an affectionate remembrance, paying them, though not without some grumbling. The farm was mortgaged at the time, and only hard tugging and self-denial had enabled him to clear off the burden. On the morning after the last payment he allowed himself the luxury of idly leaning a whole sweet hour on the old farm gate watching the smoke curl upwards from the chimney. He told Sarah afterwards that he was sure every slate on the roof knew that it was free. They shone so brightly in the morning sunshine, whilst the windows, he said, winked, each one of them, as if congratulating him.

The mortgage had encumbered the farm owing to the romantic tendencies in the nature of Robert's father.

Benjamin Gibson could not come up the lane in the evening without thinking that every bit of glass that shone was a diamond, though why people should go about scattering diamonds in a Greenmeads lane none but himself could have told. He purchased bargains, but the bargain was always on the other side of the blanket.

The same romantic tendency caused him to set out one day with a huge box of clogs, and travel with them into the heart of Wales. His idea was that in the mining district clogs would be much more comfortable than shoes, and that if only some one could introduce them, there would be a growing demand. He expected to make his fortune.

After three weeks he arrived back at the farm, leading a ragged donkey up the hill—the only thing he had to show in exchange for the two hundred pairs of clogs he had taken with him.

How he had fared he would never tell, but only shake his head, stating solemnly that the Welsh miners were a tough lot.

In his last illness he confided to Robert that if he got better he had a splendid idea for making money, but death robbed him of any chance he might have had of doing this. His wife Lisbeth was not long after him.

He had been a sore trial to her.

Benjamin had all the impulsiveness and imagination of a child, with the tenacity of a Napoleon when once an idea got hold of him. He would ask her for her opinion with the mild countenance of a lamb, and disdain it with the scorn of a lion.

When he was dead, she wept for him as if he had been her wayward son. She had hovered a little in her decision between him and Samuel Taylor, the blacksmith, finally settling the matter by putting the question, with all its responsibilities, to the church steps on her way up to her pew in the gallery. The last step being Yes, and a church step in the bargain, she took Benjamin, and Samuel walked before the procession from the church on her wedding-day, playing his fiddle with genial good-will and philosophy.

It was a hard knock for him, but he made the best of it, marrying plump, rosy-cheeked Janet, her younger sister, two years afterwards, mostly because (people said) she laughed in the same vowel as Lisbeth.

Robert's father had his tea sweetened for him, his tie put straight before he went to church, and needed a lot of care generally.

When he was gone she scarcely knew how to pass her time.

Sarah was almost a woman and a born manager; Robert looked after the cattle much better than his father had ever done; and Will, Will with his comic songs and patent shoes, which she hid inside his everyday footgear whenever the minister was coming—Will went away to Canada.

"Sarah," she observed one afternoon as she sat mending stockings by the kitchen window with its line of colour from the scarlet fuchsias, "Sarah, I sometimes think that I was a bit hard on your father. He was a good-hearted man. I can see him now, his face fairly beaming, planning what to do with that fortune when it came. He never wanted aught for hissel', only for us! I feel fairly choked when I think I used to tell him to mind t'pigs, Sarah. I believe," impressively, "that he was one o' those folk the minister talked of t'other Sunday—geniuses. He said they were absent-minded."

Sarah knew then that her mother's illness was more serious than they had suspected, for in anything like good health she would never have been under such a delusion.

Mrs. Gibson lived several years after that, however, though she never scolded with the same vigour, or laughed with the old heartiness.

Sarah had long before her mother's decease taken on the complete sway of the household, as Robert had control outside the doorstep. She had received one matrimonial offer from a village shopkeeper, a widower who had an idea that she would be a good manager.

"I don't go in for anything risky," Sarah answered him, over the counter. "Marriage is no better than a German lottery. When I want excitement, I'll buy a bicycle and ride down the hill for my pertaters."

Her voice was so decisive that the shopkeeper applied for a housekeeper the week after.

This proposal was a valuable asset to Sarah, for it gave her considerable power over Robert.

If he hinted that the breakfast bacon was a trifle overdone, she would ask him what would have happened had she married Walter Smith, and he felt humbly grateful.

Once only did he wax savage, and say, "Damn Walter Smith," and then it was upon the occasion of her wishing him to marry Elsie, the girl on the farm on the other side of the hill, because of a dream she had had presaging death to the dreamer, according to the "Complete Dream Book." The prize pig dying the week after, Sarah felt easier in her mind, and let the subject drop, seeing that it really annoyed Robert. As a matter of fact, she did not wish to place the reins within anybody's hands, no, not even to give them over to Elsie, who was her ideal girl, practical enough to turn a dish-clout into a dumpling.

Sarah had the sterling qualities of her mother— common sense and forethought—and though somewhat hard qualities, they were none the less sterling. Sometimes she suspected Robert of having inherited the taint of romance from their father, though not in a sufficient degree to make him a poor and careless farmer. Besides, Robert loved the land as his father had never loved it. With his feet on the sods and his head against a space of sky he was as happy as a trout in its native pools.

The convictions that Robert was a bit romantic were founded upon such incidents as his giving a passing tramp a copper. Sarah believed in relieving deserving cases, but had no faith in these people from nowhere, and predicted Robert's bankruptcy and ruin every time he gave a penny.

She had a sincere affection for him, which showed itself in this curious habit of scolding at him. Perhaps there is as much affection in a good, sound scolding as in a kiss; it is only a difference of expression. Robert often heard her voice running on its grumbling course as unmoved as if it was the murmur of the meadow stream, or the ticking of the grandfather clock in the corner of the kitchen, thinking his own thoughts to the sound.

He would have been mightily surprised had any one suggested to him that Sarah was a "nagger," for he took her tyranny as something he was born to, knowing it was affection, after all. Once she had tried to be very nice and kind to him, and after a week he had anxiously inquired if she was ill and if he hadn't better call in a doctor.

On one occasion they differed—as to whether the lamp-wick should be cut or picked clean. Robert clung to his point with gusto that evening, and Sarah left the house in a huff. When she did not return by seven o'clock in the evening he set out to seek her. He discovered her having a dish of tea with Matty Burns, with half of a daisy-mat beside her teacup as the result of her industry.

"I was beginning to think you had drowned yourself, Sarah," he said, as they climbed the hill together, and his voice trembled.

"Any one that could think *that* o' me must have romantic notions," derided Sarah. "Some day you'll make a fool o' yourself, Robbie, for I know it from that remark."

Romance was a constant dread of Sarah's, being a thing to be fought against tooth and nail in herself and others. If you listened to Romance there was no telling what you might do, for you left the common-sense track of everyday life, where butter is so much a pound. She looked after the fuchsias in the window-sill and they throve under her care, because she managed everything well, and hated to waste, but she had no more tender feeling for their lovely purples and reds, nor sorrow over their dropped petals, than a hippopotamus would have had. She voted against the appointment of the new minister because he talked so much poetry in his sermons, and poetry was not common sense. Let her have an honest, plain-dealing man like Mr. Crawshaw, she said, who made the road to heaven as straight as a pikestaff and almost as narrow, and called sin sin, and a spade a spade, and not all this talk of circumstances, brotherly love, and stars. Stars wasn't no business of ministers at all. They ought to look after their flock and see it didn't stray instead of walking into rain-pools as Mr. Wallas did because he was a-studying of the night skies. Wasn't it romance that made Polly Flyn get into trouble, took John William Lawson soldiering so that he got killed in the Boer War when he might have lived to be seventy, and wasn't it romance that made his mother take his death so to heart she drowned herself in Willoughby's pond a few weeks after?

Wasn't it romance made girls be whispering of lovers together instead of darning their stockings and saving their money against old age, and repaying the kindness of their parents instead of marrying the first pair of trousers that came along?

Of course it was!

Most sin and wickedness came from romance, from Eve's time downwards, for common sense ought to have told the foolish pair that having so much they could have no more.

This morning Sarah sat watching her brother as he ate his rasher of bacon hastily.

"You'll have indigestion, Robert," she warned him, "if you gobble like that. There's a day tomorrow, as the man said, and if there isn't it doesn't matter."

"I'm going to the city on a bit of business," said the farmer, fastening the tags of his shoe-laces in a determined manner, and with that Sarah was obliged to be as happy or as miserable as she pleased. There was a lack of confidence about Robert this morning that suggested something he was afraid of sharing with her—something uncertain and romantic.

It was long since the villagers had seen Robert Gibson so smart. They were accustomed to his battered Bluchers, rough tweed, and the flowered silk handkerchief which he wore as a compromise between respectability and comfort.

This morning he wore a fine black coat, dark green breeches, silver straw Trilby hat, and he had in his tie a horseshoe pin for luck.

Emily Hutchinson, who was sweeping her flagged passage (a kind of rivalry existed between Barbara and she in keeping their "fronts" clean ever since Emily's Jimmy fought Barbara's Lewis), prophesied that something strange was going to happen, judging from appearances. When a man like Farmer Gibson, a steady, reliable citizen, whose movements were as good to tell the time by as the clock, and better than most clocks—when a man like this was seen early on a working day dressed as if it was a "feast" day, his green breeches did not presage a funeral, but a wedding.

"Sin' he got his fause teeth, I've been down on him," admitted Barbara Green, shaking her head sadly. "'Tis a sign of falling away and vanity of the flesh when a man gets his third set o' teeth; against all the laws of Nature, as I tell Sanders, who has been on for following in his steps, saying Gibson looks years younger. In bygones they weren't ashamed o' getting old—now it's hair-dye, fause teeth, and no wrinkles. A sin against the Lord, that's what I call it—when the Omnipotent is making His power felt, up steps the devil in the form o' an artificial teeth seller and says, 'There's a chance yet—be young.' What will their great-grandfathers say when they see them enter the eternal kingdom, aged ninety-one, and not a honourable silver hair to show for all that struggling and moiling? 'Twill seem as if they have sat down all their lives and made merry with the devil. But they do say"—a trifle inconsequently—"that you can get 'em at Bringford on the instalment plan."

"I do wish bonnets had not gone out," sighed a sweet-looking woman, with a faded voice that sounded as if it came through the telephone. "These lollopy hats don't suit my face, and strings were so snug under your chin!"

"You haven't got much o' a face, 'tis true," put in Barbara Green. "You are very chinny-boned, Mirandy. What you want is some emulsion."

"Nay, nay, there is nothing ails me," said the woman with the far-away voice, and the tears sprung to her eyes, and, turning, she smiled artificially and went inside, closing her little green door gently. The echo of a cough reached the little group, leaning on their brushes as if waiting for inspiration to suggest the next topic.

A little bird chirped and flew away, followed by his mate.

"In the family," said Emily Hutchinson, meaningly. "Then they pinched so—and now 'tis all dribbling in doctors' bills. She doesn't speak to Sally Fisher for saying the word—cut her dead ever after. There's a bill up near the Town Hall in Bringford saying it can be cured. I don't know. If it can, 'tis worth the bonnets going out and the teeth coming in."

"When your time has come it has come," cried 'Liza Smethurst, stoically. She could not bear people to be sympathized with. "And rally to me"—with her great arms akimbo—"what's life wuth when you reckon it up?" Then she spied the greengrocer's cart creeping along the lane and ran in to get her potato bag.

"Have yo' noticed anythin' new about 'Liza?" said Barbara Green, looking slowly round the group. "'Cause I have. I'm not as green by nature as I am by name. It's not only seein', it's smellin'—poor thing, she has got running fearful often with the jug."

"Well, I never!" exclaimed Matilda Greaves, who had never done a bad action in her life—nor a good one either.

"I'd never have believed it. They were brought up—"

"Brought up?" squeaked asthmatic Mrs. Jones, eyeing the other scornfully. "Dragged up, you mean. Poor thing, she's her nose over the wash-tub from Monday morning to Saturday—and a lazy, good-for-nothing spending what she earns."

"But a woman—a woman should be patient," sighed Matilda.

"Old maids' husbands are always easy to manage," retorted the other.

Unconscious that her reputation, the only wealth she possessed, was being filched from her, 'Liza Smethurst went back into the house with her potatoes.

She sat down and began to peel them rapidly, looking at the mother-o'-pearl clock with concern. Her little gossip meant that it would be almost midnight when she tumbled into bed after her work.

A boy of seven, misshapen and pallid, sat watching her peel away, almost like a machine.

"How sharp you go, mammy," he said. "You can do them sharper than anybody in the world. Sharper than"—he paused as if choosing some worthy opponent, and said at last, "God!"

'Liza threw down her potato-peeling knife, wiped her hands on her sack apron, and said, "Harold, child, if you say that again I'll hev to whip you! T' parson would think you'd heard it at 'ome. Who did you hear say it? Tell me quick!"

"Nobody," he said in affright, for he had never seen his mother like this before, angry with him. "Harry told it to his own head."

She snatched him up in her huge arms, kissing him passionately, the fear fading out of her face.

"'Tis the stuff the infidels talk in Bringford," she murmured to herself. "But—thear, he's only a child." Then to her son, who was pulling at her apron, she said in compunction: "Must mammy tell a bonny tale?"

His face lit up.

She took him in her lap and began.

"There was once three little piggies, with curly pink tails, and wee squinty eyes, who wanted everything to eat—"

"Like daddy?" interrogated Harold, and she said, with a shadow on her face, "No, no, these were greedy piggies, and walked on four legs and paddled in the dirt all day till their pretty pinky tails were black. One day their mother said, 'Come, piggies, it is time you all go out into the world and seek your fortunes.' Out they started, and then they came to three roads. One piggie went to the right, another to the left, and one right on. The first little—"

The sound of heavy steps interrupted the narrative, and the next moment a blotchy-faced man flung wide the door.

The fear on the two faces seemed to exasperate him. "This is 'ow yo' spend your time, is it?" quoth he. "Don't speak, or I'll shut your faces. Harold!" (the lad started as at the crack of a gun). "Come away from your mother—women aren't fit to train childer, bring 'em up like toffee dolls. Come and shake hands with your father."

Harold slunk away.

"Come here, when I tell yo'!" yelled his parent. "Now what's the good of having childer if yo' can't make the devils heed. Come here, 'twill be better." He snatched up a large belt from a chair-back.

'Liza's eyes flashed, but she said nothing.

But when her husband raised his arm as if to strike, she took the bread-knife from the table.

"Touch 'en if yo' dare, and I'll put it clean through thy heart an' tha' hes one," she screamed, and just then the door opened and a neighbour came in, drawn thither by the noise.

"That's the sort o' wife a man has. Is it any wonder he goes wrong?" snarled the man. The neighbour withdrew.

"Fetch me a quart o' ale from the Cow, and don't gossip and let the foam go off," he said; and she obeyed, but took the boy with her, leaving him in the sanded passage of the inn, staring with all his might at the picture of the fighting cocks upon the wall.

Mrs. Green saw her pass her window.

"'Tis only too true," she sighed, genuinely sorry, "and by the flush on her face she'd had one at the bar."

The minister called that afternoon to see 'Liza, after having visited Mrs. Green.

He sat down on a chair she dusted for him, and she listened in a puzzled way whilst he spoke of the wine that stung like an adder, though it was so red and warming.

When he had gone she thought deeply.

"Why, they must ha' thought that I went to the Cow for myself!" she murmured over the tub to the splosh-splosh of the old-fashioned peggy washer. "Now that is a terrible thing to think! I've half a mind to tell 'em of it, the hussies, for they must have set him on. But—no, 'tisn't wuth it. The boy knows."

Harold sat amongst the dirty clothes, listening in a dazzled delight to the tale of the three pigs with the curly pink tails. When it was done he went to her and cuddled her.

"When you die," he said with innocent eyes, "you will sit on the right hand of God Almighty—Maker of heaven and earth, and mammy?"

"Yes, dear," she said, stroking the opaline bubbles from her glorious woman's arms.

"Will—will the three little piggies be there?"

"Yes," answered his mother absently. "Toss me the soap, there's a lovey."

Carrie, however, had gone back to the city thinking that all happiness was to be found in the country, where the meadow daisies were white and golden, and quite distinct from the park daisies.

How surprised she would have been could she have seen Farmer Gibson speeding towards the grey city that seemed to her now as a hot, dark cage to a bird that can see a green bush beyond.

Jane Wilkins, the charwoman in Greenmeads, whose husband was dead, yet still lamented, had promised to sit up and find out what time Robert Gibson returned home.

Blissfully unconscious, the farmer plodded his way through the streets, Carrie's address tucked inside the band of his hat. An agreeable young man walked with him from the station and piloted him safely through the throng and maze of streets.

"Come and have a drink," invited the handsome stranger, but he shook his head, answering, "Nay, I've business to see to; I may when 'tis done with—it all depends. Could you tell me the way to there?" He took the scrap of notepaper from his hat-band, covered the mystic words "*blew eyes*" with his giant thumb, and held out the rest for his companion to see.

"Carolina Brown, Oysters, Ardwick," read the young man as if he had never heard the name before in his life. "Let me see. We'd best go this way."

Just then a policeman passed, eyeing the young man rather narrowly, and he cursed inwardly. The farmer noticed nothing, walking along with an air of wellbeing.

"There's your street—walk right on," cried the Manchester man, jokingly, slapping him on the back. "Good luck and good-bye!"

"Thanks for your kindness," answered the farmer, gratefully. "If ever you should be in Greenmeads— (picnickers do come, betimes)—you call at Hilltop Farm, and our Sarah will make you as good a cup o' tay as was ever brewed in this world."

"Old fool! Green as his breeches. Carrie Brown, my dear, he's sweet on you. I'm in at this. She must have got on with him when on a visit to Clara's Well. I'll have my finger in this pie."

"Devilish pleasant fellow," said Gibson to himself as he plodded along, not unlike a Dutch clipper as he went through the crowd. He sometimes used an oath or two of this type, to feel his manhood intact within him, after Sarah's scoldings, and because he had a sort of feeling that roughness, even a spice of wickedness, kept a man a man.

He began to feel shy as he got near to the number of the door. When he had reached No. 180 his heart was going like a sledge-hammer, but he did not stop.

"Brown, Oysters," he read over the door in would-be stylish sign-painting, and peeping in at the window saw mountains of East Rivers and Blue Points piled on the marble slab.

"Nice morning," said a pleasant, businessy voice, with the shrill music some birds have, and on the other side of the counter he beheld Carolina Brown.

She was busy getting the oysters he ordered ready, and the brief glance she had given him was not keen enough to detect in the face beneath the Trilby the countenance of the Greenmeads oppressor, though she thought there was something familiar in it.

The landlord had been suggesting to Carrie that the rent ought to be raised, and Carrie and he had been having a wordy battle.

When he had gone, she had wept a little, because even now it was hard sometimes to manage, and because he judged the shop was doing rather better this year he wanted to raise the rent. Because she thought her eyes might be a bit red Carrie did not talk to her customers this morning in her usual "cocky" manner. She was holding imaginary conversations with Mr. Lawrence— long conversations in which he came off worsted every time—as she opened Farmer Gibson's oysters.

"Nice day yesterday," insisted the farmer, swallowing an oyster. Carrie was getting his change, and had her frizzled head over the till.

"Awfully nice," she said, absently. She noticed that duchesses and people like that said "awfully" a lot, and used it in the shop when she wore her best hair-comb and enamel brooch.

Then there was a pause, broken only by the panting of a motor.

"It 'tain't worth ten shillings, with that little hole hot as blazes you calls a kitchen," she was going on mentally as she counted out the coppers.

"It was a nice day the day afore, too," said the voice again, startling her, for she had almost forgotten his presence.

"Yes. Sixpence, seven, eight, nine, ten, eleven, one shilling, and one makes two," she said mechanically putting the change down.

"Partickler about dinner-time the day afore yesterday," he persisted, and Carrie started, and looked straight up this time, with the shadow of the summons clouding her face, to stare right into the farmer's sunbrowned one.

"It'll be at least five pounds and costs," he said admiringly, then wiped his mouth on a huge country pocket-handkerchief, edged with Paisley pattern.

Carrie gave the sort of cry a spider will cause.

"Six more oysters," he commanded. "And don't look at me like that. I'll pay for what I get and—I ain't a bad sort," putting his big hand on the little red, rough one covered with rings *à la mode* Duchess of Dinglemore.

She snatched it away.

"Summons me, if you want," she said, her blue eyes flashing, "but don't think you can come and insult me because I trespassed on your old hill."

"I only want to be friends," he said quite pleadingly. "And I'm a straight-up man, Carolina"—with a solemn face all at once. "I've never played crooked with any woman, not one." Then he laughed. "Because it wouldn't ha' been any good if I had; they can beat a man into fits at that game. Yes, by Jove," and he slapped his knee. Then he finished the last oyster, and looked round the small shop, adding, "This ain't a place for a nice girl like you, Carolina. There's a little farm wants a mistress, girl, for Sarah's gettin' too old for the work, and then I like your face, 'cause it's so straight. You can have lots to spend, and I'll look after you. And now you know my business, for I'm a straight-up man, Carrie, though we've all of us our faults, as the man said who was a bundle and had only one virtue, which was—he never went out "without his wife."

"How was that?" inquired Carrie, smiling, with feminine curiosity.

"'E was paralysed," chuckled the farmer, slapping his knee and enjoying his own joke.

"You might be paralysed yourself some day," began Carrie, prophetically; but humour tickled her out of her gravity, and her laughter rang out with the farmer's.

Very different was this proposal from Lord Digglemore's in her novelette. This was a kind of take-me-or-leave-me business. Lord Digglemore had talked of dying if he was not accepted, but Farmer Gibson only ate oysters, calmly wiped his fingers, and sat down in the blue-curtained little alcove with the marble-topped tables, whistling "And to be a farmer's boy," whilst she made up her mind.

Several customers came in, ate oysters, and departed. The farmer peeped at them all, himself unseen. He could hear her discussing the weather with each one, and catch the jingle of the cheap bangle with the six-penny-pieces attached, the first bit of jewellery she had possessed, bought with a whole year's savings when she was a scullery drudge for the Follingtons. What a miserable time that had been, for all the other servants had poked fun at her because she looked such an old woman in her cap, and there was the terribly hot moment when the "missis" caught her drinking water from the jug as she took it for Miss Molly to wash her hands in her room, and made her go back, wash the jug out three times and fill it again—all these memories connected with that little bit of paltry jewellery. It had comforted her in her sorrow, when she was as a captive in a strange land, rebelling futilely, and before its possession she had beheld it in the jeweller's window, in its satin-lined box, and fancied she should outshine

Miss Molly when she wore it. After hard days, days when all had gone wrong, she had retired to her room at the top of the house, and reverently put it on the scraggy, red arm, and heard it jingle with a holy look.

The last customer was an Italian, who stopped his mirror-covered ice-cream cart bedight with sullied gilt eagles, before the door, eating his oysters, with his eye on the cart and the miserable donkey that drew it.

The farmer was tapping his boots with his stick meditatively, when she peeped in at him. She had been weighing everything up in her mind as she talked of the weather to her customers.

It was the best offer she had ever had, or that she would ever have, in all probability. She was no chicken, for she looked younger than she was, with her fair hair and complexion, bright blue eyes, and hopeful smile. She was twenty-six in September.

The days were long days, from eight in the morning to eleven at night, excepting the half-day when she went to the picture-show across the way and ate chocolate.

All day she was opening oysters, talking of the weather, agreeing with the divers opinions of various customers, parrying the insults of drunken ones when the hour got late, and when the last customer had gone she had a mountain of pots to wash up for the next morning, with the same old song over again.

The farmer ceased tapping "The Farmer's Boy" on his No. 12 shoes, and looked up.

"Well?"

"I'll think it over," said Carrie, as if she did not already know that she intended to close with the bargain. Still, she thought it might be best before really promising to see Fanny Winklesworth, who was very clever with the cards, and see if it would be wise.

Fanny was so good at these things, for had she not told Rose Mary Jones once there was *tears* for her, and

sure enough Rose Mary's Fred got entangled with a
dressmaker and gave her the go-by, because she was
only a flax-girl. Rose Mary had come to cry on Julia's
bed in the hot little kitchen where the dresser seemed
on top of the fire almost, though both Fanny and Julia
said there was "oceans of room."

Perhaps Fanny would see if she would have a happy
life at the farm, but Carrie knew despite any advice
that she would marry Mr. Gibson. "Every day I shall
sit on that there hill an' look at the sky," she said to
him a little later. "'Course I shall have to sell the shop
afore I can come," with her mixture of practicability and
dreaminess that was so confusing and charming.

"Right," he answered comfortably, squeezing her
hand in his mighty paw. "Say, Carrie, you might call
me 'Bob' instead of 'Mister,' as it sounds more at-'ome-
like, somehow."

Suddenly he gave a little exclamation of anger and
astonishment.

"What's the matter?" inquired Carrie.

"My watch!" he gasped, and then she made further
inquiries, eliciting the fact that he had been directed
to the shop by a "nice, smart, young feller." His attire,
conversation, and looks were described, and Carrie's
face went a trifle paler, but the farmer was so engrossed
in his loss that he did not notice it. She poured out tea
for herself and him in the odd cups she had picked up
cheap, then the bell rang, and she had to hurry away.

Mr. Gibson was in a fit of despair when she came
back.

"I could tell 'im in a crowd of a million," he vowed
fervently, "and if ever I come across 'im I'll tak' it out o'
'is hide!"

Then he told Carrie that the watch had been his
father's; the only good bargain his father ever made,
as he died without a will, having refused to believe till

the end that he would die. Willie and he had agreed to wrestle for it, fair and square.

Willie had said, "I'll hav' the twenty pounds, Bob, and thou can tak' the farm (loaded with debts Carolina!); but as for the watch—a genuine Lever—we'll wrestle for that."

On the top of the hill which Carrie had rolled down so gaily, the two country men had fought for possession of their dead father's watch—Willie because it was worth something in hard cash, Bob because it was his father's, and he knew that if Willie got it, it would soon be out of the family. The wind had rustled the grasses on the hillside, and the murmur of the stream sounded between their heavy breathing, but they wrestled fair, and then Willie found himself lying on his back, and knew that he had lost.

"I'd as soon have lost anything as that," sighed the farmer dolefully, his massive face quivering a little. "Ever since I can remember aught I can remember that watch. There ain't its match for time-keepin', either," he continued, as if ashamed of lamenting it for purely sentimental reasons. Carrie noticed that his eyes were grey, dark grey, and could be fierce and tender.

She laid her beringed hand on his shoulder.

"Just you leave it to me," she said almost sweetly, "I'll get it back for you. Just you give me 'is description, and I'll get the police to spot 'im, an' see if I don't send word soon as it's all right."

"You are clever," said Mr. Gibson, his face lightening; and for the first time it crossed her mind that perhaps it wasn't quite "fair and square," as he would say himself, to marry him to get out of the oyster-shop. Then she reassured herself by telling her conscience that he had never asked her if she loved him—only to be at the head of his farm because Sarah was getting old. She determined to be a good wife—feed the pigs and make him good dinners—in return for the position and freedom he would give her. It would surely be a fair exchange.

"That clock's too slow," she hinted, as he sat in the corner rocker as content as a squirrel in summer, "There's a train leaves Victoria at seven-twenty; would give you a quarter, an' you'll catch the car at the corner."

"Don't you think you might kiss me, seein' as we're almost engaged, in a way, Carrie?" he asked, twisting his Trilby.

"Not I," she said, reddening; "but you can kiss my cheek, seein' I ain't quite made my mind up yet."

When she shut up shop that night, and sat munching a frivolous cake and sipping strong tea without milk, she regarded the wall-paper steadfastly.

"I don't love 'im, that's a cert.," she said audibly; "but I'll be good to 'im, an' I'm a good cook. I've had my bit o' fun, like the rest, and never naught wrong. Things might end worse than settling down on a nice little farm. An' the sky was so nice."

Upstairs, as she undressed, she sleepily regarded the almanac of a country lover helping his sweetheart over an awkward stile.

"That feller's a bit like 'im," she thought, as she unlaced her stays. "Drat the knots! Yes; the same sort o' eyes, honest and like a dog's, fierce and softlike. Not such big han's an' feet, though. I'll tak' that picter wi' me, but I won't tell 'im as it's like 'im. 'E might laugh. An' I don't love 'im."

In a few minutes she was asleep, dreaming she was in the country climbing stiles, and that Fanny Winklesworth had bet her a cheese-tart that she didn't get back in time to open the shop for the theatres.

Meanwhile a weary woman in a country cottage was holding a vigil behind her white blind and the hanging Star-of-Bethlehem plants. She was half asleep. The clock had struck twelve when heavy footsteps coming down the country lane, white in the moonlight, roused her from her doze.

Peeping, she saw that it was indeed Farmer Gibson, and that her vigil was over. She looked at her clock on the mantelpiece.

His shadow was on the bright road, his hat on one side of his head, as he swung along singing at the top of his voice the following pathetic words with the joviality of a comic song:

"Daisies white have covered o'er
All my heart can e'er—(hiccough)—e'-er hadore,
Shall I never see—see—thee—thee—more,
Sweet—Sw-ee-et Belle Mahone?"

Only twice in his life had Gibson been known to overstep the chalk-mark of sobriety. On one occasion it was from excess of joy, as he had paid off the mortgage which encumbered the farm; and the other time was when he had been chosen as one of the jurymen on poor Molly Smith's child, the youngest of seven, the eldest not nine, burnt whilst Molly ran for an ounce of tea from the village store. Bill, her good-for-nothing husband, had been drunk in the Red Cow at the time, but because he was a man the coroner reserved his reprimand for the mother, who was the responsible person. Molly took washing in too to make ends meet. She had said nothing to all the sharp words of the coroner, telling her she was the indirect cause of her child's death through having no fireguard, which he was sure was cheap enough; and because Gibson could not get her anguish-smitten face out of his head he had taken "strong drink to make him wink." Then there had been the awful sight of the child's charred body, too, which he had remembered for weeks.

Jane Wilkins described his geniality next day to a little group of gossips.

"In t' middle o't' road, at twelve hay-hem, singing like a lark," she cried impressively. "When he had sung what I telled you"—with a sweep of her hand—"he began to *swear*, and ask where his watch was; and then he shouts, atop of his voice, 'Six oysters, Carrie, my blue-eyed darling; write to-morrow!'"

"Awful!" gasped the little group.

"I followed him down the lane to hear his talk," continued Jane, having the time of her life, "and it was a treat. Then he went over the stile, up the hill, and all the way up I heard him singing that one tune and shouting the chorus enough to waken the very dead with his 'Wait for me at 'eaven's gate.' Whilst it's my opinion he's going exactly in the other direction," she finished piously. "If that Carrie comes here, we must all give her the cold shoulder, say I. As if there ain't decent girls in his own place as would make him good wives, any one of 'em! 'Far fetched is nothing worth,' as the saying is."

They went into their little houses, the sweet sunshine all about the lane. But a vendetta had been sworn over their unromantic brooms. Some of them had marriageable daughters.

Chapter III

WHEN WOMAN MEETS WOMAN

"HELLO, Car.! What brings you 'ere?"

"My legs," she answered shortly. Then, "Ain't there some place where we can talk away from this lot?"

"Sorry there's no drawing-room, pet," answered a mocking voice.

"We'll have to get in the open to talk away from these. These are my pals. Allow me to point them out. There's Cartmel, who was a doctor once, till he went stony through the drink. Said he ought to have been a farmer by rights, but his folk thought it wasn't genteel, and put him to cutting folk up. He says there's no God, but when he's very sick, down-and-out, he says his prayers—but he's mostly drunk when he says 'em. Cartmel!"

A fat little man came from a corner where he had been reading a newspaper.

"This is Carrie; Carrie, this is Cartmel," said the dashing one. "You couldn't lend me a twist o' bacca, could you, Cartmel?"

"Sorry, old chap, but—" began Cartmel apologetically.

"Oh, well, never mind if you don't care to," laughed the smart one.

"I reely haven't got a bit," said Cartmel pathetically. "See!" and he turned out his pockets with the air of a martyr.

"You're awful mean," said Carrie scornfully to the handsome young man. "Think everybody's as mean as yourself, too."

"He's all right—all right," pleaded Cartmel, and went back to his seat in the corner, to laugh immoderately over *Quips and Cranks*.

"He's a poet, is Cartmel!" said Carrie's companion. "When he's drunk he reads his poems to us, and we all scream with laughter. They are so bloomin' sad, you know, and Cartmel is so gay as a rule. But they're not bad; I've seen worse in books that were praised to the skies."

"Why don't 'e sell 'em?" inquired Carrie, her business instincts rising.

"He wouldn't. He wouldn't show them to us only when he's drunk, old chap. He don't look it, but he's reserved."

"Ain't poets reserved?"

"Not they," scoffed the man. "They write about their love-affairs—only they call the girl a different name—for all the world to read. Bad taste, I call it. Cartmel, now, has to get the sadness out of him; but he keeps it for the benefit of his special friends—when he's drunk, like a gentleman."

The scene was a low lodging-house in Ancoats, over whose door hung a red lamp with the words, "Beds, fourpence. Men only."

Carrie had climbed irregular stairs before she entered this room full of smoke and unkempt figures. There was a strong scent of rancid bacon and red herring on the air. Sometimes a blear-eyed wisp of manhood would pass into the searching rays of the sunshine, a frying-pan in his hand and a hungry look on his unshaven face. When he had done cooking he put the knife he had bought for a penny into his pocket, lest it should get appropriated. It was cosmopolitan and democratic,

44

that knife, cutting tobacco and pigs' flesh with the same meditative hacking movement.

It was Sunday morning.

Church bells were contradicting and wrangling with each other from a score of steeples. The strong rays of the glorious sunshine shone in at the windows of the long room, making its dust a path of gold-motes and its bareness not quite so bare.

A man huddled over a pot of beer lifted his head to hear a woman's voice in the place, then took a long drink to inspire forgetfulness.

A woman's voice made him remember that he had kicked his wife to death, only she lived just over the time, or he might have swung. As it was he had done time—paid the debt; what was there to bother about? It made him remember that Polly, his daughter, was on the streets, and Tom in the Penitentiary, because sand-hawking did not pay so well as stealing, and was no sort of job.

"See that man there?" asked the handsome one of Carrie, jerking his thumb in the direction of a thin, ill-looking man crouched over the fire as if it was winter. "He plays the fiddle like an angel. Only, the other day, he was drunk and fell asleep on the flags, and some one pinched his fiddle. He has never spoken a word to any one since he told us of it."

"What drove 'im here, then?" asked Carrie, the anger with which she had entered the room clearing away before the light of human interest. From her childhood she had loved to study faces.

"His wife."

"Bad 'un?"

"Nay; she just died, and after that he simply wandered from place to place, he says, trying to find rest, and never finding it. He went all to pieces. Some men are like that—can't get along at all without a woman to fuss over them; which I call pretty weak."

"And some men," said Carrie, her face flushing, "care too much for their bloomin' little selves to worrit about other people. Just you come out. I'm going to talk to you, Charlie."

When they got into a quiet, narrow street she faced him suddenly.

"You pinched a watch the other day!" she cried, never taking her eyes from his.

"Well?" As he threw out this ejaculation he was stuffing his pipe with the Best Flake, which he had had all the time he asked Cartmel to lend him some.

"You've got to give me the ticket, that's all," she answered hotly, "or I'll give you in to the police."

He laughed.

"It wouldn't do, little girl. How would that farmer lover of yours like to know that his *fiancée* was connected with a thief? It wouldn't do, Carolina; for that's what he had written on the paper. You was clever to find out that it was my doings, though. You have brains, Carrie, only you've got a muddled idea that there's honesty in the world. There ain't. It's the fudge they teach at Sunday-school. There may be germs of it, but they're undeveloped. Tell me this, Car."—a little fiercely under his languid manner—"where's the difference between snatching a gent's watch from his pocket and snatching bread from the mouths of hundreds because they ask for a rise in starvation wages? The flax-girls are out! My! they ain't got much blood in 'em, but what they have is *red,* the red that makes revolutions. Nobody calls their boss a thief, because he lives in a villa. I only rob the overweighted of superfluous luxuries; I leave the poor alone."

"What price me?" asked Carrie fiercely.

"Oh!" he answered, looking her in the eyes, "you're my own."

She sighed and winced.

"Ain't you ever goin' to lead a decent life?" she asked wistfully.

"I tell you, little girl," he responded bitterly, "there ain't no decent life—not in all the world. No, Carrie, it's humbug. What did a decent life offer me? You remember the furnace, like hell, where I once was fool enough to sweat and moil, and we used to get 'gassed' at intervals and be carried out to revive—to revive, to go back to hell, and moil and burn; and if we asked for a rise of wages—twopence—twopence a day, mind you, it was like drawing blood from a stone! That's what your decent life spells! I know this life ain't right, either. I sponge! What's a sponge? A sponge is a thing that sucks up, Carrie, sucks life out o' other lives, and I'm that. But I am honest in knowing it. Most men don't acknowledge it to themselves, and there are many of 'em bigger sponges than I."

"Well, what about the ticket? What's the price," said Carrie, sighing deeply at the problem of things. "Ten shillings?"

"How lucky you came," he remarked, as he pocketed it. "I was wondering how I was going to get my Sunday dinner. Say, Carrie, when you are quite happy in that farm (he told me to call for a cup of tea some time!) think of me here, and give me a lift now and then. If you don't—"

"You won't dare to come to Greenmeads," exclaimed the girl. "I'll send you all the pin-money I get—only keep away. I've been a good friend to you, Charlie, and I can't think you're so mean as to ruin me like that. Keep away."

"Send the money regular," he said, as a parting shot, "or I shall be bound to put in an appearance."

She did not look round as she left the street hurriedly, fierce anger in her heart, or she would have seen that the old callous cloak he wore had dropped from him now there was no one to see.

"It *is* mean," he thought, climbing the stairs, "to sponge on Car., but I can't help it. It's the jungle law—

the survival of the fittest, the upholders of society praise so, where you've got to crush down nobler feelings, or miss a meal. No wavering—or we go under. Now what shall I have at din.?"

Charlie was Carrie's brother.

He had the same kind of cocksure manner, a little exaggerated, the same kind of blue eyes and fair hair, but in temperament he was like his father, whilst his sister took more of the nature of the hard-working mother, who had dragged herself wearily along to the Maternity Ward of the Workhouse to bear her last child—the child she had smiled wanly for, when they told her it was dead. Carrie and Charlie and Clara had all gone along with her, for their household sticks had been sold for debt.

The children had gone about the ward telling the nurses that their father had gone away to America, with a feeling of importance, though they knew nothing of America except that it was away.

Carrie remembered her mother lying in that room, and their being lifted up by turns to gaze upon the pale face. Charlie and she had quarrelled about her afterwards, as the nurse pulled them away.

"I finks she's awful crushed," Carrie had whimpered. "She'll smother like the cat in mad Willie's oven, if they put the lid on. Where's the little doll she's got come from?"

"It's a baby," Charlie had told her. "Doctor grows 'em in his garden."

Then they had looked out on the ghost-like trees in the grounds below, with the snow coming down.

Charlie had suddenly begun to cry for his mother, blubbering so loudly that the nurse had come.

"Hush, you can't make that row here," she said severely. "Want your mother? Well, you can't have her. She's asleep. Play!"

But they had not played.

All the afternoon they stood and watched the snow coming down, nestling together, and once the porter, a short-necked, comical-looking man, came in and looked at them.

"Here's a book," he said, "with pictures of Jack and the Beanstalk. Poor little kiddies," and he had walked hastily away.

Clara had made friends with another girl, a girl with bandages on her hands because of eczema, but Charlie and Carrie had looked at the snow together, and quarrelled about the pictures in the book, saying, "'Tis" and "'Tisn't" till they were tired out, and it was too dark to watch the snow coming down.

The next day it still snowed, and the next.

"What's that? Look!" and Charlie and she had pressed their faces against the window, watching the coffin carried along—a black line in a world of whiteness.

Suddenly Charlie had given a piercing scream.

"It's mamma. They are putting her in the dirt," he said, with a dim memory of having once been with his mother to see a neighbour interred.

The matron, keen, clever, and hard, came upon the scene.

"Come, come, we can't have this noise. Look how good your sister is," pointing to Clara, playing in the corner.

"Clara," answered Carrie to the nurse, "don't belong to *us*. *We's* pals."

When Charlie had screamed himself hoarse, Carrie had stolen to the window. All was white now again—the black line covered from sight.

Tea came round, and Charlie was hungry, and she gave him her cake as well.

He never mentioned his mother after.

Then they grew—Charlie was put to a trade, and Carrie trained for service, whilst Clara had been taken out of the House by a relative because she was her namesake.

Carrie thought of all this as she walked away—indeed, she never saw her brother without these memories quickening in her mind. She judged him, and then she looked beyond him and saw the little boy screaming himself hoarse against something unknown and terrible, and saw herself holding his hand, and promising to love him always, and beyond the snow falling ceaselessly as if to cover something.

Charlie had been his mother's boy.

Carrie gave him her cake always when he seemed sad, and once—when he threw his toy at the nurse for scolding him and then ran away so that Carrie was suspected and shaken for it—she shut her lips firmly, and crept to the window after getting her breath back, looked out, out there, wondering if what they had put into the earth knew, and loved her for it.

After leaving her brother, vexed with him for his meanness, yet proud of him against her will, for his handsome and elegant appearance, Carrie went to the pawnshop to get the watch out.

A baldheaded man in red velvet waistcoat with nap well-nigh worn away, gave it to her, after testing the sovereign she gave him with his yellow teeth—as if to prove its goodness.

"Think I'm a forger?" scoffed Carrie.

"I wasn't sayin' nuthin'," said the man in the red waistcoat. "I've been done that often—"

"You! You was born with one eye open," said Carrie, and slammed the door.

She rubbed the watch carefully on a bit of silk, and afterwards burned the silk to free it from the atmosphere of the baldheaded man. Putting the watch in her drawer she locked it up, and, sitting down, got out a packet of stationery.

"A postcard will go for a ha'penny," she murmured.

Carrie was careful in little things to be careless in others, and just now wanted a new costume.

She addressed the card to Hilltop Farm.

Sarah looked at it the next morning as Jack Cole, the postman, delivered it. Then she reared it against her brother's cup, as he had not come down. Then she thought she heard the stairs creak, and wondered, and finally took it up, turned it over and over, and read these words:

"DERE MISTER GIBSON,

"I've got what you lost. This is also to say I will take the place you offered me the other day. No more at present.

Yours,

"CARRIE BROWN."

Sarah Gibson was so upset on reading this mysterious message that she allowed the toast to burn, and put boiling water into an empty teapot. Then she leaned disconsolately against the mantelpiece.

She could not have thought it, she told herself.

Sometimes, when she had grumbled at having so much work, Robert had threatened to bring a housekeeper in, but she had never taken him seriously.

After all these years, during which she had worked like a slave and made herself many enemies through keeping designing women at arm's length, Robert was turning her out—for a hired servant. Hired servants! Creatures who told every manner of thing out of the house, and gave the kitchen plates away to their poverty-stricken families! A mist came before her eyes, making them hot and sore. The stairs really creaked now.

He was coming, she knew, and her form lost its drooping lines and stiffened into proud scorn. She gripped the handle of the hot teapot and looked straight across at him as he stood in the doorway, a solid figure stretching himself, his jacket on his arm.

"Got a cold?" inquired the farmer genially, dropping into a chair, and hearing a little sniff.

Sarah made no reply, but poured out his tea.

Even the dark-beamed kitchen looked gay this morning, the sun was shining so brightly. The short blue curtains at the window looked more blue, the geraniums more scarlet. Beyond the blue curtain shone a yard or two of green hillside.

Bunches of dry, sweet herbs hung from the rafters, with a flitch of their home-cured. Oaten cakes were drying over the clothes-rack, whilst inside the flashing steel fender stood loaf-tins, with the white dough beginning to swell smoothly.

The big Airedale, Jack, half rose as his master entered, emitting a long, far-away rattle from the depths of his interior—then crouched on the homemade rug once more.

The farmer felt ashamed of his conduct on the previous night, as Sarah preserved rigid silence. He had a dim recollection of her standing in her green nightdress prophesying that he would end up at the gallows foot, and looking not unlike an executioner herself to his disordered imagination.

He was stirring his tea round and round, sheepishly trying to find some apology for himself, and did not catch sight of the postcard laid beside his pot.

"I'm sorry I came home late last night," he got out at last.

"But the fact is, Sarah, a stroke of good business turned my head."

No answer came from Sarah. Her arms were folded, and a thumb was wagging below each elbow in a manner that alarmed him. To do her justice, Sarah was not aggrieved at Robert's little outburst, though she thought it her duty to remonstrate with him. She had faith that she had brought Robert up right, and that he would turn out right, despite his deficiencies. It was the mysterious card and his prior mysterious business which had put her out.

Robert heaved a sigh.

It was worse when Sarah refused to talk than when she refused to stop.

Turning to his pot of tea for comfort, he spied the card, seized upon, and read it; then, forgetful of Sarah's presence, raised a shout that made the rafters ring. Half of the joy was for the recovery of his father's watch, and the other half for Carrie's well-understood message. Phlegmatic as he had appeared to that romantic young woman, after the gushings of Lord Digglemore, the farmer had really taken a great fancy to her.

After his shout he turned to look at the kitchen, as if imagining her young figure flitting about in it, and Sarah in all her bulk and rigidness met his sight, and he blushed, like a criminal caught red-handed.

"I never thought I'd see the day when a housekeeper would be brought to Hilltop," said Sarah, smiting a fly that was walking recklessly on her bare forearm.

"I'm bringing no housekeeper," cried Robert, looking innocent of such a heinous crime. "I'm only going to be married."

"Only," repeated Sarah, turning deathly pale, and she tottered over to her mother's old rocking-chair and sat down, swaying herself to and fro in mute anguish.

"Wasn't you saying the other week that you was sick o' havin' every hand's-turn to do yourself?" queried Robert, scratching his head in perplexity. "An' that you wouldn't mind my settlin' down—"

"Yes," interrupted his sister, "I said Elsie Thomas was a fine strapping girl with plenty o' common sense and money. Money? Why, she doesn't know what she's worth! I could ha' got on with her without a—"

"Well, *I couldn't,*" said Robert hotly. "I can't stand big women—they flabbergast me. (Sarah sat straight in her chair; she was not small herself.) "Mother was a wee bit o' a thing I could toss up to the rafters. Sarah"—pleadingly—"we two are not poor, and needn't worry too much about money. I'm hale and strong and the farm is clear of debt, and a man can't have more'n enough, Sarah."

Sarah's thumbs worked faster than ever.

"Humph!" she said, with more contempt in that little grunt than it is easy to imagine. Robert's patience went helter-skelter as he made a quick comparison of Elsie and Carrie.

"Elsie has a voice like a rusty kettle kicked round the lanes by brass-nosed clogs, and a skin like a nutmeg-grater, she has. In fact, Sarah, I wouldn't ha' her to wife for as much gowd as this hilltop is deep. I've waited a long time, Sarah, you'll mind—I'm no boy—and having waited, I'll ha' summat I can look at when I come home after a hard day on the land, and feel lifted up by looking at."

"Men! They can't see no farther than a bit o' pink flesh," said Sarah, witheringly. "Beauty's only skin deep, Robert."

"But ugliness goes to t' bone," he retorted. "Carrie's none so good-looking that a chap would lose his eyesight by looking at her, but one part of her face doesn't seem to belong to somebody else."

"Elsie can't help her looks," cried Sarah, warmly.

"No," acknowledged the desperate farmer. "But she could keep inside."

"Elsie nursed her grandmother when no one else could bide nigh her for the smell," went on Sarah. "And the way she brought up that suckin' pig when the sow died was a picture."

Robert felt a little mean in having said that Elsie should keep inside now. Doubtless she was as innocent of wishing to marry him as he was of wishing her to do so.

So he sucked his brier pipe, and the anger cooled out of his heart.

There was silence for some time, broken only by the bubbling of the giant kettle on the bar over the affectionate crooning (or was it asthma?) of Jack, the Airedale, with the creak of the old rocking-chair and the crunching of the burned toast between Robert's large white teeth. Sarah spoke first.

"Who is this woman? An' remember that mother left me t' clock, an' the single bed, an' the—"

She had hit Robert in a sore place this time. She knew well enough that her brother had not the slightest intention of her leaving the farm, and did it from the absolutely selfish desire to give pain. In her jealousy of this unknown woman, suddenly coming out of nowhere, she wished to wound Robert through the deep affection he had for herself, for family love is often as selfish as sex love.

The big fellow sat there, a vision of his sister driven out by Carrie in his foolish head, a vision of Sarah with her multitudinous cardboard boxes holding the heavy silk and beaded clothes long since out of fashion, waiting some crowning event that never took place, going down the hillside.

"Now, Sarah," he said in a disturbed way, "you know me different from that. I want you both. Carrie will get along all right with you. Lord bless us, there are enough o' rooms in the old house," and the pot he had taken up in his horny hand trembled.

"Who is she?" reiterated Sarah.

"She's Carolina Evelyn Brown," he answered, his face lighting up as he spoke, "and she sells oysters in Ardwick Green, Manchester."

"Manchester!" gasped Sarah. "Did I bring you up all these years to be snared by a woman from Manchester? They had a barmaid fro' Manchester at the Cow once, and a fine blossom she was! Robert, why didn't yo' go a bit farther—to Egypt or Siberia for a wife? 'Far-fetched an'—"

"I picked her up on my own land," put in Robert, quickly. "She was just a-growin' there like the buttercups and daisies, and seemed to belong to the hill as much."

"Buttercups and fiddlesticks!" snorted Sarah. "Well, I've got the churning to do."

"Hi, Sarah," called Robert as she was passing from the kitchen. "She has relatives here, so you can't look on her as a foreigner. You know, her sister Clara lives in the third house, Cherry Tree Row."

"But nobody knew them before they came," said Sarah, and whisked away.

"Jack!"

The dog rose and came to lay his nose between Robert's knees.

"It isn't going to be all plain sailing, Jack, old boy," said the farmer. The dog blinked expressively. "Lord, what sense dogs has, and how they stick to you what comes or goes! You may get drunk, or married, or any manner. Jack, old chap, I'd sell the last slate on the roof to buy thee a licence. I wonder when she'll marry me, Jack. Shall I go and see?"

Jack barked suddenly.

On the Saturday he took Jack with him to see Carrie, and after a few anxious sniffs Jack decided that she would do, and sat down near her feet, though he barked every time the bell rang. Carrie gave Robert the watch back, carefully explaining that she had got it by a hunt amongst the pawn-brokers' shops, and that she had threatened to give up the pawnbroker as a receiver of stolen goods if he did not tip it up.

"You are wonderful clever, Carrie," said the farmer. "I expect it comes of living in the city."

After a little while they had all settled, picking up the plans between the pealing of the shop-bell. Robert was careful to explain to Carrie that Sarah was a little out of the common, and had ways of her own. She had been mistress of the farm so long that it would be hard for her to play second fiddle, but give her time and she'd be as good as new butter and as nice as ninepence, he said. She had a warm, faithful heart underneath, he went on, and Carrie would get on with her, he knew. Human beings fondly think that their best wishes will breed success.

Robert made the masculine mistake of supposing Sarah would see Carrie with his eyes when once she got over the shock of his marriage.

Carrie sold her shop (five pounds for the fittings), and spent the proceeds on the wedding-dress. It was a romantic creation of gauzy lace over sky-blue, and Julia, her friend in Ancoats, sitting up in bed to look at it, closed her eyes in reverence as Carrie unfolded it in the long box.

"Poor folk only gets married once," said Carrie. "They can't afford no divorces, and so they might as well make a shine once in their lives. Did you ever hear of the navvy who said to his pore old mother, when he saw her dead in her coffin, 'Why, mother, what a h—ll of a swell you are! I hardly know you'?"

"Oh, Carrie," said Julia, between being shocked and amused. Then, "How I wish I could come to the wedding. But at two o'clock I'll shut my eyes, and see you in that frock."

The little wedding took place at Greenmeads Church on a sunny afternoon. All was very still, excepting for the cawing of the rooks in the tall trees, whose swaying shadows were thrown on the aisle floor. Robert met

Carrie at the station, and as they walked along for two miles to the church he told her that there his mother was married, and his father christened, and that he himself had been christened there. She forgot the gauzy dress as she listened to him, and a little fear far down in her heart stirred again, and the whole affair seemed more than a mere business deal. The cawing of the rooks during the service seemed to mix in with it and the running sound of the minister's voice, and it was only when old Matty Thomas gave a loud sneeze just in the most solemn part that she felt relieved, and as if she could laugh. As they left the church, with Nell Fish and Albert Jenkins, who had "stood" for them, a poor thin woman with a shawl on her head came nearer to get a glimpse of the bride's dress (the talk of Greenmeads for weeks!), and Carrie saw that she was about to be a mother.

Miserably overworked and tired she looked, but her face lit up with envy, admiration, glory at the sight of the dress, with its hints of exquisite colour through the mysterious folds of lace.

"Who is she?" whispered Carrie to Robert.

"Who is who?" he asked, turning his head, and following Carrie's eyes, thus seeing the draggled woman, and answered, "Oh, that's Annie Whitehead. Her husband is the biggest brute in the place. She used to be considered the village beauty."

Caw, caw, caw!

The mournfully insistent cries of the rooks sounded from the trees as they went down the churchyard path between the graves.

"Robert," said Carrie, "what does she stop with him for?"

"Who? Oh, Annie, you mean? 'Spect she likes him, spite of all. 'E hasn't a friend, not even 'mong his own folk, and hers don't have dealings with her because she stays with him. It's strange, but the worse he goes, the closer she clings to him."

Carrie shivered. If that was what marriage meant—

Then they were covered with confetti, and passed through a little throng of people, mostly very old or very young, expectant of matrimonial joy opening the purse along with the heart of the farmer. A cab which should have been there to take them to the church managed to arrive to take them back along the road to the little grey stone wall, and the cabby, somewhat drunk, pocketed the extra tip with stumbling thanks, and Robert flung out of the window to the throng that had followed them a shower of small change.

"Hope you'll have much happiness," shouted one after another as they passed over the stile, whilst others more impudent shouted that they should come up to the farm for supper.

Carrie listened to the talk of Nell Fish as they climbed the hill to the farm somewhat absently. The thin, anxious face of the woman in the church haunted her. It seemed more wonderful to her, that sort of love, than the other she had read of in the novelette. By and by Nell got linked with her sweetheart, and Robert and Carrie walked behind, the wind blowing freshly in their faces, and a deep blue sky in front of them. There was a load on the woman's mind. She looked at her companion.

His eyes were shining with joy—the deep joy that comes late, like warm, long days of sun after grey ones of toil in a wet spring. There was no mistaking the fact that to him it was more than a bargain—an exchange of goods for work. Carrie knew that should she be struck with paralysis as she climbed the hill Robert would gather her life up, maimed and deadened as it was, in his strong arms, and tend it like a woman, without a murmur. A mist came before her eyes.

"Robert," she said, with a voice shaking a little, "if—if you treated me like that woman's husband treats her, I should feel like giving you a rat powder!"

Robert's laugh echoed genially and happily down the hill, and over the stream at the foot, startling a bird who was teaching her second brood that year to fly.

"I shouldn't ever think of treating a dog as Whitehead treats his wife," answered Robert, gravely. "I'm a reasonable, rational, human being, Carrie, and don't ask miracles—for Annie is a miracle. I'm not a toffee angel, but I try to deal fair, and I like fair myself. I'll be able to put up with a lot from you, 'cause I chose you for my mate as soon as I heard your voice—so long as you're straight with me, of course. There's the farm, Carrie!"

She felt relieved, seeing that he was not asking for anything extraordinary, and some of her old buoyancy came back, though it felt queer to be helped up the hill. All her life she had been "on her own." She could have got on better without Robert's arm, but she did not tell him so, and tried to make her quick, short steps come in harmony with his long, strong stride.

"I never thought marriage was anything so mixed up as this," thought Carrie. Then she stole a glance at Robert's face as he plodded up the hill.

"He isn't a bad working partner," she thought again. "And he's rather nice—"

The farm, square and strong, and with something suggestive of Robert about it to Carrie, stood against the sky. He didn't say anything at all as he opened the door, and helped her in, because he found it a trifle hard to say anything about what lay nearest his heart, unless he had made it come nearer his tongue's tip by a few pints of Wheatley's best. He was the exact opposite to Lord Digglemore, who always talked most of the most sacred things.

But the welcome home was written large in his honest eyes, and in his broad, beaming smile, that seemed to introduce her at once to Sarah, Jack the Airedale, and the geraniums.

Sarah shook hands with her sister-in-law in a way that entirely satisfied Robert, and showed her where to put her hat. In fact, Robert was so pleased with the way in which their meeting went off that he escaped into the scullery, and shook hands with himself as he did when the Anconas laid their first eggs.

When he came out Carrie and Sarah were both talking, leaning against the dresser.

"'Tis grand weather," said Sarah, and Carrie answered that it was remarkable weather.

"Of course, I knew that Sarah couldn't help but like Carrie," said the farmer to himself, and went off to talk to Nell Fish.

But the two women knew (and each knew that the other knew) that it was going to be war.

Carrie seemed altogether too cocksure for Sarah's liking—an oyster-girl from the city ought to show a diffident and humble attitude, she considered, particularly on her first arrival. It was a great thing for her, coming to the comforts of a prosperous farm, and she ought to have said something to that effect. Truth to tell, Sarah would have despised Carrie utterly if she had taken such a course. She did not count the fact that Carrie was coming to help with the work of the farm, and earn her porridge just as much as she had ever done in her life.

Carrie, on her part, was repelled by the visage of Robert's sister.

The iron-grey hair and cold grey eyes sent a shiver down her spine, and the way in which she smoothed her blue apron down irritated her as much as Carrie's manner of taking the pins from her hat had disturbed Sarah.

Jealousy ages old sprang up in each of their hearts—jealousy and thirst for power.

The unimaginative pride of the discoverer was in Carrie's heart, and the bitter enmity of the old native in the older woman's breast.

"Take a chair, and make yourself at 'ome," invited Sarah, and Carrie sat down on the chair that Sarah had not pointed out to her. "You'll be comfortabler here," urged Sarah, but Carrie smiled in her little, frivolous way, and stayed where she was.

"We'll ha' to wait until they come," said Sarah, reaching the linen bag for the tea-urn from a metal teapot in the cupboard.

"The guests," explained Robert, in answer to Carrie's look.

He told her a little of the different characters and lives of those invited, as they walked up and down the garden paths, and he pulled her arm through his. A bee frightened Carrie out of her wits almost, though Robert vowed they were harmless, bonny creatures.

He took her round to the sties, and showed her Peter the pig, and was disappointed in her wanting to get away. Then they went round to the henhouse, and he explained the method of feeding.

"The white ones are nice," said Carrie, admiringly. "Let us feed 'em, Bob."

"They should ha' their feed just afore they go up," answered Robert, "but come in, and get a tinful of meal from that bag. Now," as they came out again, "throw it."

"Oh, Bob, they're fightin'," cried Carrie, and fetched out another tinful of corn, though Robert winked at this breaking of the rules.

Just as they turned away from the hen-house Robert snatched a kiss, a very respectful kiss, and forgot the hens entirely.

"Robert, they've come," said Sarah coldly, and Carrie's blush faded into whiteness—the pallor of anger. She suspected Sarah of having watched them all the time. "Robert," said Sarah, *sotto voce*, in the little scullery, "I'd be obliged if yo' wouldn't make a fool o' yourself before everybody."

Robert laughed loud, unabashed.

"'Tis not every day a man has a chance o' being a fool, Sarah," he answered. "Carrie, here's your sister Clara come up, and the childer would like to see the pigs. Come along, and we'll introduce them to the hens."

"Some other time," said Carrie, slowly, and then she smiled, and he forgot that her voice sounded chill.

The way in which Sarah cut the bread for tea, so quickly and deftly, made Carrie feel like a guest instead of a bride in her own home. Nothing of this showed on her laughing face, and she chattered frivolously. When Sarah begged her to make herself "at home," there was something in the tone of her voice that suggested an opposite wish to Carrie.

Sarah's glance at the confetti which had fallen from the crown of the bride's hat made Carrie think she was itching to reach brush and shovel to sweep it up, and she was not far wrong, for order was a strong point of Sarah's.

The sun and shadow played amongst the window-plants which had been brought home by Robert's father twenty years ago. The birds in the tree at the gable end called to each other, and between her fits of light talk, Carrie sat as one in a dream, amongst all these strange people. She felt sure that it was a dream, from which she should start awake with the shop-bell pealing like mad, to hear the crunch of the sanded floor under some heavy foot.

Robert's face, however, was very large and real whenever she glanced at him across the table, as was also his genial laughter which shook the table and made the cups and saucers rattle, until the cups and saucers rattling made Jack bark.

The few guests who had arrived were villagers, dressed in their best, who spoke very slowly, mostly about people who were dead, it seemed to Carrie. But after tea there was an inrush of uninvited guests who announced their intentions to stay to supper. These guests were less formal, and asked if there was to be no dancing. David Grimes, an old man from a neighbouring hamlet, had brought his fiddle, and the table was pushed back against the dresser.

Some of the young women who had come to dance had dreamed for years of taking possession of Hilltop Farm and its master. They were intoduced to Carrie and hoped she'd be "'appy."

Carrie knew the talk for what it was worth.

She was a stranger in a strange land, but meant to fight it out.

Clara had had to return home after tea was over through a severe headache.

Yes, Carrie meant to fight it out. The old spirit that had brought her clean and straight through the perils of an unprotected girlhood rose in her heart as she glanced in the women's faces. If they scorned her, she would scorn them. They would see who would eat humble pie first, she thought.

Robert sang in the joy of his heart "Little Brown Jug"; joined the country dance, and chose Elsie, the detested, as his partner; and blew the whistle for old David to stop playing at the end of the movements, for old David was deaf as the proverbial post, though his wife had been dropping eel-oil in his ears for years, and still did it with unabated faith. David said he had unluckily left his music- book at home, and there were only two tunes he could remember without the book, besides the "Country Dance" melody. When the company was gone, Carrie could still hear the painfully monotonous bars of that pathetic melody "The Captain with his Whiskers," and the yet more famous "Tar-ra-ra-ra-boom-de-ay."

One by one the guests departed.

Sarah took her candle and left the two sitting by a bonny fire. When she had gone, Robert pulled the chain and extinguished the lamplight, so that there was only the rosy luminance of the fire. The shadows dancing on the wall seemed to listen to what they said.

The great clock ticked deeply, sombrely, or so it seemed to Carrie. It would have been more fitting, she thought, if she could have heard the wheels rolling over grey pavements outside. It seemed as if she and Robert were alone—alone in the silent and sleeping world.

"Carrie," said Robert, "you haven't even kissed me yet," and he drew up his chair to hers, and sat with his arm round her shoulder, more like a schoolboy than a grown man. Love had made him suddenly a boy again.

She touched his cheek a moment with her fresh, roguish lips, and he was content.

"You're sure you love me, Carrie?" he said. "Better than anybody you've ever known?" There was a jealousy in his voice, for all those years in which he had played no part.

She nodded her head.

It was true that she liked him better than any man she had met. Her hand lay passively in his, and a contented feeling stole over her. His touch did not seem strange, but like that of a friend met after long years. Yet this was not love, she thought, such as she had read of.

"I mustn't keep my little wife up—late hours dropped now, Carrie," and he took their candle and stamped the fire lower in the grate.

Sarah heard them coming up and pass her door.

Under the quilt her face was wet with bitter tears. For the first time for years she had gone to bed without locking up, and she felt as a queen deposed.

"Good night, Sarah!" called Robert's happy voice, and the floor shook with his step as he went past.

"Good night!" said Carrie, in sleepy tones, but only silence answered.

"She is asleep," whispered Robert, and walked more softly.

"What's that?" cried Carrie, in the middle of her sleep, waking suddenly, and Robert saw her listening face by the pale dawn. He had been making out the outlines of throat, brow, and cheek for some time, in quiet delight.

"'Tis only Jack," he answered tenderly; "he always lies on the mat outside my door," and he drew her face close to his own, watching her till she dropped to sleep again. He saw the day steal into the room, the objects brighten in the glow, and heard the fresh calls of the birds and the murmur of the leaves about their window. Once when she flung her hand over the coverlet he put it over her again, as if he was a mother covering a child. With wide-open, shining eyes he stared into the full glory of the daylight, wondering that he had never noticed so fair a coming of the light before.

"What's all that rustling?" cried Carrie, waking, the mists of sleep yet in her eyes. "I've heard it ever so long."

"It's the poultry brushing themselves up for breakfast," Robert assured her, and she looked at him a moment, then discovered that he was joking, and burst out laughing.

"Tell your grandmother that," she retorted.

Sarah was sitting at the table when they came down.

"Jam or marmalade?" she inquired, trying to keep the quaver from her voice. Never had she experienced so miserable a dawn.

"Jam," answered Carrie, the smile dying from her eyes at the hard tone.

"The wife said 'Jam'", said Robert, and served her himself—as if she was a baby.

Chapter IV

THE GREEN HILL

ROBERT had to go to Bringford to the horse fair after breakfast, as one of his horses was quite worn out.

He kissed Carrie in the little porch looking out on the garden, with its display of stocks and asters glowing gaily in the wind.

"You'll be all right till I come back. Sarah'll show you round the farm, and tell you all sorts of funny things about our village. You won't be lost?"

"I shall be all right," she cried cheerfully, and waved her hand to him all the way down the hill. Then she went in, stood in the middle of the kitchen, and said, "Is there anything I can do? I'd like to make myself useful."

Her sister-in-law said there was nothing, with a stiff tilt of her head, so after standing by the window for some time, listening to the clank of Sarah's clogs, Carrie went and stood on the doorstep.

"Old cat!" she murmured. "Well, I mustn't take her seriously. I'll just go and roll down the hill a bit and see things upside down. The same old sky."

In the afternoon she inquired of her sister-in-law how far it was to Bringford.

"Four miles or so," answered Sarah, and when Carrie got ready and went out, she remarked to the coffee-grinder, "To think of it. She's gone after him!"

Bringford Horse Fair was an old institution. It brought hundreds of people together once a year, and there was much cheating and drinking of ale.

Carrie paused in the main street and bought some penny-winkles at a stall, and watched the horses being run about. She liked the horsy smell about the street and the funny men shouting at the tops of their voices.

The rain came on, but Carrie followed a crowd and came to the busiest part of the town.

A grubby man stood on the edge of the flags, watching her face as she munched a sandwich. Carrie thought he looked hungry.

"Have a bit?" she asked, holding out a sandwich, and he answered, "Rather—with you!"

She flushed.

"Nice day for a walk," he said, winking expressively.

"Not if my husband knows it," she answered, looking at him. "Think I was gone on you 'cause I offered you a bite? Why, I'd ha' done that for a monkey at the Belle Vue. Does your mother know you're out?"

The man laughed coarsely, but blinked a little at her withering tone and flushed, scornful face.

Carrie was vaguely surprised at herself for being so angry, most of all that her heart was beating furiously.

Looking up, she saw her husband leaning out of a window opposite, watching the horses with a keen, eager face. Crossing the street quickly she made her way to his side.

"Why, Carrie!" he exclaimed, then, "Come up the stairs. I've paid for this room. If I'd guessed you would like to come I'd have brought you this morning. Sarah never would come."

It was another link between the two.

He told Carrie a good deal about horses that afternoon, and they walked out of the town leading brown Tommy, as fine a horse as had graced the fair.

When they got on the road he swung his wife up into the saddle, and thus they went back to Greenmeads.

Sarah was out on their return, but there was a brown dish on the top of the oven.

"She has made a 'whistler,'" said Robert, sniffing, on opening the door. "No one can make whistlers like Sarah," and he explained the dish.

"Oh?" said Carrie, jealously. "Fancy that now! And it's a whistler because you whistle for the meat, is it? I'll remember."

"Rolls down the hill in the morning like a child, and rides home like a queen in the afternoon, and talks to him about horses all the evening," said Sarah to herself the next day. "And I brought him up for this!" She went into the scullery.

There was Carrie, sleeves up to her elbows, cutting up potatoes and onions with minute care.

"I'm making a whistler," she said, with a smile. "Bob likes 'em."

"So he does," answered Sarah, and walked back into the kitchen, where she stood regarding John Bunyan as if he had done her a grievous wrong.

Chapter V

STORMS BREAK

CARRIE had been married three months. It was a chill November day, with lowering clouds ranged across the sky, threatening to break on the hills. She was shelling peas in a brown dish, as she sat in the chimney nook, and had on an old lindsey skirt she had brought from the shop, with a blouse, too, that she used to wear. She could not look down at the dish in her lap without seeing the familiar pattern on her breast, the lilac spray with its one green leaf, and it gave her a feeling of homesickness for the gritty shop, the faces of the customers, and the long line of cabs that waited just off the kerb; for the throng, laughing, talking, eating nuts, pouring in and out of the theatres across the way.

Hilltop Farm seemed to be Robert's home, but not her home. She felt that she wanted some things of her own—her own pictures, the bright-coloured almanacs she had accumulated and framed in rushes, fastening the corners with blue ribbon, her own strip of faded carpet that had done such good service by the bedside, and the old alarum-clock with its gay little bustle, that seemed to say "Wake up! Wake up!" with a peal of shrill laughter, and the same sort of voice that the hawkers in the street had, a bustling city voice.

Greenmeads was sluggishly dull. The old clock, like a black upturned coffin in the corner, seemed didactic and reproving, like Sarah. Over the settle, with its Paisley print cover and cushions, was a motto in wool and silk warning the beholder to take count of the golden march of the hours. A picture of John Bunyan engaged in writing "Pilgrim's Progress" was matched on the other side of the dresser by Milton dictating "Paradise Lost" to Cromwell, and in the bedrooms such cheerful subjects as "The Judgment Day" in steel engraving looked from the wall, with little mottoes bidding one to fear the Lord and to be not weary in well-doing. She had got into the routine of the farm work now and did it faithfully and well, and was comparatively happy when she was working; but sometimes in the evenings, when Sarah sat silent and rigid, knitting as if she would never cease till the crack of doom, and Robert was working late in the orchard, a feeling that she could scream would seize her.

The brooding silence of the hills, the stillness that floated up from the drowsy village as she stood sometimes for a moment on the farm threshold, oppressed her. Particularly on grey days such as the present, her spirits were heavy. Between being born and buried nothing seemed to happen in Greenmeads, or so it seemed to Carrie, now that the first glamour of the place was gone. The nearest picture-palace was five miles away, and on the rare occasions she had visited it, coming back to the quiet farm with a confused series of comic-tragic subjects in her mind, Sarah had given the pans an extra banging to show her disapproval, and Carrie had settled herself in the cosiest chair with a yellow-backed novelette to show how little effect it had upon her!

Their battle was a silent one, and was of omissions rather than commissions, and Robert, man-like, seeing not the absolute signs of recognized warfare, refused to believe it was brewing. Such are the wars between nations—silent, imperceptible things at first, until the most incredulous cannot deafen his ears to the growing menace.

Sometimes she would have a walk down to see her sister, but Clara was disappointed after her first visit to the farm, when Sarah was like a death's-head at a feast, and cast the atmosphere of a cold-storage on the kitchen as she had tea with Carrie. What was the good of having a sister who was mistress of a farm if one couldn't come when one liked? said Clara, as if she had been hardly dealt with.

Robert was more than kind, and, finding out his wife's love for reading, always brought her a book back when he visited the town to buy his provender and hen meal. The short-sighted man in the market-house, who sat bunched up, and parted with a book as a miser with his money, got used to the strong, thick-set figure and the ruddy face under the broad-brimmed hat. Robert himself had a great disdain for this meagre man, who coughed as he sat doubled up in his chair, and parted so regretfully with his treasures. But after a time he discovered that the meagre man knew exactly the kind of book that suited Carrie, and he then admitted that probably he had not been born in vain. He regarded him with a pitying scorn for all that, wondering how he would look driving a plough through deep furrows.

He further extended his kindness to the Brown family by little gifts to the children—a bag of nuts, or of rosy apples from his own orchard, or a spinning-top from town.

One day Robert brought a brightly coloured Hans Andersen, so beautifully illustrated that Carrie felt she could not give it to Billy, but kept it for herself.

Her pride prevented her asking Clara to come to the farm often; for all that she felt the farm ought to be her home as much as, if not more than, Sarah's. The village wives and maidens looked on her with scarcely veiled contempt as one whom they knew nothing of, an outsider and stranger. After a few dutiful attempts at making friends with them she grew as contemptuous in return as they were. Hate begets hate no less than the reverse.

So Carrie roamed about a great deal after her work was done with Billy and Joe. With the children the moors around never oppressed her, and they sat often on dry beds of rusty heather opening round eyes to the wonderful tales of dear Hans Andersen.

Sometimes she went into the stables and talked to Robert as he brushed brown Tommy down; but as that handsome creature proved both a kicker and a biter Robert refused to have her in during that operation, after the discovery.

A restless feeling to which Carrie was entirely new sometimes took possession of her when she was not working. "It is the country," she thought, "after the busy shop."

On this November day Carrie had promised to take Billy and Joe to Stonybrook, where they would gather scarlet hips to string for beads. From the farmhouse window she watched the lowering clouds. She had made the smooth, flagged floor, with its rich golden-brown tints, fresh and clean as brush and soap and water could bring it. A batch of bread, crisp and light, was cooling on the white-topped table with half a score of homely muffins. She had dusted their bedroom, and the peas she was shelling were for the broth for supper. Robert had gone to Bringford to see about purchasing a new horse, for his own favourite had suddenly died, after a few hours' illness.

As Carrie shelled the peas she watched the clouds swoop into the sky, like so many huge, dark-winged birds, and knew that a storm was gathering.

The oppressive atmosphere made her head ache. She felt she must go out if it rained cataracts. Sarah was more than flesh and blood could tolerate, for never a word had she spoken that week but what was absolutely necessary in the working of the household. At night as the wind went round the house she was knitting or patching, like an automaton, and Robert's arrival was generally belated now, as the days were shorter, and there was so much to see to. When he did come in, with his breezy presence and his cheery "How's things?" she sometimes felt she could kiss him almost, without being asked—if Sarah hadn't been there. Not that she loved him. Loved him, indeed! When you loved a body, your voice got into your throat and wouldn't come to the tip of the tongue, and your heart beat double as fast as it ought to—so the books said. She had none of these symptoms. She only felt that it was pleasant to feel he was there—there was an air of freedom in the kitchen that was elsewise absent from it when only she and Sarah were in it. Robert somehow saved her from Sarah—Sarah of the sphinx-like face, who knit and knit and knit, as if she would never stop.

Once or twice Carrie had tried to say that Sarah need not think her an interloper, that they could be friends; but one look at her face scattered the softer thoughts. "Old cat!" she would say mentally, and wish Robert would come in. "Of course she thinks I married him for the farm!" and then the restless pain would wake in her heart, and she would walk to the garden gate. "There you are, Bob!" she would say jovially as he came up the hill.

The smell of his rough coat, the damp, fresh touch of it as he came in from the outdoor world, was reviving. His funny way of humming, all out of tune, as he dropped into a chair, would make her laugh to herself, whilst acknowledging that if he had not done it she would have been sorry. She began to study his character in her shrewd woman's way, as well as his tastes in the culinary line. It was interesting, and it gave her an advantage over Sarah. She beat down her prejudices and pride to make friends with his few friends.

Crowing Molly, the washerwoman, who lived in the little house with the handrail along the stone steps, was one of Bob's cronies, because far away back in the past she used to give him toffee made specially for him, and used to amuse him by imitating all the sounds of a farmyard. She told Carrie she had done it to keep her from moping, and to keep the soap-suds out of her mind, though they'd got into her bones, and Carrie would sit rocking in a chair whilst Crowing Molly was by turn a cow, horse, ass, hen, dandy cockerel, or a lark, singing lost in a world of blue. To win Crowing Molly she had sought far and wide for a mangy cat, bringing it back at length.

"They said you were proud," Crowing Molly had said wonderingly. "Aye, I am fain to get Tib back. It isn't much of a thing"—looking at the animal critically—"but when I've done a hard day, and I'm having my supper, the thing looks at me like a Christian."

She told Carrie stories of Robert when he was a boy, and of his pulling a child from the Bringford Canal and coming to dry his clothes on his back by her fire, fearful of what Sarah would say. Also stories of herself when a girl, and her dream of going out to Salt Lake City with Polly Flyn, who never wrote, though she had said she would, after she got there. She should have followed certainly, but the sow she wanted to sell died, and she couldn't get the money, and Polly never wrote.

Carrie would sometimes turn the mangle, bringing a pasty for afterwards, and by and by Molly got to know that if she talked about Robert when he was a boy Carrie was fully repaid for her labour.

It was a new light into Robert's character to Carrie when she learned of his jumping into the canal, though he couldn't swim. It irritated her afterwards to hear Sarah scolding at him, as if he was an ordinary human being, when he ought to be wearing the V.C.

"Fetch the coals in sharp, or we'll be frozen," Sarah would say; or else, "That smoke touches my tubes, Robert. Lean your chair the other way." A hot defence for her husband often trembled on her lips, but she held herself back whilst he was there, and the psychological moment passed.

Some weeks ago she had surprised him by going down the wet hillside in the gloaming to meet him as he came from the unromantic task of gathering up the poultry. She had fled from the farm that day—to the farmer!

The damp weather had come on again now. In the lanes the children had been singing to the rain, bidding him "come again another day," but he still abode.

As Carrie shelled her peas she glanced again and again at the dark clouds, a little dissatisfied shadow on her face that finally opened Sarah's firm lips.

"You aren't thinkin' o' going out, and them black clouds over Blackstone, are you?" she asked, emptying more flocks into a new cover for the bed. It was Sarah's boast that she never had done, or sat down five minutes with folded hands.

"I am," retorted Carrie, almost defiantly. "I must have a breath o' air. I'm smothering."

She pushed the peas from the shell with her finger as if she would sweep all obstacles away in similar manner.

Sarah flushed.

Carrie had once got her face read by a physiognomist (at a cheap rate, because the physiognomist was down in the world), and had been told that she had a respect for old people. Sarah would not have believed it for all the wealth of the Indies. Carrie would have retorted that she had a respect for *people*, providing they weren't near relations of the porcupine.

Carrie felt her cup of wrath running over, and indeed it ran into fiery words as Sarah said laconically, "Yo' wouldn't get mich air afore yo' married our Robert, I'm thinkin'. And what there was would be no good."

"It takes less air to keep you going when you're your own boss," answered Carrie, bitingly. "A bit o' bread and water an' a sniff o' smutty air along wi' freedom is better than a rich table in prison."

"Which means," stuttered Sarah, in her indignation and astonishment, "that you consider this place"—scattering the flocks willy-nilly, so that more went over than into the cover—"that you consider this a prison? That comes o' reading yellow rubbish."

"Yes. I consider it next door to Holloway, where they puts Suffragettes, except the winders are bigger and there's no forcible feeding—an' you do the cooking for the jailers," Carrie said, with sudden vehemence, the anger of the last few months sweeping her along, furiously, joyously, and setting every pulse of her body tingling.

"Well!" exclaimed Sarah, still sticking to the flocks, but scattering them willy-nilly. "If hever I heard the likes o' that now! You coming from nowhere into here"—looking round the farm kitchen proudly—"and no one saying a wrong word to you—"

"Nor a kind one either," almost shouted Carrie, on a huge wave of white wrath. "Out o' nowhere, you say, 'cause I was poor—but I'll let you know that the Browns are as good as the Gibsons, any end up, old girl. I don't wear false hair and palm it off as my own." (Sarah stiffened. It was her own hair, but made up from combings of bygone years, and consequently darker.) "I'm not too stingy to give a beggar a penny—a poor old blind man that can't see sun, moon, or stars—and asking him questions in the bargain, as if he be a liar! A poor old blind thing with his face black and blue with the explosion, to be asked where he come from as if he wasn't from God's hand, same as yourself, *if the devil didn't make you*"—thinking she had been too complimentary. "Oh, I'm sick! A look's as good as a nod to a blind horse, and I've seen how I wasn't wanted at all, though you weren't honest enough to put it into words. I go out to be on my own again, if you want to know—to get away from you, where I can breathe."

"We never had rows in this 'ouse, not till this very day," said Sarah, grabbing a handful of flocks—white as a sheet with not having the chance to get a word in through all this.

"No, 'cause your brother is meek as Moses and long-suffering as Job," cried Carrie. "Now is there anything you got to say, 'cause I'll hear you now. Spit it out—it has been stuck in your liver for weeks. Out with it!"

With the last word she set down the dish of peas, then flung the empty shells behind the fire as if they were Sarah, and with arms on her hips and the glow of battle in her eyes, stood—waiting.

"You weren't cut out for a farm," said Sarah at last. "You'd have done better on the stage, *Mrs. Robert Gibson.* Just you wait till your husband comes home, hussy," shaking the flocks down into the bolster-case with a half-hint as to Carrie's doom.

Carrie laughed heartily till the old black rafters echoed.

She was delighted to have upset Sarah's stolidity and to have spoken out three months' buried thoughts. It was as natural to Carrie to speak out and have done with a thing as a thunderstorm is natural in the phenomena of Nature.

"Sure of him, you think?" said Sarah, grabbing another handful of the flocks. "After walkin' in a 'ouse fitted up like a pallis, with nothin' to buy, to talk like this—to a woman old enough to be your mother."

"To be my grandmother," agreed Carrie exasperatingly.

Sarah choked.

Speech did not come easily to her.

"I don't want a 'ouse," said Carrie, touching on her last words, "I want a 'ome. A bed in a bare room and odd cups to drink out of, and nothin' that's cost much, but it can be a 'ome. Where you can work, and spill water on the floor without somebody looking as if you'd flooded the world—that's a 'ome. Those birds, they just build their nests out o' nothing—pinching a bit of string here, a wisp of feather there, and patches it up with their own slavver, and that's a 'ome."

She had stung Sarah as much with her eloquence as Sarah had stung her with silence all these months. She was happy—deliriously happy.

Going over to the old mirror, she looked into the glass and smoothed her hair.

A rebellious face looked back at her.

Beyond her she saw Sarah, vainly trying to look calm and disdainful.

"Oh, the fun there is at the fair for one penny," she sang with lightness that was like a slap in the face to the granite-like woman she had struck to the core.

The mirror did not reflect a mass of yellow frizzed hair now. Carrie had ceased to curl it by the fierce, hot tongs, to please her husband. Robert said he couldn't "abide to see her wrap it round the tongs, burning the golden beauty out of it, till it was like a dry husk waiting to be shed." Sarah had gone down the hillside to visit her friend, Jane Wilkins, when she heard that from her corner. Comparing a woman's hair to fields of corn was to her the high-watermark of idiocy.

It was getting to be brighter and softer already, but Carrie did not feel quite at home with it yet. It was so apt to wander over her forehead instead of standing stiff like a haystack, as it used to, except when the wind was really boisterous, or the rain fell. Deftly untying her apron she folded it neatly and laid it on the old settle.

Very soon she was out and down the hill, with a vision of Sarah, still stuffing the bed-cover with the endless flocks, and giving each handful an angry shake.

A little figure in a grey cloak with plaid silk hood she looked, walking more quickly than a real, country-born woman ever does; walking a little more sharply, too, because of the spiritual upheaval that had taken place. The plaid silk of the cape Robert had bought her caressed her face lovingly, as if bidding her not to be so angry. She felt a little remorse as it touched her cheek. It was almost as if Robert was pleading with her not to be so angry. But she was angry. Her heart was like a flaming coal, and she could not see the full beauty of the stormy sky with its purple-black clouds swooping like eagles over what portion of it was clear when she set out. Behind those clouds was a brassy coloured light, reminding her of the picture of "The Judgment Day."

On and on, through the gap in the grey stone wall, down the lane, past the hedges smelling of autumn leaves, and the little cottages where lived the women who looked so suspiciously upon her. Then the smoke of house-chimneys and scattered farms was left behind.

Her feet were upon the narrow sandy path running through the moors. The melancholy sound of the pale rushes bowing to the sweeping music of the wet wind mingled with the call of the peewit, wheeling round and round above her nest. Sometimes a cloud of grouse flew out from a tuft of coarse grasses. The swish of their wings was close to her face, and as she paused startled, they went swiftly past with shrill cries.

The soul of the solitude, wild and sullen, greeted her like one who understands.

On and on she went.

The wind sank almost to silence, save for a fitful moan anon in the hollows. A sense of trouble brooded over the moors. The birds were quiet now, as if waiting for something. The pools were dark and still, save when they caught the lurid reflection of a brassy lined cloud or were shook by a turbulent swell of wind that refused to be hushed. Sheep huddled together behind an old stone wall bleated plaintively, as if appealing to that awful something whose presence they felt. The grey boulders that had once been covered by fathomless salt-water looked more cold than their wont, and the sky grew darker save where it was rent by those hell-like chasms of weird light.

Over the piled sods behind which the huntsmen had hidden in August whilst they turned the moor-fowl into bunches of bloody feathers redder than the heather, sounded now the trumpet of the swiftly riding storm.

The dark breast of the moors shook with a mighty clap of thunder, and the storm rode faster, with a terrific rapture, the lash of the lightning curling snake-like through the gloom.

A few large drops of rain splashed upon Carrie's face, and she suddenly realized that she must have come many miles. As she paused to look back the moors were lit up by sheet lightning, the still pools, black ling and heather, furze-bushes and whitened rushes illumined so suddenly that it seemed as if magic had painted them suddenly upon the darkness. She covered her face with her wet hands and shuddered. Faster came the rain, dripping from the heather, beating the silver cotton grasses limp and helpless, making the grey boulders wet, whilst away down in the hollows the thunder growled its threats.

Yet there was something in the wild moor made still more desolate by the storm that gave her a savage joy. It seemed to lie defiant and determined looking up the cloudy sky, and to echo the menace of the storm with majestic wrath. Stumbling over the sodden ground she beat her way through the slanting rain, her boots soaked with the drippings of tangled, wet grass. Sometimes she went over brown bog-patches where local tradition had it that witches had once built the midnight fire to boil the evil potion, since which no living thing would grow on the accursed spot.

Physical weariness began to grip her, and she forgot her grievances.

She looked down on her soaked garments and wondered if she had better dry them at Crowing Mary's fire, as Robert had dried his on his return from the canal episode. A little sigh left her lips as she recalled her own fireside in the kitchen behind the shop, the grate with the half-brick cunningly pushed in to throw out heat without burning extra coals. Only the glory of those days of independence was now remembered in this backward vista, and the fatigue was forgotten.

Dog-tired she paused, looking as well as the smoking rain would allow across the sad, colourless landscape. Had the ground been less sodden she would have sat down to rest, taking all the risk of rheumatism for the relief.

As she glanced around for the signs of any habitation, with a low laugh at her plight, the gleam of a fire burst like a scarlet flower through the greyness. She looked again, almost thinking it one of the witch-fires Robert had told her of, and as she did so she saw a dark figure pass between the brightness and herself.

Curiosity and the pelting of the rain urged her forward, overweighing the grain or two of fear in her composition. As she neared the fire she raised her voice, calling shrilly as the city hawkers do:

"Hi, hi! hillo! hillo!"

The dark figure before the fire rose from the crouching attitude he had assumed, straightened his back, and seemed to scan the landscape. Perhaps the smoke was in his eyes, or they were weak and short of sight, for he settled down again, and Carrie once repeated the shrill cry.

Then he perceived her, and as she drew nearer the shed his position was not unlike that of a watch-dog making ready to spring. Still she held on to the path which seemed to have been made by the wet grass being trampled low by a single pair of feet. When she got within five yards of the fire she discovered that it was within a stone shed, which had evidently been used at one time as a dwelling-house. Time had utterly demolished it save for this one room, with only three of its walls and a portion of the rotten roof remaining.

Who was this wild-looking creature, she wondered, standing stock-still and gazing at him through the mist of falling rain. Just then the fire flamed up suddenly, and to her astonishment she saw that he was no other than Peter Moss, the man who had carried her bag on that far-away morning when she came to Greenmeads for the first time. He was regarding her suspiciously, even menacingly, and she felt it would be policy to propitiate him.

She had only seen him once or twice since her marriage, but once she had given him a few harebells which had seemed to attract his wandering fancy as she met him in the lane, as he was carrying home a basketful of clean clothes to the vicarage. His sister took washing in to eke out her husband's scanty earnings, and report said that she made Peter do the bulk of the work.

"Do you know me, Peter?" she asked ingratiatingly, and as cheerily as if it was the first warm day in spring after a severe frost and a sloppy thaw, though she felt starved through her whole body.

"You live up at t' farm," mumbled Peter. "But what do you want here? This moor is mine, I'll have you know, and I want no partners in my hall. None. Only the

83

moorfowl may come, to be fed every day. They do not come nigh enuff to suit me, but they'll come some day and perch on my shoulder—some day!"

"Patience is everything," said Carrie, soothingly. "To be sure they'll come, Peter, some time before long."

"Eh?" he growled, looking at her face as if awaking from some dream, and the old suspicion stamped on his features. Then a wilder look leaped up into the blue eyes, as if a great lamp was lit behind them.

He sprang forwards, laying his thin hand on her shoulder in a fierce clasp that contradicted its usual limpness.

"Have they set you on to track me?" he almost screamed.

He looked steadily into her eyes as if he would read her soul. Carrie laughed, though her heart was beating fast.

"Why should they?" she inquired pleasantly. "What good would it do them? Besides, I wouldn't do it, Peter. Not really. I like to creep into a quiet place sometimes, that I do. What a nice place it is, too. What a fine table" (this was a slab of rock he had put in the middle of the shed), "and how cosy with the firelight."

"Do ye think so?" he said, following her every word, and his claw-like clasp falling from her shoulder, to her great relief. "It's a fine place to me. Better nor a pallis."

His countenance lit up with the joy of masterdom, as his eyes ranged the shed, with the soft, grey smoke curling everywhere, and the big hole burned in the turf by the fire. In the corner was a bed of ling and moss, and on the slab of grey rock was a hunch of crusty bread, a jar full of water, and a cluster of bilberries. She followed his glance, and when it returned to her again, met it with one of admiration of his habitation.

"My hair is so wet," she said, flinging back the coloured hood, and gazing wistfully at the fire. "May I not come in?"

He scanned the face and meditated.

"Yo're a foreigner," he said, "but—wasn't it you gave me them blue flowers in the lane? Then if you come in, happen yo'll tell me o' t' new milkin' machine up at t' farm. You won't tell 'em, will yo'?"—pointing vaguely through the slanting rain in the direction of the village. "When I gets sick o' they I comes here. I look after the birds on this moor, an' they know me. I pick the berries and bring my bit o' bread, and sleep on the rushes. They always ask me where I've bin, but I never tell 'em. No, no! Sally wouldn't like me to come here, particularly on Mondays, when she wants me to turn the mangle— would she now? But I can't stop to turn the mangle when I hears the birds calling, and the big winds blowing, and know that at night the moon will turn all the watter into silver. Nobody knows it's silver but me, or they would come and take it away. Yea, take it away and leave the moon no looking-glass to see her bonny face in! Take it and squander it, and lend it, and buy things with it, and the moors would be all dark and lonesome. So I never tells." Then he seemed to wake as from a dream, and to realize how wet she was. "Come in, come in," he said proudly, and Carrie entered the poor shelter, into which the rain sometimes slanted wildly, sputtering into the fire, making it hiss as if in hot anger.

The man looked at the slender figure kneeling by the fire, shaking out the masses of yellow hair which had got wet even through the hood of the cloak, and made more wet by her standing listening to his ravings before he asked her in.

She put her hairpins in a little heap at her side, and dried her tresses, and Peter forgot his scatter-brain thoughts as he watched her bind them up again, with fascinated eyes. Then, warming her little chill fingers, she began to talk to him. He became confidential, but it was not easy, garrulous confidence without check.

Slow and painful was the process by which he gave up secrets he had hoarded so long in the dim recesses of his crazed brain. Sometimes he would stop and look at the face looking dreamily into the fire, and at the firm, almost square-tipped fingers, and the frank, blue eyes, as if measuring how much to tell her.

He told her how he lay down on the bed of rushes on the nights when he was absent from the village, and saw the stars shine through the gaps in the roof, with a fierce, deep joy—how he waited for them, looking up and seeing them come into the spaces that were all dark, and how he forgot the red glimmer of the firelight as they came with white, mystic beauty. He did not quite put it into those words, but the broken, slow fragments of speech were eloquent with a rude poetry—as much in what he did not say as in what he did. He told her how he got up once when the winds were howling and tried to find where they went and hid themselves; how he followed them into a cave high on a hillside, and knew that that was their home. Then with a last struggle to keep the secret (a vain one) after a few looks into her face, he told her his great ambition;—the ambition that had been in his heart since boyhood. Some day, he said, he should climb up to the top of Blackstone Crag and wait for the coming of the stars, and then he should be able to reach them, for it would be but one short leap, and he would never go back to the village again—never!

His face glowed with joy as he unfolded his plan, and she could not find it in her heart to rob him of his delusion, which had comforted him in dreary days in the little drab scullery where he turned the mangle for his sister, whose scolding tongue brought him sharply back to common things when he was dreaming of the moors.

Besides, he would find out his error whenever he climbed Blackstone Crag, and know how far away the stars really were.

Afterwards she was to remember his exalted look for long years, and to recall his saying that he would never come back to the village again with a thrill at the weird prophecy, so strangely fulfilled.

She watched him curiously as he fumbled within a rudely made box near his primitive bed.

"I found it on the way," he said, pointing a wavering finger, and holding in the other hand a murky picture-book. "It was trodden wi' the moor sheep, but I washed and dried it. I reads it o' nights by this fire—the pictures, you know. They worries me no end till I finds what they mean."

He turned over the pages and told her his weird fancies about the pictures, and Carrie remembered that in her pocket she had the little Hans Andersen with the blue backs.

The rain had almost ceased to fall, and the sun shining out made the gorse-bushes blaze with the treasure of diamond raindrops they had gathered. Pools of lovely, intense colour came into the sky, and clinging moss on high boulders on the hills bloomed vivid green in the flashing sunlight.

Acting on a sudden impulse Carrie drew out the book, and began to tell him the story of the China Shepherdess.

"'Nother!" he said, like a child, with a child's rapture in his man's voice that was comical and pathetic.

So she told him the story of the shoes that danced away.

Bird cries came from the moor now, and she knew that even if she hastened back to the farm she should scarcely get back in time to pour out Robert's tea.

"There, you may have it for your own," she said, putting the blue book in his hand, "and tell yourself stories from the pictures"; and as she pulled up the hood of her cloak, stepping out into the sunlight, he was poring over his treasure, like a miser over his gold. But as her shadow crossed the page he raised his head.

"Come back," he called, and as she did so he went once more to the box near his bed, and after a little more fumbling drew out a withered rose.

"I found that, too," he said. "It ain't so nice as it was in the smell, an' not so white in the look. It was white as milk when I found it! But it's a rose, a real rose, an' you may have it."

He beamed again at her thanks, and settled down over the book with a glorified look.

Then she hurried back along the sandy path, past the pools that had been dark and still as she came, but were now full of blue and emerald.

What a strange adventure!

She had heard Robert speak of Peter Moss's disappearances, sometimes for a week at a time, and how neither threats nor coaxing could extract from him information as to his whereabouts and doings during his absence. She wondered if it were right to tell. Sniffing the gorse scents and the sweet, sharp smell of the wet brown earth, and drinking in the colour of the sky, now getting tinged with sunset pomp as she approached the village, she decided that it would be mean to divulge the secret of Peter's dwelling. The poor soul did no harm to any one, she argued. It was an innocent whim, surely, to leave the mangle for the moors several times a year, and call the moorfowl his chickens, and think of reaching the radiant, far-off stars.

So engrossed was she with the strange scene she had left, that her own domestic unhappiness only came into her mind with the sight of the farm as she climbed the hill.

The windows were aglitter in the sunset. The garden was a mass of autumn colours, made more fresh by the showers, and all seemed at peace without. A speckled hen with bright, red comb fluttered away as Carrie walked up the path. Through the closed door she could catch the chink of teacups. After a brief hesitation, mastered by a toss of the head, she put her hand up on the latch, and, passing through the glass porch, entered the kitchen.

Robert was getting his tea. For the first time he did not look an affectionate welcome as she entered.

There was something restrained in his manner as he pushed the teapot towards her and as she sat down after taking off her outdoor garments. With a mumbled excuse he went out to fodder the cattle, leaving her to get the tea alone.

Sarah sat in her stiff-backed chair with the air of a martyr waiting to be burned at the stake.

With one disdainful look at her, which said she knew she had been telling Robert her own version of the tale whilst she was not there to defend herself, Carrie withdrew to the farm window. She sat looking down the hill, till the green of it began to darken, and she heard the birds in the tree at the house-end call sleepy good nights. Splashes of burning gold and emerald, fiery blotches of crimson, came into the sky, showing over the geraniums with their mad red flowers, and the fuchsias with their purples and blood colours, vivid as if they were trying to outrival the sunset.

It grew darker.

Robert's steps sounded under the window, paused, as if hesitating, then swung round, down the hillside, so that they could not be heard for the silence of the soft grass. Carrie realized that instead of coming to sit in the firelight as was his way, after the toil of the daytime, he had gone down into the village.

Anywhere, she thought, to be away from her! That cat, Sarah, must have added even more to the truth, and now that she thought of it rationally she had not quite spoken the truth, without anything being added to her words. She should have said that it was Sarah she felt was her jailer—not Robert. Indeed she had grown to look on him as her good comrade.

Sarah could see the little proud face outlined against the light of the sunset sky, whenever she looked from beneath her scant lashes.

As the last rays of daylight faded she did not see Carrie wipe something away as if it was a wasp. It was a large round tear. Yet Carrie was not sorry for the "row." She regarded it as inevitable and felt glad she had told Sarah "off," as she called it in her own mind. She felt morally cleaner and better for the honest talk. She was only sorry that she had unconsciously stabbed Robert by mixing plural and singular together. Then she shook herself, took her candle, and went to bed.

"He is going to be as nasty as she is," she thought. "I could fight her, and win my place. But if he begins—".

Then she got into bed and made herself sleep.

Chapter VI

THE LOST PURSE

A WEEK passed away, somewhat slowly at Hilltop Farm. Every dawn came heavy with rain, and the evenings closed in soon now. Carrie sometimes found herself wondering with an almost guilty feeling how the little oyster-shop was progressing under the new management, and how her friends were getting along. Particularly she wondered how Julia and Fanny were progressing. She had written twice to Julia, telling her of the farm, the pigs, and how good her husband was, and what a cat Sarah was, with the candid confidence that only exists between two women when they are really good friends. Julia had dictated the answer to Fanny, after she came from the flax-mill, and Fanny had cleared a corner of the table, and written back the Julia-ish epistle in her large, sprawling handwriting, that told of her large heart. Carrie wept as she read the letter. The sweetness it breathed forth in the sometimes misspelt words was so like Julia. What a good, patient soul Julia was, she thought, and then with her eyes full of tears laughed as she thought of herself as compared with poor Julia who lay in bed day after day, week after week, staring at an ugly brick wall that was not even a cheery red, but had turned black with many years of Manchester fog and smoke. She could see in her mind's eye the pleasant face, with its soft brown eyes, and the two long plaits of hair, brown as the eyes, lying over the pillow, when Julia's head was aching. Sometimes, when her head was cool and free from the neuralgia, those long, thick plaits would be piled on Julia's head, and then they looked like a coronet, and gave her a royal look. Royal indeed was Julia! She was an uncrowned queen of innumerable nights of pain and unrest, governed by the bright, brave spirit.

Ten long years she had lain thus, unable to lift a cup to her mouth, and yet people in trouble came and sat by her bedside and went away comforted. In answer to their inquiries as to herself, she would say that she was all right, and had only had one heart attack that week, or something equally remarkable.

Carrie always remembered a passage of Scripture when she thought of Julia, which compared a patient soul to a quiet pool filled with waters. Once she had spent half a day at a seaside town with Robert. They had walked along the shore, and Carrie had seen a sand-locked pool, still and beautiful, as it caught the quivering lights and shadows of the sky, and the white glint of the wings of the stormy gulls passing over it. The passage of Scripture came to her mind with redoubled force. Julia was like a pool filled with waters. Shadows and sunbursts, and stormy birds of passage, pain and sorrow went over her, but the pool was always limpid and lovely, and filled the minds of those who beheld it with wonder and love, giving them rest.

This evening Carrie sat finishing one of the novelettes preparatory to sending a whole batch to Julia.

Sarah was not very well, having a swollen face, which she was continually bathing with hot camomile flowers and poppy-head water.

Robert had a cold and had gone early to bed, refusing a remedy Carrie had proffered. The tall clock in the corner pointed to seven.

"I'll just run down to the post office," said Carrie, laying her book down on the white-topped dresser which was religiously scrubbed with sand every Friday morning, until it was smooth as ivory, and fair as new-fallen snow in contrast with the two green hair mats on which stood two glass decanters that had only held wine twice—once at the funeral of Robert's father, and then at that of his mother.

The post office was a quaint, old-fashioned shop where you could purchase marbles, tops, and whips, home-made toffee, and tarts of unbelievable size, and cakes familiarly termed "tram-stoppers" by the people of the hamlet. You stood behind the door to lick your stamps, and your head collided with scrubbing-brushes and gridirons, hung from the ceiling, and if you got a really severe knock Betty Lever would sell you sticking-plaster, or green salve to remedy the fracture. Betty Lever had a bad leg and a long tongue, and always sold her stuff to a customer with proud condescension, giving her paper bags a twist that was characteristic, and saying, "*I* never puts alum into my stuff. Is there anything else? Those pies? They are twopence, an' you couldn't make them for the money. I really loses on 'em myself!"

"How dun yo' manage to sell 'em, then, Betty?" inquired old Billy Buff once as she said this.

"Well," answered Betty seriously, "it's because I get such a big sale, yo' see, Billy," and he had gone out laughing.

She had a stepson, an epileptic. His father had died within a week of their marriage, killed at his work as quarryman. Despite the remonstrances of her relatives, Betty did not send Philip Lever to an institution, but set up a shop with her husband's club money, made the big pies, and toiled for his unfortunate boy as if he had really been her own flesh and blood. She was a great gossip, and had done some little mischief with her tongue, though she was close as an oyster about her own affairs. Carrie often ran down to the post office where more of anything was sold than stamps, just to parry wits with Betty Lever. Betty would try to make Carrie say something detrimental to Sarah by suggesting that Sarah was getting older, and that there was nothing in the world so queer as folk.

"Only other folk," Carrie would say. "I say, Betty, is it true that you are going to be married?" and Betty would look up nonplussed at any one daring to ask her questions. Carrie had been thinking it would be a change to run down and tease her a little. The farm kitchen was oppressive.

Sarah never lifted her head from the dish of camomile as Carrie announced that she was going out.

Then Carrie remembered that they were not on speaking terms, and bit her red underlip fiercely. During the week the swollen cheek had made unconscious calls on her sympathy. She had a little humiliated feeling at her heart that Sarah had not answered her.

Putting on her cloak she soon had the farm at her back. The big, white stars glimmered through the darkness, and besides the gap in the stone wall dividing the hill-land from the lane was the yellow flicker of the lamp Robert had told her they had had to fight two years to get, and didn't get then until Leyland Parker, coming back from the town drunk, had broken his gay young neck by falling in the gloom, whilst the servants at the Hall had waited up for him in vain.

After she had gone Sarah cleared away the fomentation articles, and walked over to the dresser upon which Carrie had laid her book. She picked it up with an expression of disgust, and a murmur of surprise, that Robert allowed his wife to read such stuff. Turning the pages she read a few sentences, here and there.

"'Lilian's wine-brown eyes sank before the fiercely burning glances of the Earl, and a blush like an Alpine after-glow stole over her beautiful brow. Her heart beat so rapturously that she was afraid he would hear it.'"

"Humph!" grunted Sarah. "I expect her stays was laced too tight, the young hussy. It would ha' been more seemly on her if she had emptied a bucket o' water on him. Lord in heaven, what rubbish!"

To inspect the book more closely, she sat down to the task, putting on her glasses, with audible comments from time to time. (Sarah had once lectured a woman in the village to herself, going through the quiet lanes, and on looking round had found the woman close on her heels, having heard every word.)

By and by the pages fluttered less frequently.

After ten minutes Sarah awoke to the awful fact that she had read a whole chapter of the ridiculous stuff with more than ordinary interest.

A flush suffused her sallow skin, and throwing down the book as if it was some evil thing, she took up her knitting.

The trails of ivy round the window began to tap, tap, tap, and between the scene came the restless moaning of the winter wind. A stream of light, the mingling of fireglow and lamp-rays, flowed down the hillside into the darkness. Far away, too remote to send its rush and roar, even as the faintest echo, to the quiet farm, a train would speed along the metals, making them pulse to its heart-beats. Ever behind it streamed a golden cloud of smoke, like a pillar of fire, filling the darkness with glory.

As Carrie returned from her errand, she caught sight of a train gliding like a fiery snake through the shadowy valley, and wondered if it was going to her beloved city—her city of grey mists and shop-windows, and arc-lights, and ideas.

Betty Lever had been asking her innumerable questions, and Carrie had parried them no less skilfully than Betty had thrust them forth. Betty's weapon was no sledge-hammer, but of stiletto-like fineness, but she had found Carrie a tough customer. Her way of answering, "Well, it might be," was so aggravatingly cool.

"From Wimbleton to Wambleton is fourteen miles, and from Wambleton to Wimbleton is fourteen miles," warbled Carrie, having picked up the strain from Robert, who had told her a story in connexion with it.

"But how far is it to Mrs. Gibson's?" inquired a man's voice out of the darkness, and she gave a quickly suppressed cry.

It was Charlie's voice.

"What do you want?" she inquired, turning to the dark figure filling the gap in the grey stone wall. "Wasn't it a condition that you stayed away? What will 'e think if he hears of my being talking to a man? And you know I won't introduce him to you—you'd only want help from him! Oh, you—"

Then she saw Jane Wilkins's figure silhouetted against the yellow luminance of Betty Lever's window.

The man observed her start.

"Go away. I'll see you later," she cried quickly, for Jane was coming down the lane, and the sound of her clogs could be plainly heard.

He took the hint, and disappeared into the night.

Jane Wilkins was surprisingly affable as she caught Carrie up. She told her that she was on her way to the farm to see how "poor Sarah's" face was, and said Carrie would be company for her up the hill.

There was nothing for it but to accompany her, or rouse suspicion. Carrie thought that she must make some plan for slipping out again when the two women were busy talking.

"Come in, Jane," invited Sarah, and soon the little, hard-featured woman was basking in the glow of the farm fire.

Report said that she sometimes had not much of her own, but Jane never said anything to uphold such statements, and no one dared to repeat them to her.

Carrie, even in her mental distress, could not help noticing how nice Sarah could be with those after her own heart.

By and by, as they were in the middle of the interesting and mystical subject of how Tommy Fields lost his warts by following the advice of a pedlar and tying worsted round a pin and dropping both by moonlight in the ashpit, Carrie hoped to slip out almost unnoticed.

"Are you goin' out?" inquired Jane, her sharp eyes shining in the lamplight like a mischievous squirrel's. "Don't let *me* frighten you away."

"I'm fetching two apple pasties for t' supper," answered Carrie, and they heard the porch door slam behind her. When she reached the spot where she had stumbled against her brother she walked a few yards, looking about her to see if any one was near to eavesdrop. Then, placing her fingers in her mouth, schoolboy fashion, she whistled shrilly.

Out of the darkness came the sound of the easy, familiar steps she awaited.

They retired to the blacker shadow of a clump of trees.

"Now, what is it you want?" she asked sharply, though in a low, suppressed voice. "And be brief. How selfish you are, Charlie, to come here at all."

"How selfish you are, Sis," he echoed bitterly, "to have a snug nest, and not want me to join—your only brother!"

"Don't get sentimental," she said ironically, "or you'll make me sick. I read you like a book. I see through your meanness, but I help you—only, don't think I believe that sort o' rot. How much do you want? I've sent you a sovereign he gave me for a new 'at by to-night's post."

"I want five pounds."

He heard her gasp of astonishment.

"Impossible!"

"That tale's off. You must be able to get at more than five pounds. But," his voice grew gloomy, "if you can't, I shall have to go to jail. I took that amount from a gent's pocket, and had a rollicking time for a week. But he found and recognized me, only I bluffed him by saying I was out o' work, and would repay if he gave me time. I've only two days."

"Well, you'll have to go," she responded in a hard, set voice. "I haven't got five pounds in the world."

"He has!"

"Well, I can't beg of him. We've quarrelled. Besides, he'd wonder what I wanted with all that money. I send you all he gives me."

"Didn't he say, 'With all my worldly goods I thee endow,'" insinuated the melodious voice, and Carrie realized that her brother was asking her to rob her husband. True, she didn't love him. They weren't even good friends just at present, since her tiff with Sarah, and that dragon's report, but she wasn't going to rob him—even for her brother.

"You may go. It's the best place for you," she mocked, but even as she spoke the words came the picture of the pauper funeral long ago. There was a little brother sobbing bitterly, his hand in hers, and days through which they clung together, amongst strange faces, in a long, bare room.

He was so handsome and clever too. And what would Robert think of a brother-in-law who had been in prison?

"I can't help you," she repeated, and again came a picture of the days when Charlie was very small, and stood on a wooden stool at his mother's side, handing her the buttons to stitch from the card as she bent over the pile of shirts.

She felt in her pocket.

"Take it," she cried impulsively. "It is all I have. It's the 'ousekeeping money for two weeks, but take it. I'll say I lost it."

"Carrie, old girl—" he began, and just then they heard the deep bass notes of a dog's bark, making the hills re-echo.

"It's Jack!" said Carrie. "Jane will be coming back. Go."

Without a word of thanks he disappeared.

Carrie was mounting the stile as Jane came up to it on the other side, lantern in hand, throwing into half-light, half-shadow her thin face, topped by its heavy, black bonnet that she still wore for her departed, though he had been dead so long, and his death was, as the funeral card said, "a blessed relief from suffering"— certainly for Jane.

Jane always said that he had his little faults (like 'em all), but when he was in work, and when he was sober he was the best husband in the world—a statement no one contradicted, for no one could recall seeing him in both these states of well-being at once. Neither could they contradict the statement that he always wiped his feet on the mat, a great and rare virtue in Jane's estimation.

Her little, bright, deep-set eyes were rather suspicious now as they turned on Carrie's face.

"Mercy on us!" she panted. "We thought you was makin' those apple pasties, and growin' the wheat for the flour to mix 'em on."

"I've lost my purse," answered Carrie, in a grief-strangled voice. She hated to lie. She had come to the farm with the intention of being quite straight, even if she was not dying with love of her husband.

"Lost your purse?" echoed Jane. "Good Lord a-me, whatever was you doing?"

Something in the tone exasperated Carrie. They had never trusted her, these country women, she thought, just because they knew nothing about her, as if that wasn't as good a reason for trust as distrust.

"What do you think I was a-doing?" she flamed out, with her face wilder than she knew, and more beautiful, too, under the gay colours of the hood. "Think I was playin' hop-scotch down the hill in the dark with it? Think I lost it purposely?"

"Nay, I thought nothin'," said Jane, faintly. "Suppose I shines the lamp on the lane and we look for it." Carrie tried to be as truthful as she could.

"I lost it somewhere near that chestnut," she said. This was the spot where she had talked with Charlie, and had slipped it into his hand.

So Jane and she turned back, searching, one with hope for a time, and the other with mingled amusement and shame to see the rusty old black bonnet bobbing about, and the lantern making its grotesque shadow dance on the lane. Sometimes the wind almost blew out the light of the lantern, and then Jane would cover it with her cloak, and heave prodigious sighs, and repeat Scripture, and all would be dark.

"How do yo' know you lost it nigh the chestnut?" cried Jane once, looking up suddenly, and seeing a flush creep into the woman's face.

"Didn't I feel it in my hand just as I came near?" cried Carrie, disdainfully; and Jane thought things she did not say.

"It's no use," said the elder woman at last, her face quite blue with the cold, and her teeth chattering. "It's clean gone, wherever it be."

Was it fancy, or was there a double meaning in those innocent-sounding words? Carrie glanced at her face, illumined a moment by her lantern, and could not decide.

"Well, good night, and thanks for helpin' me look for it," said Carrie, and they took their separate ways, for Jane refused to go back to the farm and have an apple pasty now, as it was so late. She went to her little cottage, and Carrie up the hill, the dog following her. It was surprising how fond the dog was of Carrie, the latest inmate of the farm. It was another cause of grievance to Sarah that Jack would follow her brother's wife as soon as herself.

Little did Carrie dream that Jane after having a bite of supper in her own little house, and warming her starved fingers at the handful of fire in the shining, well-blackened grate, again issued forth, a little figure in the dark, lonely lane, with the rays from the lantern shining like the will-o'-wisp by the chestnut tree, to see if she could find the purse.

Once she picked up a handful of wet, brown leaves, then threw them into the dyke with disgust. Here, there, and everywhere flitted the weird figure, even diving into the damp dyke at the risk of getting amongst snails, her pet horror, holding high the farm lantern. The cold wind cut like a knife. Once it sent a sharp pain through her shoulder-blades, and she remembered that Dr. John had warned her to be careful. But with compressed lips and sharp, determined eyes she kept on with her search. Why?

Was it that she wished to return the purse, with the honour of having found it? No. Neither was it that she wished to find and retain it, for she was strictly honest. It was not to help Carrie, for she disliked her rather than otherwise, and thought her a young upstart out of nowhere, with the narrow prejudices of one whose life has been spent within a circuit of ten miles of the place she was born in. The strength in these country hearts was built on knowledge of their own place, and ignorance of those outside it. The old tribal feelings still lingered there. Almost everybody was related, if only distantly, and it was not safe for a stranger to pass his opinions on any individual, or he might unconsciously be talking to a cousin or half-cousin—and a third cousinship was a strong link!

Jane did not believe that the purse was lost at all, now. She thought it an artful city dodge to get hold of money to waste on novelettes and other rubbish and was determined to bottom the mystery, and run the fox to earth.

Round and round she went, looking intently on the path, and amongst the fallen leaves of the chestnut.

The church clock struck nine.

How cold she was! Why shouldn't the purse have been lost? she argued once or twice as the wind grew icy. Perhaps Carrie had been mistaken about having it in her hand as she passed the chestnut, and it lay on the hill near the farm, to be found in the morning by the inhabitants, for no one else came that way, unless there was a tramp on his way to Manchester. Why shouldn't the young woman lose her purse as well as any other?

Just as these thoughts passed through her mind and as she was thinking of giving up her search, she saw something sparkle amongst the leaves she had turned with her umbrella.

Forgetting the snails, she was soon grasping it, and holding it full in the rays of the bright, yellow light.

It was a man's signet-ring with a large blood-stone in the centre.

Then, with triumph in her heart, Jane went home. In some mysterious feminine way she guessed that Carrie knew some one who had lost that ring. She had fancied before she joined Carrie at the stile that she heard the sound of retreating footsteps, and now felt convinced in her own mind that her imagination had not played her false. Some one was leaving Carrie just before she arrived with her lantern, and that some one was a man, and either a lover or a husband who had to be paid to keep quiet.

In the light of her own kitchen, she examined the ring. On the inside were three initials, S. T. G.

Charles Brown had once stopped a pair of runaway horses in Oxford Street, and the merchant in the vehicle felt extremely grateful, and gave him the ring as some recompense for risking his life. Not that he had valued life very much just at that time—for he was just a blast furnace man, returning home after an evening walk in his working clothes, too tired almost to read the night paper.

"Guess he's a toff," commented Jane, regarding the three initials and wishing that the powers of clairvoyance were hers. "Likely enough 'tis some one hup in life, but who has now come down, and had to get a bit back o' what he'd given her. The minister said she'd an hinteresting face—and what did that mean if it wasn't that there was something at back of it? Don't all the bad folk live in the cities, and the good folk in the country, in the plays?" She looked round on the last word, as if fearful that any one had overheard her confession.

She made herself a cup of coffee, cut two slices of bread, very thick with a thin scraping of butter, and toasted her feet comfortably at the bars.

When she had emptied the cup she swung it three times round, and placed it to drain in her saucer, then took hold of the handle and looked within, her head on one side.

"There's a dog," she said at last. "One leg has gone, so to speak, and there is a hump on its back—might be an habcess, but 'tis surely a dog, and a dog is a friend. Then there is a 'ouse—yes, for sure, there's the chimbley smokin'—just like life, and 'tis on a hill. I'll go up to Sarah's to-morrow, and face that hussy with this ring. There's a letter, too—four dots, an' one for the stamp, plain as the nose on my face. I must buy some ink to write back."

She went to sleep that night after the first flush of her joy had worn off, revolving pictures in her mind of her particular friends, and their wonder at her smartness in collecting concrete evidence against the woman they all despised. Lately, though, there had been signs of relenting on the part of some of the weaker ones—'Liza Smethurst having said openly at the greengrocer's cart that it was her opinion Farmer Gibson's wife was as good as folk in general were made. But then this might be the outcome of Carrie's having given Harold pennies whenever she saw him in the lane. What luck to have made this discovery.

As she watched her candle's shadow on the wall she saw the revering looks she would receive on the morrow with modest grace.

In the morning she would arise and climb the hill with the first cock-crow and tell Sarah what manner of creature her sister-in-law was.

Before the first cock-crow, rousing the echoes of Hill-top Farm, Jane was awakened by a terrible pain.

She dared not breathe, so intense was the agony, but sat up, her hard hand pulling the nightdress together at her chest. With a great effort she got downstairs and made a mustard plaster, creeping back to bed shivering and shaking with the cold. As the wan light crept into her room she was writhing in agony, and scarcely conscious of what she did. When the sun rose and she knew in a dim, wandering way that the village would be up, she knocked at the window, and Milly Tod running to the post office for bacon happened luckily to look up and see her. But Milly's husband had to burst the lock with several thrusts of his stalwart shoulders, before they could get in. Consciousness soon left her and they sent for her cousin's wife from the town four miles away. She had often wished Jane to live with her and her husband, knowing how useful she was in a house, and disliking domestic work herself. But Jane clung to her little house and stubbornly refused to move from it whilst she had a pair of hands to win her daily bread.

Very cross was Alice at being summoned from the town so summarily. She had wanted to go to a school social that night. Jane would have to live with them now, she thought triumphantly.

As she lifted the patient's head, something rolled from beneath the pillow. It was a handsome signet-ring.

After some meditation as to where her cousin could have got it, she decided it would be safest to take it back to town with her when she went home at the week-end; for Jane would come—or she might die—and as her nearest relative Ted had a right to it, surely.

The days went by. Alice was restless and could not wait until Jane was out of danger. In her heart she did not think the sufferer would recover, and the doctor held out no hope. Carrie came once or twice with broth from the farm, and talked to the towns-woman, who poured out her opinions of her queer cousin. Once, quite unexpectedly, Carrie said a few hot words that surprised Alice, and Jane opened her eyes, but closed them again wearily.

Sarah proffered to stay with her old friend and let Alice go home after Carrie's return from one of these visits, and eagerly the offer was seized. It is true that as she hurried to the station Alice had a few suspicious thoughts about "bits o' things" being taken, but she was not a patient nurse and was glad to get away. Sarah looked faithfully after her friend, but one day confessed herself tired out, and allowed Carrie to take her place, whilst she went back to the farm and had a sleep "in her own bed."

"What a tale it'll be!" murmured the patient feebly, trying to get up, and thinking it must be late, and that she had promised Farmer Wild's wife, who was lying-in, to go up and put things tidy for her. Then she opened her eyes.

Carrie stood by the bedside, with a bowl of steaming soup in her hand.

"What are you doing here?" she cried, rubbing her eyes.

"Lie quite still. You have been so poorly," answered Carrie, gently. "Sarah will be back in an hour or two."

Jane searched into her mind, and remembered the pain, her knocking at the window, and nothing more, until this weariness. It must be true. Then under cover of the clothes she searched for the ring. It was gone. Carrie must have been too clever for her and have got it back on pretence of looking after her. She resolved to do nothing yet, but get well, and to go to have tea with Sarah, and confront her with the facts of the story.

Every day Carrie came with hot beverages from the farm, through the snow. She felt so sorry, for she guessed Jane must have got the chill looking for the lost purse. If Jane had died, she would have felt a murderess, and the weapon of a murder—a lie. Jane, as she sipped the hot soup with Carrie's arm supporting her, thought sometimes what a hypocrite the young woman was, but sometimes she wondered if she was, only it made her head ache to think.

The days slipped by, snowy and wild, and it seemed long before Jane got to Hilltop Farm to tea. She went almost buried in clothes lest she should take another chill.

At last she kicked her pattens off by the porch, and entered the familiar kitchen.

Carrie went out to feed the pig, Peter, of whom Robert expected great things at the next Bringford Fair. She looked comely and almost like a country girl in her round woollen cap, and Jane thought it a pity she was not as good as she was well-favoured. Perhaps it was the subconsciousness of Carrie's kindness during her illness which was at work, but now that she was really at the farm, the dramatic crisis she was going to bring about seemed a rather silly thing to Jane. She thought if she did say anything, she wouldn't make a fuss about it, but just state the facts, quite barely. As Carrie swung out of the door, Jane said in a loud whisper to Sarah, who was more deaf than usual, "How dun yo' get on wi' her?"

Sarah sniffed.

"She might be better, and she might be wuss. I allus reckons to look on t' breet side o' things, Jane, as the man's wife said when he killed hissel' wi' falling out o' t' tree—for he might have been killed wi' it falling on him, she said, and that would ha' been wuss. But as for trying to get on with her, or her with me, we just goes both our ways. Robert could ha' eaten her without saut [salt] when he brought her home at first, but I let him know a thing or two. I never speaks to her 'cept when company's here, and I does it then to save Robert being talked about. But Elsie—Elsie would ha' be a fitter—"

Jane put up a warning finger, for she heard Carrie's light step where the snow was cleared away before the door. She half suspected they might have been overheard, for Sarah's voice was not a whisper. Nothing could be guessed from her face, however, as she mixed the food in the big farm bucket deftly, and went out and past the window once more.

"Sarah?"

"Was yo' speakin', Jane?" asked that good lady, holding out the plate of hot buttered muffins to her guest.

Jane had been going through a severe mental struggle as she sipped the hot tea from the blue willow cup. She felt that Sarah, her lifelong friend, should know that Carrie might not have lost the purse, about the footsteps she had been almost sure she heard, and about the man's ring that had so mysteriously disappeared again. Yet the remembrance of Carrie's ungrudging patience strove hard with this, and she was swayed almost equally by her two obligations. She also remembered that when she married her husband, his people did not take kindly to her because she was a servant and not a good four-loom weaver, and because she wore edging on her underclothes. In this fit of conscience she drank five cups of tea—and those blue willow cups were not doll cups. Sarah preferred solid things to dainty ones.

Carrie meanwhile was leaning over the sty watching Peter eat his meal. She guessed that the two women were discussing her and kept away, smiling scornfully to herself. After a while she grew weary of this occupation, and somewhat starved, yet she was too proud to go in and disturb their conversation. For some little time, in fact ever since Robert had changed in his manner towards her, she had been getting tired of the battle, and more inclined to give up the fight than glowing for victory. Some of the heart seemed to have gone out of her, as the country folk there would have put it. This afternoon, catching Elsie's name as she entered, and guessing its purport, she had felt homesick and heartsick. How sweet it would be to be back amongst people who did not look on her as an interloper! She remembered as she watched Peter grunting round his food that she had not been down to see her sister, Clara, for a few days, and that Joey had the measles. It would be a nice walk. It would also give the two women in the farm kitchen a chance to say all they could about her.

Half-way down the hill she paused and looked back at the farm. The sun was setting red in an ashen sky, and made the windows like fiery gold. At the end of the gable was the great tree, swaying its arms madly, as if rebelling against the will of the wind.

Something worked up in her throat.

She loved it all, quiet as the place had been after the city. No one could help but love it, it was so beautiful. If she had been happy there it would have been paradise. Unhappy though she had been, her heart clung to it, but she hated to be despised. Her pride was getting stronger than her love of conquest.

"Why should I ever come back?" she thought, and it would not be put away, that troublesome question. It was in the sound of the wind, and the hoarse whisper of the brook just breaking its chains of ice, and written upon the fair patches of untrodden snow that lay away from the footpath.

By the time Carrie reached her sister's house, and was gazing gloomily into the fire, with Joey on her knee, Jane had unburdened herself of the story of the ring she had found, and her belief that Carrie had some lover whom she was in the habit of meeting clandestinely, and to whom she had possibly given the purse. Sarah had told her before of Robert having his watch stolen, and of Carrie getting it restored. Jane now communicated the happy thought to Sarah that perhaps Carrie herself had stolen the watch and given it back to him.

Sarah listened and rose to draw the blind.

She was smiling.

"Nay, I don't think she is dishonest," she said. "Our Robert wouldn't be taken in by one of those sort, after the way I brought him up. She isn't the kind I care for; but I believe she's straight. Besides, the ring could be anybody's," with aggravating unconcern in her voice.

The contrariness of human nature made Jane forget all her previous relenting thoughts of Carrie. "The ring disappeared from my house when Carrie came to—"

"I came before Carrie, and there was no ring under your pillow then," said Sarah. "I don't like her, but truth's truth. You're being misled by romance and imagination," she went on with the severity with which she detected this taint in anybody.

"You are actually taking sides with her," exclaimed Jane hotly, gathering up her skirts.

"Truth's truth," reiterated Sarah. "And I won't stand by and hear my sister-in-law accused of being either a thief or a red woman. She ain't sly enough, Jane."

"You're as changeable as Bringford weathercock," muttered Jane, as she unlocked the door of her little cottage before dark fell on the hillside, and on the sleepy, straggling village.

There was a letter behind the door. It was from her cousin's wife saying they were glad to hear she was better, and that she had taken a ring from under the pillow, thinking it unsafe to leave such valuables to strangers, as it might be a temptation. She also stated that she had taken two honeycomb quilts, thinking Jane would come to live with them after this illness, which would be sure to rack her constitution up. The letter was a little sermon on the way her queer, independent ways upset her long-suffering relatives, and on her selfishness in living alone and their having to come running away when she was taken ill, instead of being comfortable and coming to live with them and do bits of things, that she, Alice, might go to the mill instead of doing them herself.

Jane lifted her head from the letter, which she had read kneeling on the shining steel-topped fender, by the light of the fire which she had poked into a blaze.

She looked slowly round on her household gods. Her eyes rested on the chest of drawers, with its two staring china dogs, with heavy gilt chains round their necks, and with the ball of glass that was an egg-boiler and snowed till the egg was done, set in the centre. Over the drawers was the picture she had bought in the days of the Cotton Panic, leaving threepence each week at the shop till it was quite paid for. Lovingly she glanced over all her possessions, with her mind's eye diving into drawers and boxes upstairs, even to the lumber-room, her back getting straighter and straighter each moment.

"Not till I can't move a finger," she vowed, anger leaping up in her heart against these waiters for dead men's shoes, these relatives who would also like to rob her of her priceless independence.

Then she read the postscript.

"PS.—But for that upstart creature from the farm—the young one—you would be here now. Ted came to fetch your things, and had ordered the ambulance; but she said she'd rouse the place if he touched a stick. She talked a lot of impudence, and said your death would be at his door if he moved you, and that there would be bother. If I were you I'd have no dealings with her; she seems dangerous. Ted said so."

Jane was crying softly by this. Carrie had saved her household gods from being scattered, maybe her life, and she had done her this ill turn. Putting on her things, she climbed the hill to the farm, and told Sarah other and different theories about the ring, and her sorrow for what she had said. But Sarah, contrary by turn, for all her warm defence of Carrie, had believed some of Jane's imputations. The girl had been very fond of strolling about by herself, and never gave accounts of her whereabouts. Perhaps she had some old lover who hung round, knowing she was unhappy here. She did not say all this to Jane, who was strangely penitent; she told it to her own soul. The honour of the house was safe with Sarah, who would have as soon thought of pulling down the rafters of the old home as of undermining the honour of the family name. Whatever her inner convictions were she would deny them, and be the last to blacken the name of the tribe.

Feeling considerably relieved, Jane went home.

Shadows began to thicken in the old farm kitchen. They flickered like ghosts on the walls and amongst the old black rafters.The wind whoo-ed round the house so drearily that Sarah, unimaginative and practical as she was, shivered, so plaintive and like a homeless thing it sounded.

Robert came in and had a late tea, but Carrie did not come; and after some desultory talk and the reading of the paper he grew visibly uneasy. His uneasiness grew into alarm when the farm clock struck nine, and he went down the hill, through the gap in the wall, along the lane, till he came to her sister's house.

"No, she has not been here," said Clara, from a few inches of open door-space.

He waited up for her till eleven.

To Sarah he said no single word of his grief at this strange behaviour, feeling, with a throbbing sense of injustice, that she had never really given her a warm welcome though she had not shown open hostility. Taking his candle, he went to bed. Sarah fastened the farm door, but not with the old, proud sense of joy. She felt that she was barring out some wanderer, and under her calm exterior her heart misgave her. If the girl had a secret lover and had gone away with him, would she be any to blame? The thought disturbed her usual self-satisfaction. Then she, too, went to bed; but only to listen for footsteps that never came, and to the stormy, outcast voice of the wind as it came sweeping up the valley. Tossing and tumbling on the yellow, old four-poster, she rejected the idea that Carrie had committed suicide as soon as it entered her head. No; the girl had too much common sense, for all her fiery, long-winded speeches and the novelettes.

Morning came, but no Carrie.

As Sarah went to feed the pig, Peter, she read on the boards in front of the sty, written in a large hand with white chalk—the large, flourishing hand she had seen only once before on a postcard—these words:

"I was a Stranger, and ye took Me not in."

She brought Robert to read, and they knew it was Carrie's farewell message. It wounded more deeply than any bitter thing could have done.

"She did not care for me, and you made things too hard for her," said Robert, bitterly. "There was no one else when she married me, I could swear. But she was a wild young filly, and needed a gentle hand. But—let her go. If she had cared she would not have been driven away so."

Yet Sarah could hear the blame in his quiet voice, and winced. She felt that she could not bear it, and told him of the suspicions of Jane about the purse and the queer coincidence of the signet-ring found in the hedge.

"Well, there's the work of the day to do," he said drearily, like a man stricken. "Do not talk to me about her. Let her go."

He learned later, from the station-master (though he did not tell Sarah that he had been to inquire), that his wife had gone away that morning, taking a ticket to Manchester. She must have been at Clara's last night, after all, and have crept back to write that message on the pig-sty. She must have come very softly, for he had been listening all night. But—let her go. It was only going back to the old times before she came, he thought.

When he went out about his work, Sarah's face twitched to see the rasher of bacon untouched on his plate. Turning up the chair cushion to dust, later on, she came across one of the novelettes. Almost sacredly she put it by in a drawer of the white-topped dresser. The page was turned down half-way.

"She may only have gone to frighten us," she thought. "She may want to finish the tale when she comes back."

But the days drifted on, and there was no word from the absent one.

Robert found that it was not quite like going back to old times. A great desert lay between those old happy times and these, for then he had never known and loved Carrie, and therefore never missed her. He brooded on her voice, her face, her sudden, birdlike movements; her pungent sayings, that were yet not malicious.

The days dragged as they had never done in the old days. And through it all ran the thought that she was perhaps laughing in her old careless way with another man. He could not go to seek her; it was too late.

Chapter VII

"PADDLING YOUR OWN CANOE"

CARRIE saw Greenmeads recede through gathering tears that refused to be blinked away.

White mists lay on the December fields, trees were leafless, and the pools were dark save for a glint of fast-fading gold where the wind had tumbled dead leaves from the boughs above. She sobbed, her grief quite beyond control, as she caught the last sight of the church spire, with the background of wild hills rising above it. She thought in a bewildered way that the rooks would still be cawing in the wind-shaken trees, just as they had done on that sunny afternoon when she was married.

At the next station a commercial traveller got into the compartment, and she struggled for composure, and won. She rolled her handkerchief into a hard little ball, turning it round and round in her hot hand, and making plans for the future.

The commercial traveller hazarded a query as to whether she minded his smoking.

"No," said Carrie, and looked out of the window, blinking back another rush of tears resolutely, and recalling Robert's instinctive route to the pipe-rack after his day's work.

"Little Waketon!" shouted the porter, and a jolly little woman with a fat, tiny girl got into the carriage.

She made Carrie laugh by telling how she dodged the railway company. It was a very simple plan, but there was a touch of genius in it. Instead of a hat, her girl, who was seven, wore a little white fur bonnet, which was just kept on her head by the strings. When they went away for the week-end, they took the child's hat in a paper bag; but she went and returned in the little bonnet.

"Me, with six; what could I do?" she asked Carrie. "It isn't as if the porters got it; is it, now? And if they make you pay—well, you pay; and if they don't, 'tis a savin'."

The fat little girl swung her feet and opened her round eyes and looked quite a baby as the guard said "Tickets!" at the next stop.

The familiar line of cabs was waiting by the kerb near the little park in Ardwick Green as if it had never moved away since Carrie had left, but was still waiting for customers. The little butcher's shop, too, with its large letters informing the public that it was patronized by Royalty, came into view.

All these old landmarks struck her with a sense of the unchangeableness of things, and also with a queer sense of great changes within herself, leaving no marks for the outside world to read. A few months ago her outlook on life had been very simple. You took the best respectable chance you got, did your duty, held your own, and laughed at things lest they should laugh at you. Now it seemed a puzzle to know what was one's duty, what was your own, and how to get the necessary humour to laugh at troublesome things.

A sensitive pride had suddenly sprung up within her being, making holding on to things, fighting for them with the tongue, seem an impossible and vulgar thing. In a moment this gathering pride had culminated, and made it utterly out of the question to ever think of crossing a threshold where she was in the way, where she interfered with the harmony of the household, where she was mistrusted and despised and misunderstood. Better to go back to her own place, fight the old fight for existence, have her old friends.

She had on a hat Clara had lent her, so that she need not go back to the farm. True, she had crept back to write the inscription on the sty, and as she wrote had heard Robert cough in the upper room. She had seen his shadow cross the white blind, candle in hand. All the way down the hill in the dark she had watched his shadow, with a bitter feeling that he ought to have taken her part, and that he would have told Sarah that she was to be secondary queen only after she came, if he had cared for her as he professed to.

However, she thought, she had burned her boats behind her now. She did not regret it.

Her thoughts as she went along were of the shop. She wondered if the widow who had taken it on were tired of the long hours and grubby work, and if she would care to sell it back. Carrie had only ten shillings in the world, but hoped to be able to borrow a pound or two to purchase the fittings and pay the rest afterwards.

Great was her surprise on reaching the old corner to find the window empty and the shop being rebuilt to the whistling of "Bonnie Mary of Argyle" by half a dozen workmen.

The man on the ladder, tapping away, with his blue jacket spattered with dust, looked at the woman in the hat with draggled feather who seemed so interested in their work.

"Say, what are you making of it?" inquired Carrie, catching his eye on her.

With the hammer in his hand he paused, staring down into the interesting face with the bright blue eyes, straight little nose with the inquisitive tilt, and the dimples at each corner of the impudent mouth.

117

The scrutiny aroused Carrie's wrath. Why couldn't the man answer a civil question and have done with it?

"Think I'm a bloomin' dummy?" she asked angrily, colouring to the roots of her fair hair, and yet wondering dimly why she did such a thing. "This shop was mine—once. What's the matter it's being altered?"

"No offence," said the workman good-humouredly, giving the stone a cool little tap. "Maybe I liked the turn of your nose, Polly—"

"It ain't Polly, then," said Carrie.

"What is it then?" he inquired, swinging skilfully round on the ladder. "Come now, what is it?"

"It might be Matilda, or Agnes, or Martha Jane," began Carrie, with the old spirit of fun waking for a moment.

"'Tain't," he said decidedly. "It's something short, sharp, and hot. You ain't got a Matilda face."

"Never mind my face," snapped Carrie, "but answer your superiors" (with a twinkle in her eye) "civilly when they ask a civil question. What's to do it's being knocked about like this, my old shop? Where's the widow gone that had it after me?"

"Had to clear out, she had, when the Young Men's Cheerful Club wanted to buy it. Why, what's the matter?"—for Carrie's face had whitened visibly.

There was no chance of getting her old business back.

Did it mean going into service again? She set her little white teeth at the thought, with the old wounds she got at the Follingtons quivering anew.

"Nothing," she answered the workman. "Only I thought of getting it back. Thanks for your information."

"Here, I say, Polly!" he sang out, and she looked back. "If it's work you want, I can get you some. My sister has a cook-shop here in Manchester. She's good to get on with, and wants help. How about that?"

He looked anxiously at her.

"I could call now and then," he went on, rather sheepishly, "to see how you liked."

"I ain't got any references," answered Carrie, with the old flashing smile.

"Your face'll do for me," he retorted quickly.

The smile died suddenly out of the woman's face. She remembered that Sarah had not taken her on trust. It was queer how a man would trust her quicker than a woman, and looked farther and deeper, giving credit for what he could not see.

"I don't want service," she said soberly. "But it's awful good of you to say that. Shake."

She held up her ungloved, toil-worn hand, and he noticed the heavy ring on it, and wondered all day about her, and where her husband could be, with a disappointment covered up from his mates by the whistling of old songs.

All that day Carrie wandered about Manchester, looking in at the shop-windows and trying to revive old enthusiasms. It was no good calling on her friends until evening, for they all went out to work, either as printers, shirt-makers, or flax-mill hands.

As the whistles sounded, echoing drearily over the interminable, drab streets, and the people poured out like pale phantoms by the light of the flickering street-lamps, she called on one or two of her friends, telling them her predicament. All were sorry, but none had any plans to give, or asked her to stay at their home even overnight! She had called on those who were best off, and hope was faint indeed as she went along to the poorest of her friends, Julia and Fanny Winklesworth. The streets were narrower, grimier, as she went along, and full of neglected children. Dull-eyed, tousle-headed women sat at their doors shouting to each other to get above the roar of the traffic. It was difficult to think they had once been young, fair, and had dreams. Carrie shuddered. Would there ever come a time when she looked and felt like that, she wondered? The future was too big and dark to think of—she must get some work.

Through a black little entry, then into another street, and she was soon at the house of the Winklesworths. It had a clean doorstep, and in the window was the model of a green glass ship struggling through a stormy, green glass sea. Always struggling, always making no headway, was that ship, and might have been taken as symbolical of the worldly affairs of the Winklesworths. Yet it never sank, as many lives had done in those narrow streets, to be washed up, broken, hopeless wrecks to make men shudder.

Soon the story was unfolded, and Carrie was bidden stay there, to share such humble comforts as they had. Fanny said she would see if they could do with another hand at the mill, and after tea went upstairs to make a bed as well as she could on the floor in the spare room. Carrie had to have hers, she said, and after a battle Fanny came off conqueror, because the former was too tired to argue.

That evening Carrie pawned the Mizpah brooch Robert had bought her once when in Bringford, and added a little to her ten shillings, so that if she got work in a few weeks she could pay for her board with the Winklesworths.

In the morning she got up and drank from the same pint pot with Fanny, a draught of hot strong tea without milk before they went into the damp, dark streets. Arm close in arm, they struggled along in the teeth of the wind, which sometimes almost threatened to extinguish the street-lamps. Sometimes they clung together against the wall of a house, laughing because it was just as easy to laugh as cry, and because there is a grim humour in fighting against things and getting the best of them, to the working-class mind.

Only the clatter of the clogs was heard in the lull of the wind—tramp, tramp, tramp, sounding mysteriously out of the darkness, and hurrying more quickly like the ending of a musical march as the shriek of the whistle gave its warning that the doors would soon be closed. Little feet of half-timers, fresh from school, and the feet of grey-haired women who had borne children, buried children, had grandchildren, yet still must follow the call of the whistle. Gay women, melancholy women, grumbling women, silent women, struggled along against the wind. Women who clung with a scream, half of terror, half of mirth, to the arm of some man worker when the strong gusts came, and women who clung by preference to a lamppost, firm-rooted, then went on with bent heads. Most were silent, and those few of glib tongue and ready joke found little response from saturnine companions. Breath was precious!

In twenty minutes some of them—indeed, most of them—had risen in the dark room, dressed, swallowed the draught of tea got by the aid of the gas-jet, and were at work a half-mile or more away.

"How's your feet? Mine are like clay," said Fanny, as they entered the long room. "But when all the gases are lit it'll be better. My mantle is nearly gone, and the boss is a mean old crow, for I've told him twice about it. My eyes are worth more than the gas-mantles, don't you think, Carrie?"

"Rather," laughed Carrie, looking round at the machines, standing silent like ghosts in the dimness of the half-lighted room.

"There's the lift," said Fanny. "It doesn't work till the engine moves, and if you go down just when the engine's stopping you might get caught there half-way."

"And then what?" inquired Carrie, with the breathless curiosity of one who has never worked amongst machinery. "Do you get killed?"

"Killed!" and Fanny laughed, though it was early on in the morning to laugh, and her feet cold as clay, "No, they bring a ladder, and you've to climb out, *and they might see your stockings!*"

"Has any one ever been caught?"

"Mercy Winkles, once, and she wouldn't be got out, but stayed there all the dinner-hour, though she cried all the time."

"I'd have risked my stockings showing before that," said Carrie. "Wasn't she awful hungry?"

"Yes. We didn't half give her some humpy. But she couldn't help it. And she went to be a nun after. I think she'll have cried harder to get out o' there than she did to get out of the lift; but she was a good sort, too. Used to give the bacon from between her bread to the other girls, and say it was to get used to being without. She used to bring nun books, and read 'em in a corner, and once Matty Walmsley took one away and left the *Comic Cuts* instead, and she went into a passion, then pulled up, and crossed her hands on her breast. We all think she went that way because she couldn't get her work off, and the boss was always on her bones."

A young man in a blue overall now came up.

"Mornin'," he said, and lit one of Fanny's gas-lights.

"Mornin'," answered Fanny. "I say, Joe, couldn't you sneak me a mantle? You'll see me labelled Blind, playing a Jews' harp in the street some of these days, if you don't. It's no use asking 'im," with a stress on the last word. "An' it was broke when I got it."

"All right. I'll come sooner to-morrow, but don't say anythin' to the others. It 'ud be as much as my shop is wuth," and he passed on, lighting up, and whistling "*We all go the same way home.*"

"He's decent," said Fanny. "If we'd him for a boss now—"

"He'll always be at the bottom," said Carrie, practically. "He gives way," and she sat on an upturned tin, rubbing her hands.

Soon the majority of the toilers were in their places. The great wheels began to move, slowly at first, then gaining speed, and the quick sound of the machines setting to work, the bump of the lift as it reached the top, bringing some hurried toiler, made the air resound to movement.

Fanny went to the boss as he stood looking round to see if each worker was in her place.

"A new girl?" he echoed, and then saw Carrie, and stood weighing her up, as if she was a new machine waiting for his inspection.

"Done any flax work afore?" he asked.

She shook her head.

"Oh, well, there's no harm in learning," he said indifferently. "And some of these are going to be cleared out. Are you sharp?"

Carrie wavered.

Some of these girls were going to be cleared out, when he could get others to take their place who were sharper. She had a guilty feeling.

"Yes, she's awful sharp," cried Fanny. "Needle sharp, as she'll show you," and dragged her away, whispering afterwards, "Now, what did you look like that for? Why didn't you speak up for yourself? If you don't here, nobody else will."

But Carrie soon found out that this was not wholly true, though every one had it for a maxim.

After a time Carrie got used to the monotonous grumble of the machines, and could catch Fanny's instructions above the pulsing sound.

Breakfast-time came, and they discussed lovers, dreams of the previous night, the latest murder, and the series of pictures then running at the picture-palace.

How soon reappeared the boss to shout out "Get those machines on, you lazy devils!" for it seemed only a moment to Carrie since they had sat down. Really it was half an hour by the white-faced clock that the girls had subscribed for (and often wished they hadn't, for the time seemed longer through their watching it when they were tired). But when there are things to set straight, so that there are no arrears when the engine starts once more, and the hot water for the tea is to be fetched, and you have a seat to find and fix, and you feel you must rest two little minutes before beginning to eat, how quickly the time flies!

Then came the scrape of the machines being set on again, and now gossip began to spring up and enliven the toil, as if the food and drink had loosened their tongues, and given courage.

Sometimes the toilers on one frame would attempt to sing, and those on another would set up a conflicting melody, until the boss, heralded by the bump of the lift, silenced both parties. He would stand regarding them cynically, in absolute silence, and everybody would look perfectly innocent, but a trifle shy, then he would swing round on his heel "as if it had a swivel on it," Carrie said, and go away as if they were beyond his contempt.

Very often they were love-songs they sang, for many of them were still young, and those whose dreams had been shattered by short rations, the daily grind, and the ironies of a ready-made existence joined in them just the same, as if trying to believe them. Veronica Jones sang solos, without being asked, though she was often requested to desist. When she sang love-songs the girls winked at each other, and knew that she was thinking of John Mirby, who worked in the other room, and sometimes came round with an oil-can to stay the shrieking of some crank-wheel near the roof.

"You wouldn't think to hear her bawl like that that she'd fainting fits," Fanny said to Carrie, passing up and down the length of her frame. "She often has to be carried out. Mind! You'll catch your hand if you do that again! Don't put it down there, put it this way."

And so the day wore on, not quite so long as those that were to follow it, because of the spice of novelty. Whispered conversations went on at times, mostly between friends, partners on the same machine. They were generally about boys they knew, if they were young girls. Going past them for something Fanny required Carrie would hear something like this.

"Oh, an' what did 'e say?"

"'E says, 'Never mind your old man. He got married, didn't he?' An' I says, 'Yes, an' 'im only nineteen,' and—"

Then Carrie would overhear, "That's the new one. Hush!"

They would continue the conversation in a louder key, gradually shouting it out when the length of the frame divided them, utterly careless of her presence.

Some of these girls thought the men and boys in the other rooms wonderful creatures.

When Carrie began to feel less awkward at the tasks Fanny set her, and had a little time to look round, she felt that she loved the girls. Poverty has no deceit, and they got to know each other quickly. Some thirty girls and women worked in the long, whitewashed rooms, and when they were really serious, singing some old hymn tune, or a popular ditty of the day, there was a sense of brave, beautiful fellowship about them, transforming them from so many cranks in a mighty machine into living souls. Some of the girls told her their little love-stories.

When a worker came with her head half-covered with curling-pins, her companions would ask her where she was going to-night, and who her pal would be.

The "golden hours" they spent with their sweethearts were mostly passed in the picturedromes, where the youth smoked Woodbines, and spat with the air of a duke newly arrived at his inheritance, and the girl chewed nuts, and was glad of the semi-darkness that hid the moisture in her eyes for the deserted Indian girls.

Such were the bright oases set in the desert of toiling and moiling, and the struggle to make both ends meet.

Some had only their working dresses, and these brushed free of the fluff had to do duty on all occasions, and were washed by instalments. They could not roam far abroad, but loitered in their own doorways, looking wistfully and scoffingly at the Sunday-dressed crowds, and waiting for the dusk to fall—the kindly, romantic dusk. The more fortunate ones, with a dress laid aside for Sunday—fought for with primitive savagery at a sale—walked with their young men along the Ashton New Road, backwards and forwards along that road, till it was time to part, under the stars, or sometimes in the rain, under one umbrella.

At such times a young couple found it difficult to believe that in a few hours the whistle would call them, two slaves amongst a multitude of slaves, when they felt that each other was the most wonderful person in the world! They walked on air, and saw the stars shine, and even poverty could not numb their hearts, but let them stray for a short time in that fairy garden whose gate opens but once, and, once closing, nevermore!

Through the following week the spirit of those few hours consecrated their lives. Every bit of work they did was for each other, not for the boss. They lived for these week-ends, and forgot the mechanical monotony of walking backwards and forwards over a few yards of hot, dusty floor that pulsed to the throb of the tireless engine, and the whirl of the spindles became an accompaniment to thoughts of each other.

Then they married, and the bliss soon died. The old painful monotony crept back, worse than ever, and once again they were numbers—links in an endless chain. Carrie loved them all—those who were courting, and those who weren't and vowed they never would, and those who were married, and brought their babies in their arms if they stopped half a day at the mill, and came for their wages on the Friday night.

Sometimes just as she had made up her mind that a certain individual was hard and selfish she would get an illuminating glimmer of something soft and tender, until she was fairly bewildered. Margaret Vane would be almost knocking her next neighbour over in an effort to make a few more bobbins in the day than that neighbour, and would spend the extra pence in a dancing doll to hang on the gas-pipe to make the whole of the workers on the frame laugh. Milly Jones, who had to be shamed into paying to the hospital collection, once took old Betty Smith's bad lot of twist and gave her a good lot instead. Once Carrie was thinking that Sarah Miller, a grass widow with two children to provide for, was a bit too gay, when that pale-faced woman with the light eyes looked up, read her thought, and said, "Some folk cries when aught goes wrong. I laughs—to keep fro' crying." Occasionally she felt dizzy, to look up and see all those hands and arms working away in unison, as if they were cogs in one big wheel.

A low hiss, the most perfect imitation of escaping steam, was the Masonic signal given to chatterers that the lift was ascending, possibly bringing the manager. Thus they protected each other. The chatter mostly came from the youthful portion, which was not made into a machine without a struggle. When the engine broke down, these young ones gave a yell of delight, gathered into the open square in the centre of the room, and formed a set of lancers, bowing to their partners with sardonic humour, squabbling which should take the lady or gentleman. By and by, as responsibilities pressed them, they toned down, their faces took on the set, staring look which marks them out even in the street as industrial workers, and until that joyous, exasperating youth died the others protected them.

They lent each other cheap books. They talked with hushed breaths of the anguish of Lady Isabel in "East Lynne," and thought Barbara Hare a trifle forward. They did not realize that there was more tragedy in any one of their drab lives than in that of the delicate Isabel. The tragedy in the lives of the people is in what does not happen, rather than in what does happen—in all they do not realize.

Fanny told Carrie as they breakfasted together of the young man she had been engaged to a long time ago, before Julia hurt her spine by falling down the worn wooden staircase of the factory—which was afterwards set to rights. "Perhaps, it was all for the best," she said, quietly munching her almost butterless bread; "things weren't so bad but they might be worse." And when she saw other people with children they didn't know how to feed she was downright thankful. The worst bit now was when half a day's stoppage made it wellnigh impossible to get the rent together, and when the young ones shouted for joy it made her feel wild.

Carrie was very often tired. In the oyster-shop she had been able sometimes to rest five minutes on the three-legged stool behind the counter, but here that was prohibited.

"Oh, you'll get used to it," said Fanny. "It does take you in the legs at first. Have you heard that he's given Mary Ellen over there the sack? Ties her knots too big."

Buzz-buzz-buzz! Click-click-click! Dum-dum-dum! The sounds of wheel, spindle, and the pulse of the engine's iron heart went on invincibly.

Carrie looked across at Mary Ellen, the pale young woman in the glasses, who always looked as if she could do with a stick at her back, like the climbers in the window at Hilltop Farm. Silently she was pacing backwards and forwards at her machine, no sign of emotion in her face.

"What will she do?" breathed Carrie.

"Don't know. She's near-sighted, and her glasses don't suit her eyes now—and she can't get more—that's why she makes the big knots. His-s-s! The boss!"

Polly Brown, who was acting the Merry Widow with a waste-can on her head, flew to her place and seized a bobbin the wrong way up.

The boss crossed over to Carrie.

"Think you'll be able to manage on your own?" he asked; then without waiting for her answer, "Over there, No. 12 frame, on Monday."

He walked away.

"That's Mary Ellen's frame," whispered Fanny.

"Oh!" ejaculated Carrie, and the happiness left her face. "*You* can't help it," protested Fanny; but Carrie did not answer.

On the Monday morning Carrie walked over to the vacant place. The first knot she tied she felt was something towards paying off her debt to Fanny and Julia. She was aware that the other girls were watching her, weighing up her skill, and pasting up the report of it in their minds. The friends of Mary Ellen talked in undertones of her dismissal, and disliked Carrie according to the degree of their liking for Mary Ellen. But in a few weeks she lived down the impression that she was at all unfair, or that she was greedy.

The debt she owed the Winkleworths was cleared off, according to them, though Carrie swore she never could clear it off, and the time stole on. Sometimes it seemed short, sometimes long, according to her mood, and she was often very tired.

But Carrie loved this life better than domestic service. She felt herself one of many—weak and insignificant enough alone, but wonderful, strong, beautiful, along with them.

She had her thoughts. They were deeper and sadder than they were before she ever saw the green hill in the country; but she felt that they alone made her life tolerable, they and her companions. Sometimes she wondered if Peter the pig would take the first prize at Bringford Fair, sometimes if Robert missed her at all, or if Sarah wore her very oldest bonnet and cloak, as of yore, only bringing out her best to air, lest the moth should feed on the shining silk, hoarding them up against some wonderful occasion that never arrived.

Eight months went by.

A feeling of dissatisfaction in Room 7 made itself felt. Three months before there had been a strike, but Room 7 had gained nothing but hunger by the transaction. The girls and women talked in little knots in the meal-hours, when they came into the long room where Carrie worked, to dine with their friends. The dissatisfaction was a murmur at first, then swelled louder and louder, but still Room 7 felt its own impotency unless the other rooms backed it up.

One day, Carrie, as they were all sitting at breakfast and had been discussing the state of things, jumped up, stood on an upturned waste-can, and made an impromptu speech, full of grim humour, fire, and a sense of justice. She asked the girls to back up Room 7, and join the Union, those who were not in it already, and fight, like Englishwomen. They listened with mirth at first, knowing her aptitude for a joke, but her fire of words at length stirred their blood.

Just as they clapped their hands and she stepped down, Dick Jones, the boss, swung out of the lift. How much or little he had heard could not be guessed, but something certainly, by the gleam in his eyes.

"He'll be down on you, Carrie, for this," said an old worker sympathetically.

"What do I care? If Room 7 gets a rise they'll enjoy it when I've gone," she laughed, and perhaps this brave, laughing speech inspired the girls and women to suffer again for the sake of Room 7.

All the workhands joined the Union, which was indeed very poor in funds.

The morning came when the toilers in Room 7 refused as one woman to work for seven-and-six. They boldly demanded a rise of ninepence, saying the machines should stand idle else. Jones cursed them all round, and told them he wanted none of their damn nonsense, and ordered them to knock the machines on. He told them that the other rooms would not back them up for more than a week or two.

Some of the other hands who had wandered in near the doorway to see the scene shouted "Won't we? Try us!"

Jones came up from the office with the verdict that there would be no advancement. They took their shawls and overskirts and filed out into the street. The throb of the machines in other factories came to them with a sound of prosperity.

Carrie and Fanny passed the first day washing up old blouses and bedding in the damp scullery. They told each other cheerfully that the battle would be brief.

The Battle for Ninepence began.

City papers reported it when there was a few inches of space between society chit-chat, the winter's fashions, and musical critiques. Preachers talked solemnly from the pulpit of the spirit of unrest abroad in the land, and regretted a materialistic conception of life that kept the toilers from the inner light. People quarrelled as to which side was in the right.

Not hearing the voices of public opinion, the strikers hung on, going paler and thinner each day, crying each time they left the strike-meetings, "Are we downhearted? No!"

From scrap meat to ham-bones, from ham-bones to butterless bread—credit refused in many cases—everything sold that could be done without, and always the thought haunting them that if they would merely consent to give in they could get meat again. It haunted them as the landlord stood on the tattered doormat and looked askance, and as the children whispered for more and could not have it—but most of all as the papers began to appear in the grocers' windows, saying in bright, red letters "Join our Club!"

But they did not give in.

The weeks crept by, each one longer than the last. They felt that they were clinging now as mariners to a spar. It was simply a question of how long they could hold on. Some were dumb, and some were vehement. Fanny was quiet. Carrie became cynical. Somebody opened a soup-kitchen, and when she heard of it she threw back her head and laughed a trifle hysterically, saying, "Isn't it good of 'em? They'll go to heaven when they die, won't they, Julia?" Once she got a day's cleaning at a lawyer's and earned half a crown. She divided it up sitting on Julia's bed.

"They were having folk to dinner," she told them. "And I'd to hurry to get done before they came. You should have seen *her* putting autumn leaves at each corner of the table, an' singing up an' down—and her frock trailing half a mile—yes, it did, Julia! She turns round and says, 'You're sure you went into all the corners? I do like things done thoroughly.' Then she gave me half a crown for having tumbled half the house about and back again! It makes you mad—but it makes you laugh!"

One afternoon Fanny and Carrie went to the strike-meeting. It was held in a bleak building showing the bricks and rough stonework inside. The rain was splashing monotonously upon five high windows. There were forms without back-rests ranged row on row, with another line running all round the four sides.

The place was half full of women and girls, with a sprinkling of men. Some had cleaned their clogs and brushed straw hats, others sat listless and unwashed, having forgotten the flesh in the battle.

Upon a little wooden platform that appeared dangerously like tumbling down whenever any one either left or stepped upon it, sat the chairman, a cosy-looking man in black. A woman in a nondescript hat, rather tired looking, sat on the other side, her hand near a small bell that rang with a harsh intonation.

The chairman rising and making the boards shake, informed them that the speaker who should have come had missed her train. As it was raining they must do their best to pass half an hour along as best they could amongst themselves.

With a little nudging from her companions Annie Swales, a consumptive-looking woman in a grey shawl which seemed to pull her head down to the ground almost, made her way up to the platform, and took her place upon it.

Swaying her thin body to and fro to the tune, she sang in a sleepy, unharmonious voice, "My Evelina, O!" Her husband, also a flax-mill worker, played the accompaniments from behind the hall on a threepenny mouth-organ. Everybody who knew it joined the chorus, and those who didn't tapped their clogs, following as well as they could in muted voices.

There was loud applause at the end of the song. A song is always popular that leaves room for the audience to join in. The chairman then gave his address, playing with his watch-chain as he did so. He assured them of the continuance of their weekly five shillings to the end of the fight. (Unanimous applause.) He often thought of them, he went on, as he sat by his fire at night, his feet in his slippers, and pipe in his mouth.

(A young Irish girl who had come from a public institution to sing for them winced just here, wishing he had a little more tact and remembering that they perhaps had no fires.)

He admired their splendid courage, he continued (they wriggled in their seats, being bored), and assured them that the men would not go in without them. ("Hear, hear," from a bent little man with a broken-stemmed pipe stuck between blackened teeth.) He recited them a little poem from Wordsworth, but they wriggled still.

He said the strike was drawing to a successful issue, and negotiations were already afoot.

Then the young Irish girl sang a couple of Greig's cradle melodies in her moist, fresh voice, and there was sudden silence and cessation of whispering.

The woman with the tired face and nondescript hat rose and spoke to them. Then she made them laugh by a funny recitation, in which a man was worsted by a woman, clever as he had thought himself. She put her fingers upon the finest chords in their hearts, and stirred them to martial music But when they had gone home she sat a long time by the table with its faded cover and the sharp-spoken bell. The weary look was more fixed as she left the building. She did not take the car, but walked miles to her home through the grey streets.

"Why didn't you ride?" somebody asked her, as she dropped into an easy chair, and she smiled faintly, saying, "I couldn't. I had no—no money."

In a few more weeks it was over.

Annie Swales's baby had died, and she was so low that she could not go back to work just then. She bought an old black skirt and bodice from a rag-cart that came round to her back door. The baby was buried in a public grave.

It was a glorious victory.

The ninepence was won. It was there, something you could grasp, use, eat and drink, or help cover yourself with.

They had suffered together to get it. It was there for

the next comers. A few weeks later Carrie was stopped for a trifling mistake in her work.

She looked up at Jones, as he gave her the notice slip, her blue eyes full of scorn.

"This is boycott," she said, in a clear, slightly raised voice.

"Nonsense!" he growled. "It's for bad work," and walked away a little ashamed, knowing her carefulness as well as speed.

"We'll come out again!" cried the girls, gathering round her. How pale they were still!

She shivered as she looked at their faces.

"Not for me," she said proudly. "I'm not that sort. See that hand there?" holding out her firm, practical fingers. "Well, those hands are mine. He can't take 'em, and they can do more than this," pointing to the machine. "Don't worry for me."

She went round to the other mills, but they all knew her. It *was* boycott.

Chapter VIII

THE CHRISTMAS-CARD FACTORY

EVERY morning Carrie got up when Fanny did going out with her, in the hopes of being able to find something to do—somewhere.

She sold a new blouse which she had in her drawer, and the Mizpah brooch had gone again. The darkness and silence of the streets, echoing only to her lonely footsteps, sometimes made her feel that she could scream—not at the darkness, nor yet at the silence, but for fear of something that seemed to loom there for such as she.

One windy morning she paused before a huge building that sent a stream of light into the dingy street. The shadows of the straps revolving were cast on one of the windows. Anon, a woman's head went by, quick, like the shadows themselves.

Looking wearily up at a creaking signboard, Carrie read in glaring letters:

Girls Wanted.

And over the door, by dint of much eye-straining, she made out,

Morning Star Christmas-Card Works.

After a moment's pause she opened the door, and found herself in a lobby, facing an office-window. Some one was talking in the office, and the conversation was continued, then a young woman in a dark velvet dress came and looked at Carrie over a buff-painted wicket-gate that barred the entrance into the official sanctum.

"Are you after work?" she asked politely enough, yet with something grating in the voice itself.

Carrie bowed her head.

"Utterly inexperienced?" inquired the young woman.

Carrie bowed her head again.

"I would give you eight shillings—for a time," said the young woman, regarding her critically. "Not that you'd be worth it—not that you'd earn it, at first; after, we could see."

Carrie bowed her head once more.

"Can you start now?"

"Now," answered Carrie, and followed the young woman from the office, through a bare, flagged room with three rude tables in it, a form, and a fire, over which was suspended a giant kettle, whose sooty covering quivered in the draught of the chimney.

Two steps led into another room—a busy, gaslit room, with four long tables down its length, where sat girls and women of almost every age, bending over pasteboard boxes.

They did not look up as Miss Woods entered, bringing the new girl.

"Sarah, show this girl her work," said Carrie's guide; and a small, brown-eyed, flaxen-haired lassie obediently quitted her stool and procured one for Carrie.

"Push up," she cried, and the workers on the table pressed nearer together, giving Carrie some half a yard of space for herself.

"You fold the insets this way, and then get hold of them like this; no, that isn't the way—just put the inset in straight, and it's quite easy; no, not that way," and she looked at Carrie as much as to say, "How stupid you are!"

Carrie felt stupid. Her toes and fingers were frozen almost. She had lived on bread for two weeks—bread soaked in milkless tea. The light after the darkness bewildered her, and the sly glances the other workers cast at her made her fumble more than she otherwise would have done.

"Thanks," she said to the brown-eyed girl. "I think I can manage now," and the power of the blue eye quelled that of the brown one. The prejudice against the stranger, unknown and unknowing, had met her again.

In one hour Carrie had learned the rules of the game, and won the respect of her mates at the table.

References to "Memory's Jewels" and "Waves of Remembrance" became monotonously sickening to Carrie after some time. The pictures ceased to attract—those bright Christmas pictures of snowy lanes with illumined houses at the turn, suggesting plenty and prosperity. She wondered if Colonel and Mrs. FitzPatrick, who were paying nine-and-six per dozen for the cards named "Masterpieces," were aware that fifty of these cards had the insets pasted within them, were carefully cleaned with the rubber dirt-eraser, packed up, for considerably less than one halfpenny, by those who were on piecework.

It struck her as unfair to the workers themselves that they were paid by the number of bundles they did, when the bundle varied in its numbers of cards from fifty to half a dozen. This caused much bitterness amongst those workers who got more than their share of fifties, and many hot looks were exchanged.

When Carrie had done a bundle, she had to make a mark thus—1—in blacklead, on a slip of paper at her elbow. Miss Woods, if she found her too slow, on counting up those marks at night, would dismiss her—on evidence of her own showing!

Miss Woods sat at the end of the table, watching, and the girls could only make silent grimaces to each other when her eye left them for a moment.

"Can't you talk?" asked Carrie once, to a mild-looking girl on the other side of her—a girl whose hair-ribbon was eternally having to be pushed up to keep it in its place.

Miss Woods was just then at the farthest table, near to the printing-press, whose grinding seemed to shake the hot, gaslit room.

"You wait," she murmured, her eyes on her work, her fingers never stopping, "You don't know *her*. Watches you like a cat watches a mouse. She's coming," and all the time the deft fingers went on inserting the slips that bore wishes of fellowship and love.

The shuffling back of Miss Woods's stool simultaneously with the stopping of the printing-press announced dinner-time. They rushed away, carrying their stools with them, into the bare, flagged room with a huge soot-covered kettle. Within five minutes, all were sitting down, eating and talking as fast as they could.

"Haven't you brought aught?" inquired a stout bonny woman of forty, with little black curls and a comfortable atmosphere. "There's a cook-shop round the corner."

"I'm not hungry," lied Carrie, looking her straight in the eyes.

"Fancy that now," she said. "Well, you might ha' a bite with me, just to show there's no ill will."

She held out a slab of bread, thick and butterless, but holding a shaving of boiled ham, and made a place by her side.

"Oh, all right, if you put it that way, but I'm not hungry; 'tis my stomach gets out of order at times," lied Carrie; and the woman nodded her head as if utterly deceived.

"Have you worked here long?" inquired Carrie, her teeth busy on the slab, so that the words were slightly muffled.

"Years."

"Oh!" gasped Carrie, faintly. Then, "Isn't she a snoozler? Is she always like that? Or has she got a gumboil this morning?"

"Oh, you've seen her at her best yet," grinned the woman. "She sacked a woman, one of the Christmas ones, yesterday. Shouts at her to get her things on, and the woman says, 'What about what I've earned?' 'Oh,' says she, 'come an' look for it when it snows green,' and the woman, old enough to be her mother, she shakes her fist in her face, and says, 'Scoundrel!' We have to sing low here all the year, do' ye see? But it fairly suits us, up to the fanlight, when one of these stray ones tells her the tale. Ha' a sup? 'Twill warm yo'."

Carrie took a drink from the pot with its photographs of the reigning monarchs set in a laurel wreath on the side.

"Twopence to see the lions feed!" said a man in a blue jacket, standing in the doorway.

"Nay," said a pugnosed girl, her face surrounded by frizzed hair, so that she resembled a Pomeranian dog (a torn sleeve hung down like a Bishop's). "Th' lioness is up above," with a glance towards Miss Woods's room.

There was a general laugh.

A boy came through the room to wash his hands.

"Hello, darling!" he said, striking a stage attitude, and chucking the girl at the end of one of the tables under the chin. She screamed with laughter.

Then the spoons and the dishes were busy once more, and occasionally some girl scrambled her way to the huge kettle.

"Mind what you're doing?" they would grumble at her as she came back with a potful of boiling water.

"How can I? Look at the room there is," she would say, and in truth every square inch seemed occupied.

"Do yo' see that girl over there?" asked Carrie's pal. "That little girl with the blue eyes and sleepy look? Her father is dying, poor little thing, and her seven-and-six is all they have coming in."

"She finds us the cards when we're one short," said Carrie. "She always gives you the wrong number!"

"No wonder," said the woman.

The child they were speaking of got up, stood on one leg yawned, and went out of the room singing a comic song of the day, and all the girls and women looked at one another, then some one said, "Bless 'er! An' a bonny face, like a little sparrer!"

"Come along. Get on with your work," shouted Miss Woods, and the printing-press began to grind once more, the girls took their stools, silent, automatic, tasselling, putting in the insets, reading the orders, putting round the elastic band, and making their mark when the bundle was complete:

"A Merry Christmas and a Happy New Year!"

Through the afternoon they worked, and when it was almost dark the gas was lit.

"Such a headache I have," muttered one girl. "And me too," said another. "I've been staring—I couldn't see!"

"I'll have less talk and more work out of you, Sally Lever," said the woman at the end of the table, leaning on one elbow, her dark eyes glittering.

Sally blushed and bent her aching head lower.

Carrie's eyes blazed.

"I want Card Number 133," said a woman of thirty, who wore a shamrock brooch on her breast, and coughed genteelly every now and then.

The child-girl of the comic song and dying father and the sleepy look asked dully, "One forty-three, did you say?"

"Put your hand out to feel you're not i' bed," sneered the girl of the brown eyes. "Pinch yourself, Mabel."

"I did once—wi' the elastic," said the child. "Shut your face, or I'll gi'e you the wrong 'un every time."

Miss Woods came round on one of her periodical voyages to take up the bundles.

Her heels dug into the wooden floor as if they had spurs attached and she was urging forwards a rebellious horse. "Come, come, hurry up!" she said, and flew down the room.

Six o'clock, and they had half an hour for tea.

"She's nice if you keep on t' right side of her," said a woman with a purple face and black bodice.

The workers looked at her scornfully.

"You've only been here two weeks. And who's going to try to keep on t' right side of her?" said a girl, passionately. "We never prate back, but we aren't going to lick her boots for her yet!"

"'Tis a very responsible position," said the purple one apologetically.

"Well, she's paid for it; we aren't," said another. And then somebody said, "Oh, shut up!" and began to whistle "The Cock o' the North."

Back again, until eight.

At one minute to eight a worker stole a sly glance at the clock. "Get on with your w—urk! I'll tell you when it's time to stop," said the voice from the end of the table.

A minute later the lights went down, each girl snatched her paper full of marks, handed it in, and, putting on her outdoor garments, went out into the street.

By dinner-time the next day Carrie Gibson had been scolded four times. She had been inquiring once how to put in a new kind of inset, when the Eye had caught her.

"I thought," said the purple woman, as they sat eating—"I thought you were going to go once when she shouted at you."

"I'm going now, when I've had my dinner," said Carrie. "Wouldn't work for a thing like her if it meant death on leaving. The only time she's looked sweet was when one o' the men came in. I hate that sort. Crushes their own sex under their heel, an' smiles at the fellows."

"She *is* a flirt," said the pugnosed girl. "Awful!"

"If she asks for me," said Carrie, holding the door open a moment, "tell 'er I had enough. Tell her to keep my bob and a half, and buy herself a temper with it. 'Tis worth it to get away."

Then she passed out into the street, with envious looks cast after her.

"Must ha' something, or she couldn't gi'e ower like that," some one said, and then the topic changed.

A very white Carrie reached her lodgings.

"I've given up," she said, sitting down on a chair near Julia's bed. "It was silly; but she made my blood boil. Some of 'em haven't any blood—no more'n a cockroach!"

"Poor Carrie!" said Julia, sadly. "I wish I was rich."

"I wish," said Carrie, slowly, "that I could crush her as she crushes them—down, down, and down!"

And Julia said, "Oh, Carrie!"

"Not for myself," said Carrie in that still voice. "To think of her and her likes, the world over, crushing such as they be, till they daren't laugh or look up! 'Tis because I love them, not just for myself."

"Perhaps she has to do it to keep her place," said Julia.

Carrie paused.

"Perhaps she has," she allowed, her wrath over, the colour in her face again. "'Tis better to be them than to be she, with all her big wage and velvet," and she took off her battered hat.

Chapter IX

THE LONG, WHITE ROAD

"I CAN'T stay and sponge on you and Fanny," said Carrie one morning. "I'm going back to Greenmeads."

"To the farm?" asked Julia, with a tone which said she thought it the best thing to do.

"No," answered Carrie, shortly; "I won't be driven back by starvation, in these rags! When I go, I'll go of my own free will, and finer than ever I was before. Sarah'd be delighted if I went back like this. I'm going to Clara, to see if she can recommend me to go out cleaning."

"You've no money," said Julia, after a pause, in which the white cat could be heard mewing plaintively for the kittens who were drowned.

"I'll manage. Shanks's pony does away with the need for tickets," cheerfully responded Carrie. "Don't you worry, Julia, for I'm old enough and hard enough to take care of myself."

Julia did not appear to think so from the look on her sympathetic face. Carrie looked considerably paler and older than when she came from the farm. There was a worn expression that warred with one of proud independence on her face. The lines round her mouth were sometimes almost bitter, despite her rollicking bravado. In the shop she had possessed a home and things of her own. Lodgings, even with two such congenial and generous souls as Julia and Fanny, were not like having even a room of your own. Sometimes she was afraid that she intruded upon their lives, and got a strange, lonely feeling. They had each other, and their father, a quiet, slow-spoken man, who had a small pension from the firm he had worked for more than a quarter of a century. Their father was a man with the heart of a child and the courage of a lion. They were people of one blood, with the memories of family life. The dolls'-house he had made them long ago, now set on the bracket in the corner, was a relic to them; but it made Carrie feel an interloper.

The world seemed callous, wide, and something to be afraid of to Carrie sometimes.

In the night, as she lay listening to the wind battering against the fire-screen made from an almanac, she had decided to go.

Julia was fumbling under her pillow. Finally she pulled out a shabby purse, given to her by an old school-mate long since dead. In the middle compartment were three crooked sixpences, which she had kept for good luck—not that anything very wonderful had ever befallen, excepting once when Fanny found a half-sovereign on her way to work, and when she had the bath-chair given to her. These two events, coming during the period of preservation of the crooked sixpences, strengthened Julia's faith.

"Lift me up, Carrie," she asked, with a shining look that made her more like the pictures of the saints of the Middle Ages than ever.

Carrie did so, looking at the purse in the thin hand, the exultation on the pain-graven countenance—the joy that was come from being able to help.

"Here," she said pleadingly, "take them, Carrie," turning the purse upside down so that the three sixpences fell upon the bed.

Then, more eagerly, looking into the protesting countenance, "They'll bring you luck."

"I couldn't take them from you, Julia," said Carrie, stubbornly, looking across the way at the smoke-blackened brick wall which Julia saw all the day as she lay in bed. Her mouth was set firmly, but her eyes were dim. When people were good to her, Carrie always felt knocked over; when they were unkind, she detested and tried to make them be just, at least. Julia's face grew overcast. She had wanted to help so much! What better lot could befall those sixpences, saved through long years, than to help Carrie along the road to her sister's.

Carrie saw the baffled, sad look, and choked back the pride into her throat.

"There," she said humbly, stroking the hand on the counterpane, "I'll take them. Thanks, Julia. If anything could bring me luck it would be this money, I know."

Then she was gone, and all the way to the highroad that was to take her to Greenmeads she was thinking "Dear little Julia" to the sound of her own steps. Soon she left the houses behind and came to the country, which lay grey and bare to the rough winds. When she had gone ten miles she was very tired. Looking up, she saw a vehicle coming, and determined to ask for a lift. But when she saw the man's face, so prosperous-looking and self-satisfied was it that the words died before they were uttered. Sometimes a child came out of a little house near the road, looking curiously at her, or a hen flew with a startled cluck through the hedgerow. She began to think of all the people who had tramped this road since it was made, and wondered if their thoughts were anything like her own. Her feet throbbed with the unaccustomed walking, and because her shoes were so thin that she could feel every stone through them. The cold, nipping air made her hungry, and as she had no food, hunger became faintness; yet still she went on. Julia's precious gift must be hoarded against the worst, not spent at the first touch of need. If her strength gave out before she reached Greenmeads, she would have to stay somewhere for the night, and must save the money for that emergency.

The rumble of the wheels on the road, iron-hard with the frost, died into the great silence. Still she held on, trying not to think of all the weary miles between her and Greenmeads.

Sometimes she passed quiet graveyards with dark trees dotted amongst the white stones, and heard the cawing of the restless daws. At noon she sat down to rest—her teeth chattering, her thin shawl pulled closely round her, watching the people pass by. They looked at her almost as if she were a tramp! The thought stirred her chill blood.

Then she began to think about tramps. Why, everybody on the road who had no work was a tramp! That was all it meant, that despised word—people for whom there was no work and no place were tramps.

She wondered whether it wasn't better to be a tramp than a flax-mill girl, struggling along on a wretched ten shillings per week, with the monotony only broken by an occasional strike, full of hunger, fierce emotions, dogged sufferings. A tramp would always have the wide, clear sky over his head, the earth beneath his feet, and no eye, mean and watchful, like that at the end of the table, upon him. There would be hunger and thirst and chances to run, but moments of joy and cheer such as were never felt in those cage-like streets.

Her eyes followed the road, winding up and down, through trees, by pasture lands hoar and grey with frost, but soon to be green with the coming of spring. She thought of the evenings, tramping alone on those roads, amongst the grey shadows, seeing the red lights of cottage fires shine upon the white silence—and shuddered. No, her heart was not big enough, brave enough. She loved a corner and things of her own—and a pal to suffer and enjoy life with.

As she rose to her feet, footsteps sounded behind her, regular, easy footsteps that neither lagged nor hurried, but came right on, out of the white silence into the white silence, unafraid. They belonged to a man, in rusty fustian, with a red woollen scarf knotted about his throat. He was forty, fat, jovial, his face dyed a rich red-brown with wind, rain, and the sunshine of many years. He was not bad-looking. In his eyes were memories of strange things he had seen. As he caught up with her, Carrie guessed that he was a rolling stone.

They began to talk. There is a bond between those who have nothing, as well as between those who have a lot. They spoke straight out from their different experiences, forgetting the bite of the cold wind, hunger, and the road hard as iron.

"Might as well go 'long with me," said the man, in comradely fashion. "'Tain't a bad life, on the whole. I've tried the other sort, but—nevermore!"

He put his hands in his ragged pockets for some little warmth, and sang,

"The Lord is my Shepherd, I shall not want.
He maketh me to lie down in green pastures,
He leadeth me beside the still waters."

"You never realize the joy and beauty of that old Psalm till you've been a tramp a year," he said seriously, his eyes beaming. "Only—it's best with a pal. Last week my second old woman died. Pneumonia. It's always that with us, or rheumatics; but you've got to die with something if you rent a 'ouse, so that's no argument against tramping. You'd like this sort, young woman. I'll never beat you, unless you drives me to it, and we'll always go halves, little or much."

"What about winter?"asked Carrie, laughing.

"Well, you gets fourpence from somewhere—though it's surprising how hard fourpence is to scratch together sometimes," candidly. "Then you gets a bed in a casual, or a shelter, and buys a red herring with the other penny, if you've got one. If you've naught" (he scratched his head ruefully)—"and it does happen sometimes; folk has no faith these days!—you finds a dyke as sheltered as you can, and that's where the benefit of a pal comes in. Two can hitch together, and keep each other warm."

He whistled again, this time from the opera of "Floradora."

For a time there was only the sound of their feet on the road. The man broke the silence.

He told how many years he had lived like this, without doing any work. The idea that he could exist without work had come to him suddenly—like a flash of inspiration, he said. But he had worked twenty years before that without finding out how easy it was, when you knew the ropes, and had frugal tastes. Those twenty years, he said, justified these idle ones, for into them he had crammed more than many a well-respected man does in a lifetime.

"Bless you!" he said, with a burst of mirth at the thought, "I worked high days and holidays, and Sundays, and overtime at nights till I didn't know where I was—nigh. Got a bank-book, and put money in and had to fetch it out when sickness came, and played the whole respectable gamut. At thirty I was a widower, with a doctor's bill as long as my arm for the departed, and as I'd neither chick nor child, and no one to care a penny whistle what I did with my life, I just tried this for a change. It was hard at first. Thought the folk stared at me; didn't like to tell a lie, but I soon got over that. Yes, bless you, I learnt the halfpenny trick, the tea trick, and get along now, having taken my degree. It's not half bad."

He explained to Carrie, as they went along, the meaning of the halfpenny trick. You had a halfpenny, which you clung to through thick and thin.

There was a scientific law which made people give to him who had, he said, as the Salvation Army people knew. It was the same law that made saving easier after the first few pounds. You went into a shop, looked woebegone, and throwing down the halfpenny with a down-at-the- bottom gesture asked for a halfpennyworth of bread, or a bit of "bacca" if you needed it. It was a mean woman who would take what she thought to be your last halfpenny. Generally speaking, where people were normal, you got your halfpenny back with the bread, and maybe another added to it.

The tea trick was similar. You took your can and asked for a drop of hot water, and got sugar and milk put in free.

He told her of amusing things that had happened to him, the strangest of which was of the parson who had told him to go into his summer-house and drink the keg of beer up, locking him in with it till morning. It was, he grinned, the worst beer he had ever tasted. That was why the parson gave him a chance.

They had now reached the signpost where two roads met.

"Coming with me?" inquired the man, cheerily, stuffing his pipe with tobacco.

Carrie laughed.

"Not me," she scoffed. "You never said anything about what happens when you are old, and see the fires shining on the road, and would give the sun, moon, and stars, to toast your toes at the fireside."

"Bless you," he cried, with easy patronage and wonder at her greenness, "we never get old. We die young, afore the bloom has gone"—with his wide grin. "A short life and a merry 'un."

"No, I'm not comin'," said Carrie. "But here's something for luck!"

He took the crooked sixpence, spat on it, and with an easy adieu, swung away, whistling into the silence.

When he had gone Carrie stood still listening to the echoes. Then she turned round, and instead of proceeding on the road to Greenmeads began to retrace her steps.

"If Bob should see me like this," she thought, and that was the thought that turned her back.

"I hate him," she continued bitterly to herself. "He could ha' found me easy—if he had wanted."

A man in a laundry van gave her a lift.

Carrie looked at the snow coming down from her shelter under the V-shaped covering.

"What made you give me a lift?" inquired Carrie.

"I'm a Socialist," answered the man. "You're my sister. If you'd been drunk—or anything—you'd ha' been my sister."

"That Socialism?" inquired Carrie.

"That's so," said the man.

"I thought that was Christianity," said Carrie, meditatively.

"I hain't no Christian! I'm a hatheist, I ham!" and his voice was fierce.

"Is it pulling them down as is up?" asked Carrie.

"No, it's only makin' 'em get off those who are down," answered her companion.

She had only a little way to walk to the car after he set her down, and then began the dreary walk to her lodgings.

Fanny opened the door.

"Oh, Carrie, we're so glad you've come back!" she said.

Carrie did not answer just at first.

She felt dizzy and strange, but stood there smiling at Mr. Winklesworth and at Julia sitting up in bed reading, and at Fanny with her curious, excited look.

Then her room, with the pictures of Moses in the bulrushes, dolls'-houses, and the table set for tea spun round and round.

"Socialism—tramps—Bob!" Carrie said faintly, and fell in a heap between the dresser and Julia's bed.

It was only for a few minutes that she lost consciousness. When she regained it she found herself laid across the foot of Julia's bed, almost suffocated with hot salt bags.

The warmth revived her. She drank a dish of hot tea.

"Carrie," said Fanny, one hour later, as she lay composed on the sofa. "Mrs. Fisher brought a newspaper in to-day, just after you'd gone, and there's something in about you."

"Me?" inquired Carrie, very quietly. Life in its full force had reduced her to this weakness, so ineffable and calm.

"Yes, you are advertised for—in the Missing Relations column, and there's a fortune for you and your brother and sister."

"The lucky sixpence!" exclaimed Carrie, and, sitting up, laughed hysterically. "Oh, Fanny, we'll have a whole week at Lewis's Sale! Won't that cat Sarah open her daylights?"

Chapter X

SARAH ATTENDS A FUNERAL

JONAS BLEASDALE sat smoking his pipe, watching the smoke curl up to the rooftree of his cottage in Greenmeads, as he awaited the guests coming to his wife's funeral. She lay in the parlour in the pitch-pine coffin which stood on the table in the centre of the room, with her hands having lain idle longer than ever in her life.

Jonas had not invited any guests, but he knew that they were coming, though he had no idea how few or how many in number they would be. Sarah from Hilltop had told him they were coming, and when she said a thing she meant it, so it must be so.

They were coming as a protest against anything strange in the burial of an old and respected villager, who had ever paid her way, looked after her own affairs, and gone to church twice every Sabbath, hail, rain, or shine.

Rose Mary deserved a decent burial, and they were coming to see that she got it.

Jonas sat staring first at the smoke trying to reach the ceiling, then into the depths of the fire which roared half-way up the chimney.

He was between sixty and seventy, but looked at least ten years older, for he had worked very hard, drunk very hard, and lived a queer, hermitage sort of life, despite all his fits of boozing, keeping his heart and his purse-strings tight.

Some people thought him a little "dotty," but he was a good blacksmith, who could put as decent a shoe on a wild young filly as any one within a twenty-miles radius.

Dark, deep-set eyes glowed from under bushy brows, giving something of the look of a savage bulldog. Children shrank from him in the lanes, and grown folk pitied or scorned him as their disposition impelled them.

Poor Rose Mary had married him when she was twenty and he was thirty-five, in a fit of spite against Wilfred Myers who kept her waiting in the rain for half an hour one evening. Wilfred, as hot-tempered as she, to show her how little he cared, enlisted as a soldier, and was killed the following year in a skirmish out in India. His old mother to the day of her death would shut the door insultingly whenever Rose passed that way, blaming her for the death of her only, well-loved, handsome boy.

But she had been punished enough for that girlish mistake.

Jonas, after a few years of their wedded life, insisted on carrying the household purse, than which there is no greater indignity to the soul of woman!

At her death he grudged her burial, so the village said. Well, either that or he had gone crazy—though many inclined to the theory that downright wickedness was the cause of his peculiar way of trying to avoid burying her. He had really tried to do that.

Only three days before the local authorities had knocked at his door. "Come in," invited a satirical, asthmatical voice from the peaceful ingle-nook.

"Where is your wife, Rose Mary Bleasdale, of this parish, who died on Tuesday last, and whom none have seen interred? Beware what you say, Jonas Bleasdale, husband of the before-mentioned, for it may be used against you."

He had cackled out a fit of laughter, which left him coughing for breath, and sounded like dried peas rattled in a bladder.

From his eyes had glittered a spark of volcanic ire as he met those of the young man interrogating him. It seemed only yesterday to him since he caught little Abel Woods stealing flowers from his garden, and thrashed him soundly. Now the young fool thought himself a man of importance because he worked in a lawyer's office.

Then silence reigned, during which he resumed his pipe.

At last he seemed to come to a decision.

"Well," he said, breaking the silence as suddenly as a gunshot and enjoying their start, "if you want to know where she is, she's there," pointing the stem of the pipe towards the grandfather's clock in the corner. They looked first at the clock, then at each other, thinking he must have suddenly gone mad with grief at his loss, for they could see nothing but shadows, and the bed-warmer glittering in the red firelight.

He rose from his chair and hobbled across the sanded floor. Opening the clock he revealed the corpse standing rigidly upright. Alas, Rose Mary, when you married strange Jonas Bleasdale in a fit of spleen, you never dreamed it would mean being hid as a corpse inside the grandfather's clock that had ticked off the long years of an unhappy life. You were ever a stickler for propriety, too. How the bows of your best bonnet would have quivered with horror at the thought of such a fate! But lie content in your poor coffin, of which he begrudged you, saying to the astounded officials that he only took you for life, with another dry, cackling fit of laughter, for your friends are coming down in their wrath, thick as the locusts upon the wicked, and will see that justice is done, though tardily.

The local authorities had contented themselves by a warning and a mandate for immediate burial, but Abel Woods called on Sarah at the farm, telling her the strange doings of Jonas, because he had heard his mother say that she and Rose Mary were close companions in their youth.

Sarah it was who, gripping the goose-head handle of her umbrella, went from house to house of the scattered hamlet, wherever dwelt a friend of the deceased woman, spreading the news of the awful scandal of the affair, and bidding them come down in their might.

Molly o' Joseph's said she had seen Rose laid out—the best sheets on the bed; had dressed her in the white stockings and nightdress saved for the occasion; and stated that all had expected seeing a funeral train wend its way up to the old Greenmeads churchyard a day or two after. Knowing Jonas to be eccentric, they had thought he would ask few to the funeral, and so the days had gone on, when, getting alarmed at the flight of time, the authorities had been informed.

Much ill will had been caused in the village by the keen competition between people to get their dead buried in the old churchyard rather than in the new cemetery. The older folk would as soon have thought of going straight to perdition as of being buried in the new place to wait the trump of the awakening angel. It was the conservative clinging to familiar soil which is weak or strong accordingly as the standpoint varies. The old Greenmeads churchyard was full of trees of long growth, making it green and pleasant as a wood. The stones were mellowed by sunshine and showers, and rich mosses clung there whilst every name engraven on the stone was that of some old family—maybe a distant relative, or a connexion by marriage or friendship. It was rich with a thousand memories. In the middle stood the old church, with its russet-red roof, like a mother amongst her children. The villagers had a fancy that when they crept under the sod they would be able to hear the singing of the choir and the rolling glory of the organ through the open window. Many had children, who had died long, long ago (when they were young mothers), laid under the shadows of those kindly trees, making the place like a garden. Sisters, brothers, fathers, and mothers slept there. It was a human longing to wish to lie down and mix one's dust with that of friends and kindred.

The new cemetery was on the top of a bare hill, with a few shrubs trying to flourish in the teeth of the northeast wind, and with the glimmer of new stones, with new names that told nothing, for the townspeople had taken a whim to come from Bringford and be buried in this quiet country place, and it was like lying down amongst strangers to be buried in the new cemetery. In spite of centuries of preaching we are but children and pagans yet. The soul and the body are so closely wedded together that it is troublesome and painful to distinguish which is which.

Rose Mary Bleasdale was going to get into the old churchyard by "the skin of her teeth" almost, said the villagers. Her mother, who had died of cancer, was at the bottom of the grave, and next her the old maternal grandmother, who had come to live with them after the paralytic stroke which turned her from an active, cheery woman into a restless, quick-sighted invalid whose only delight was to tell tales of the misdemeanours of the children, leaning forward in her rocking-chair, her black eyes gleaming as she cried, "Maria! Maria! the children are stealing the sugar, wench."

Little had any one thought that Maria, the ruddy-cheeked daughter, would die before the old lady, but so it had happened.

Hannah, the little flaxen-haired sister who had despised dolls and loved horses, lay next to the grandmother, having been run down by a passing dray. The father came next, the jolly wheelwright who used to sit after his day's toil in the bar parlour of the Red Cow, and who always sang "Roses underneath the Snow" when he had had a glass too much. Many a villager thought of him as they heard of Rose's death, and saw in memory his round, shining face that no sorrow could make anything but cheerful, and his twinkling eye fixed on the yellow ceiling of the inn as he sang in a voice full of faith:

"Turn around with br—ave hendevur,
Let your vain repinings go!
'Opeful 'arts will find for—ever
Roses underneath the snow."

Lastly, Charlie, who had succeeded his father at the wheelwright's shop, and married pretty, giddy Kitty Mills, whom he met at the fair. Kitty had allowed him to die, said report, for the dearth of a mustard poultice when he got a chill.

It was a deep grave—a real old-time grave, not the pretentious, shallow thing they make now, where you can see the bottom without risking falling in. When the wheelwright had died, his old blind mother, who lived a long way off, had heard all the night previous to the funeral of her only son the trickling of the rain. She sent word by her daughter that hay or straw must be put into the grave.

"It'll be so wet, our Willie's grave, else!" she had said, rocking herself as if she held a little child in her arms. She had been a mighty woman in her time—a woman built for service, who had worked in the fields, till her rough arms bled at the prick of the stubble, and yet paused not in her toil. She was a woman who had borne children, and baked a batch of bread seven days after the birth, and glorified in the fact that each child cost but five shillings, not reckoning the pain.

Her daughters had turned away, weeping rare tears at her simple request that Willie's grave should have hay or straw at the bottom, and to hear the murmuring voice that said, "It'll be so wet!"

Rose Mary's time had come now.

All through the years that grave had waited, quiet, in sun and rain, feeling sure of its own.

Jonas had bought no grave in the new cemetery, and could not have done so in the old for untold wealth. Every corner of it was crammed, full as an ear of wheat, the graves almost overlapping. Rose Mary had been glad to think, as the clammy sweat of death was on her, that her body would lie with her own people. She had never cared for Jonas, and of late his queer ways had terrified her.

Sarah was not afraid of him, and went down to give him a piece of her mind, after Abel Woods had been up to the farm with the strange news of the old clock and the corpse.

When she asked him how he would like to stand inside a clock, dead, and if he was not afraid of the house falling on him for such wickedness and indecency, he only laughed the old laugh that had so little mirth in it.

But he said nothing against her decision to stand by her old friend and see that the rites of burial were carried out. She took the grave-papers to the sexton, tidied the house up, pulled the blinds down, and even went to the kindness of making his tea, which he never touched, however.

He did not defy her, either, when she announced her intention of asking Rose Mary's friends to the funeral, but that might be because she stated clearly her intentions of paying for the tea. Once only he lifted his voice against Sarah, and that was when James Todd, the undertaker, came at her command to measure the corpse for the coffin. "Pitch-pine," he ordered, spitting into the heart of the glowing fire, over which he so often extended his hands as if cold.

"Pitch-pine!" echoed Sarah, in a voice that would have been louder but for the recollection of the still presence in the room beyond.

"Pitch-pine!" she said again, as if she could not believe her ears. "Oak's none too good for such a wife as she has been to thee, Jonas Bleasdale."

Some people said that James Todd in his early days would have been fain to win Rose.

"I've a board yonder," he put in slowly, "right out o't' heart of an oak, wi' the grandest rings yo' ever see. I'll make it o' that—*for t' same price*, Jonas!"

"She'll keep better in pitch-pine," answered Jonas, stubbornly, and getting up he banged his fist on the table, making the tea-things he had not used rattle like so many frightened puppets. "And pitch-pine it shall be, price or no price."

"Say dalewood, like the paupers has," ironically suggested Sarah. "You should ha' told her when you courted her as you'd bury her like a pauper. Do you mind, Jonas Bleasdale, when she and me and Mary Smethurst went down these lanes o' nights, singing to scare the boggarts," with unconscious humour, "and how you used to follow like a big, black ghost, and wouldn't go away though we laughed at you till the lanes echoed? If anybody had a told me then—"

A light woke in the deep-set eyes, such as might come into those of the lion, hearing the huntsman's gun within his sacred jungle.

"Pitch-pine is good as she deserved," he said in a volcanic burst of white wrath. "Didn't she deceive me all along, from the first? Told me she loved me, with her heart wrapped up in that Myers lad, who would have stamped on it if only he'd lived instead o' being shot dead. She's mended my socks and cooked my meat, and looked after the hearth, and the plants in the window, but she starved me for all that. James Todd, you do as I tell you, or a townsman shall make the coffin. Let her think herself lucky to get pitch-pine, for she was no better than a pauper. Didn't she marry me to spite him? (Curse him! she said she could see him as she died. Was false to me with her last breath as well as her first!) Take her measurements, man, and don't stand gaping there, and be sharp about it."

Todd complied. He was a mild man, and never pressed a point.

But the bottom of Rose Mary's coffin was remarkably thick, if Jonas had been very critical, almost as if that lovely board with the large rings in it out of the heart of the oak had been pushed in, after all.

It was a cold, wet afternoon on which the uninvited guests waited in the front room with its brown oilcloth, and the glass globes on the corner cupboard under which perched the two stuffed canaries, who had died of steam on washing days. There, too, was the old harmonium which Jonas had bought in the days of his courtship, when he was too full of joy to be suspicious that Rose Mary's quiet, shy ways were not the outcome of maidenly reserve but of indifference. He had bought it thinking of firelit evenings when she would live in the same house with him, when he could play to her singing, which he thought like an angel's. A curious character he had always been, if taking life too seriously is to be curious, but he would have laid his life down in those days for the little girl of the shy, shrinking manners. Over the sofa hung the antimacassars Rose had worked before her breach with young Myers. They still stuck respectably together, though so many things had worn away since then.

Jonas showed no trace of emotion. He talked with the guests on the weather, and about his rheumatism, wearing the seedy black of many years past. When the clock struck two, he rose and went into the kitchen to take his accustomed dose of physic, pushing the wreaths and crosses piled against the passage wall out of his way with his stick.

As James Todd screwed down the lid over the face that looked comely even in death, and younger than it had done for many years, Jonas coughed slightly. Putting in his pipe he drew heavily at it, then blew clouds of smoke about the room so that his face was hidden from the crowd, whatever it might have told.

After they returned from the funeral Jonas sat in stolid silence, which he broke only to urge the guests to partake of the fare Sarah had provided.

It may be added that they did not require much urging. They ate with a hearty consciousness of the present, and a forgetfulness of the future and the minister's voice which had just told them that all flesh was but as grass. The two main subjects at the funeral board were a ferret belonging to Jack o' George's, and the proper way of making rhubarb-wine.

They had none of them wronged the departed, and all had seen her laid away like a Christian; therefore they saw no reason why they should be doleful. If they had been Jonas, now, they told each other as they left, they would have been afraid of Rose Mary's ghost walking.

Sarah was the last to take her leave.

Jonas had left his post at the head of the table, and sat in the ingle-nook. His shadow much enlarged crouched on the wall, moving, as he moved, restlessly. The rain was pattering down with a dreary, haunting note.

"Good night, Jonas!" said Sarah, standing in the red fire-glow, the silk fringe on her best cape trembling in the draught from the doorway.

"Good night," answered Jonas, then he said, "You might pu' the shutters to for me, Sarah, before you go. Shutt' rain out, Sarah—shut it out! "

She was going again when he turned and called, "You're not in a big hurry, are you, Sarah?"

As she sat down he relapsed into such deep silence that she thought he had forgotten her presence. But after five minutes he stretched his hand to his snuff mull, gave a loud sneeze, and sat back in his chair.

"If ever yo' feel lonesome, Jonas," spoke Sarah, "slip up to t' farm and smoke a pipe with our Robert. He's a lonesome man too. His wife, the baggage, has gone away—doubtless with another fellow, or she wouldn't ha' stopped this while."

Old Jonas nodded.

"But I shouldn't like it turning over," went on Sarah, hurriedly.

"It's o' reight," said Jonas, taking another pinch of snuff.

"I shouldn't dream o' turning it over."

He was silent once again, then said suddenly, "I have a mind to tell you everything, Sarah. It's like telling it to the shadows on the wall, they listen and never speak. I've been lone a weary while, Sarah, just as much as if she'd been wedded to another man, or faithless to me.

"When I was young, Sarah, I never liked aught second best. I put my heart and soul into my work. I drove a nail as carefully as if an Empire depended on it, and thought o' nothing else. Then I saw Rose one day, fetching water from t' well, and carried her bucket. Folk told me she was engaged to that Myers lad, but then I heard it was broken off, and after following her about a bit she walked out wi' me. She told me, Sarah, one night as we sat under the hedge, with the dog-roses smelling sweet, and the moon up, and the cuckoo calling, that she cared naught for Myers. That was a lie. I never told lies myself. So we started life on that lie, to spite Myers, as I afterwards found out. Sarah, I've been a lone man, years, years, years." The rain trickled down the pane as if sobbing in a dreary, spiritless way. "Hearken," he said, lifting his finger.

"It rained when we were marrit," he continued, "and it's rained ever sin', an' it's rainin' yet. They say folk can get used to aught, Sarah, but being without meyt and that, they dee juse as they're getting used to that; but it's another lie, Sarah. I can't get used to being lonely. It's been a weary while. Curse him!" Even then it struck Sarah that he cursed the rival rather than the wife who had deceived him.

And so she left him, brooding above the fire, his lonely shadow stirring on the wall whenever he expended his hands for warmth, and all round the house the murmur of the rain, surely sadder music than anything, unless it be the sound of the storm-wind amongst the pines.

He had made Sarah take with her to the farm the antimacassars Rose had brought with her, saying they were the only things she had brought him, and he wanted none of them. He told her to tell Robert that the old harmonium was for sale, too. Poor old harmonium, with its yellow keys that had scarcely been touched, around which he had woven such dreams when he was buying it by weekly instalments, storing it in his bedroom in his lodgings, and almost driving poor Mrs. Walton crazy by always going wrong in the same place, sitting until starved to the marrow in the hopes of learning to play to Rose Mary's singing, when they were married! The soul of it had been until now only discords—silence, dust.

But the soul was there, waiting for the master to touch it to swelling harmonies, as wait all souls. If they give only discords, or lie stubbornly dumb, perhaps our hands have touched them rudely, been blind of knowledge, or touched them not at all. Poor Jonas! Poor harmonium! Is there a place in the scheme of things where you shall be compensated?

Billy Bond sent word that he would buy the instrument, to sell again in the town, where he had a second-hand shop. Soon it reposed amongst fenders, oil-paint portraits with fishy eyes, pepper-dusters with broken lids, and giltless vases.

Billy told afterwards that old Jonas had said, as he helped him to lift it from the wall, "It leaves a very nasty place, Billy—a terrible nasty, *empty* place," and that he had to proffer several shillings more before the old nipper would let him put it on his spring-cart. Another instance, to the villagers, of old Bleasdale's niggardly spirit. Like most people with a half-knowledge it was easier to think of an ill motive for his reluctance to let it go than of any higher, nobler one.

Jonas never climbed the hill to the farm.

Three weeks later he was found dead in the front room, lying in the empty place left by the old harmonium. The doctor found he had died of heart-failure, and the villagers jested about it as they got their milk from the carts, saying it was the first time they had known old Jonas to possess such an article.

It was so long since he had followed Rose Mary about in the lanes, with a yellow flower in his buttonhole, and a look of watch-dog fondness in his eyes. They had forgotten. So many things had happened to those still alive, and so many who had been young in that far-off time had emigrated, or died, or had drifted away from the hamlet in divers ways to divers places.

They buried him in the new cemetery, amongst the strangers, and in the night-time, when Sarah heard the rain dripping from the eaves of the farm roof, she thought with a shiver that he was still alone! But she was mistaken. He had joined in the tranquil fellowship of Death, where space and names are nothing, and the little green blades of grass shot peacefully up from above his bed, laughing at the summer sky and fearing him not.

His only mourner, a second cousin from Bringford, came to the service held in Greenmeads Church the

Sunday afterwards, thinking it looked decent to do so, even if she had not been on good terms with him in life. She had got his furniture and the money in the bank, and it was worth the effort of getting up early in the morning and walking along miry lanes.

The minister in his service remarked on the suddenness with which the Lord called His own, though several of the congregation were of the opinion that old Jonas belonged to a flock of darker colour than the anointed ones. The second cousin pressed her handkerchief to her eyes, and afterwards received the sympathy of the villagers (who could, however, see through her as through glass) and returned to Bringford.

Sarah, amidst all the talk of Jonas's niggardliness, surliness, and oddities, said nothing at all. As she often did this, it was not remarkable. A person once trying to "pump" her had said to a third person, after absolute failure, "Naught said means naught, they say, Jacob! But naught said means a danged lot, sometimes."

People talked for weeks after that Sunday about the bunch of daffodils set in the earthenware jar on the old man's grave. Several people interrogated each other as to the probable person to do such a thing, but Jonas had no friends, and it was a complete mystery. Whoever had put them there must have come very early in the morning, and early in the morning the ground had been sodden by many hours' rainfall. Joseph Briggs, who prided himself on his powers of detecting things, and had an idea that he should have been another Sherlock Holmes, sniffed round Jonas's grave, but saw only marks of hobnail shoes, which must be those of some seeker amongst the graves for a familiar name, for they moved past the resting-place of Jonas, as if aimlessly.

But Robert at Hilltop thought that Sunday morning he had seldom had such dirty shoes, and that he could have sworn he did not leave them in that condition the night before. It was yellow, clayey soil, too, different from the farm soil or that in the lanes.

Robert's head, however, was in such a state of confusion and aching that he couldn't have been absolutely sure of anything, or of where he had been the previous night, so he said nothing of the matter to Sarah.

How surprised he would have been could he have known that very soon in the morning, almost before the sun drank the mists from the valleys, Sarah had trudged down the hillside in his heavy shoes, hiding something under her cape, and hurrying back empty-handed before the first chimney-smoke curled up from the straggling houses.

Sarah was troubled about many things as the months went by.

Robert, for a short time after Carrie's flight, had done his work as of old, but was fast becoming careless. He spent a good deal of his time in the Red Cow parlour, and scattered his money broadcast when he had passed a certain chalk-mark of intemperance. At first it had only been his rare hour of leisure that he spent there, but now he was often in that red-curtained parlour, the glass of ale before him, when he should have been attending to the land, the orchard, or the livestock.

His steps were often stumbling ones as he came up the garden path, roaring out the chorus of "Belle Mahone" until the village dogs awoke to the echoes and barked, answering defiance. Next day he was penitent, but the thing occurred with sickening frequency until it was almost as convenient for any one on business to seek him in the Red Cow as at the farm.

Two of the cattle died of some disease, and the milk was suspected of giving the Boon children the fever. Robert sold Peter the pig for half a sovereign in a fit of drunken boastfulness about him. Altogether things were running to rack and ruin. Sarah had shuddered to hear of his kissing the barmaid of the Red Cow and telling her she should be his second wife. Even Carrie was preferable to the barmaid, who came from London, and laughed in a falsetto voice, and wore so many hair-pads she looked as if she'd the city of Babylon on her head, to say nothing of those great pins stuck in, as if she was a Japanese heathen rather than a Christian woman connected with the Empire on which the sun never sets.

Alone in the farm kitchen, with the consciousness of the farm drifting to ruin along with Robert, she thought of many things. Perhaps the death of Jonas had stirred up old memories of herself as a girl, before her heart had fossilized, and the days of youth, with its long, long thoughts, cast an illuminating flash on Carrie's own youth as compared with her age.

Listening for the tardy feet of Robert, to the deep bass of the old clock, she would think of Carrie, and confess to herself that there certainly was a bit of company in the foolish thing's presence. She saw her in her mind's eye flitting about, with the defensive attitude of the yellow head, or sometimes it would be the outline of the face bent over the book, eyes shining, foot swinging, as she had sat in Robert's great chair. Or again, she would see her kneeling on the wide-topped, shining steel fender, holding out her hands to the blaze and shivering as if Hilltop Farm was cold enough for a meat-safe. "She was only a child," thought Sarah sometimes, with a tightening of the heart-strings. "A child is afraid of silence. I should have been a little warmer and welcomed her," and when she opened her Bible and read the words Carrie had inscribed on the pigsty she wondered if she had been to blame.

One night, as the wind wailed in the boughs of the old oak at the gable end, she reviewed her negative treatment of Carrie. Without mercy she scanned her own soul, and came to the conclusion that she had been wrong.

"An old woman—a'most," she told herself scornfully, "with a six foot o' soil waiting for you in the old churchyard, and begrudgin' the boltin' o' a farm door, the clatterin' o' the farm pots, to a lassie!"

She had dreamed, too, and looking in the dream-book, which elbowed "Pilgrim's Progress" on the one hand and Josephus on the other, read the interpretation, which said that the dreamer had wronged some one. Sarah, though not of a romantic tendency, believed in dreams, signs of death, and such like facts, which she said she had proved time and time.

In the morning she went down and asked Jane Wilkins to come and housekeep at the farm for a while, telling Robert that she was going to stay at Linley Booth, a station away, with her friend Mrs. Moore, who had rheumatism. Under her breath she asked pardon for that lie. She did not want Robert to know she was going to seek Carrie.

Jane she took into her confidence.

She put on her best things, but, for all her exciting journey to come, could not find it in her heart to keep them on when rain began to patter, and went down the hill in her old clothes.

"If there's a railway accident they can't say I've owt nasty or raggy on," she said to Jane. "Such things do happen."

Jane wept as if Sarah was leaving the country, and waved her hand until she could see her no longer.

But the heart of Sarah was at rest in the thought that she had taken a bath before she set out (with Jane guarding the keyhole). It was one of her little foibles to wash her feet every time that she went down to the village for anything from the post office—the post office where more of anything was sold than of stamps. She thought it would be such a disgrace to drop dead with dirty feet, and that she should turn in her grave if such a thing ever happened.

She was indignant at the many times her ticket was punched before she reached the city, as if they couldn't trust folk, she said audibly—as if they thought country folk thieves because they had so many in their big places. She got a bed at a temperance hotel, and told the landlady she was staying there till she went back to the country, and from this room she centralized her search, telling no one of its object.

She had not the slightest guide to her sister-in-law's whereabouts, but every Sunday she went to the church, and never noticed the looks of the congregation, cast at the tall figure with the stiff back, heavy beaded garments, and, most noticeable of all, the home-made bonnet with the ears of wheat, so tumbled that it seemed as if beaten low by storm-winds innumerable.

Every night she read the words "Seek, and ye shall find."

Chapter XI

THE END OF THE VAGABOND

CARRIE proved her identity, and that of her brother and sister, coming into her money, which was more than she had dreamed of in her wildest thoughts before she walked, footsore and with nothing but Julia's lucky sixpences, on the long white road.

Charlie, however, had not got his share, because at the time she inquired about him he was away from his usual haunts, so she kept the little surprise in store for him.

Carrie set out one afternoon to try again.

She reached the doss-house. The proprietor was standing in the doorway.

"Who is't you want?" he asked, eyeing the prim little figure with a kind of brand newness about it.

"Charles Brown, my brother," answered Carrie. "Has he come back?"

"Oh, Charles Brown," repeated the doss-house keeper, slowly. "Things have been happening here, and when they did he was always in at 'em."

"Cut it short," commanded Carrie. "Has he got put in gaol? Can't you see I'm waiting?"

"Let me tell it you right through," said the man, not unkindly. "No, 'tain't gaol" (Carrie heaved a sigh of relief). "It's wuss. A fight started here—the very night after he came back, and he was in rare fettle, too, when he came back—had been living out in the country. Well, a wife o' one o' the boys came to ask her man when he was coming home again, and the boy objecting to this inquisitiveness on her part, out with his knife—in two twos it would ha' been into her, when Charles, who had also had a little to drink, tried to take it from him, and received it—full in the chest."

"Where is he?"exclaimed Carrie.

He gave her the name of the hospital. She put a shilling into his hand and rushed away.

Mortification had set in, whispered the little nurse, as they went along the cold echoing corridors. There was no pain and no hope of life.

The handsome one lay back on his pillows, new lines of weariness about the dare-devil mouth that had made women turn to look after him in the street.

It was visiting day. Up and down the wards noiselessly tripped the clean, sweet nurses, scolding gently now and then at some invalid who had crumpled the bed-clothes or flung them carelessly aside. Laughter came sometimes from the children's ward, and Carrie could catch through the window of the adjoining room brief glimpses of little white-gowned figures standing upright on their crib beds, playing with toys. Charlie was dying.

It seemed only yesterday since they were children, and quarrelled about handing the buttons to their mother, as she bent wearily over the pile of shirts. How infinitely small seemed his faults in this hour. He had taken money from her, even coaxed her into giving it to him, and once had vexed her very much by coming to Greenmeads, and intruding himself upon her life there.

Even so, if he had possessed money to spare, and she had been hard pressed, he would have been glad to aid her, she thought. He seemed just her little brother again as he slept, and she watched him—her little brother, whom she had sometimes been privileged to help. Then she thought of what he might have been.

What a splendid dare-devil he had been! Instead of being content to scrape and save so that he could eat meat twice or thrice a week, and live in a smutty street with a number to his door, he had joined the outcast class that lives on chances. This was the spirit that had discovered countries, founded colonies, and refused to be satisfied with little things and stay-at-home ways. He had sold his strength to no master for a wage. For all his little fault of asking loans from his sister which he forgot to pay back, he could rise to the act of coming between an infuriated madman with a rusty knife, whilst all the doss-house stood aghast, keeping a respectful distance, giving promiscuous advice to any one and every one to "fetch the police," whilst the knife was grasped ready to plunge in the woman's breast, bare and adrip with milk, as it was snatched from the mouth of the baby when she came to seek her partner.

He had never married and dragged a loved one down with him. He had lived in the open air as much as possible, sleeping in woods in summer, rather than sweat and moil over a blistering furnace, too tired to read at nights, almost, till he fell into the lethargy of the average workers who are too tired to be angry at all the preaching poured out for their especial benefit from every Little Bethel—too tired to love, too tired to hate, and too tired to feel a glorious joy in leaf, grass, and flower, when spring comes back to earth.

He was not little enough to haggle with masters for a rise of fourpence every few years, and be looked at as if he had asked for a man's life-blood. Realizing the corruptness of society, he had tried to shake himself free of it, by leaving it. But he could not leave. Down at the bottom the same system went on—only he risked more, and gained less!

All strong, original types, as well as the weak ones, thought Carrie, drifted downwards when there was no need for them—when no one wanted them. The people who could keep shops, saying that things were fresh when they were not *quite* fresh, watching the scales to a grain, getting a bit here, a bit there, or only being generous to catch more custom—these people were respectable, and often successful people.

What a queer world it seemed to the young woman, as she sat in the long ward, waiting for her brother to open his eyes.

In the next bed was a young man, getting well, closely guarded by a policeman. The little nurse told her that he had tried to cut his throat, because he was out of work, and hated to be a burden on his people. The recruiting-sergeant told him he was too narrow in the chest for a soldier, and when his sweetheart gave him the go-by because she thought the courtship eternal, he spent his last coin in buying a razor—which had failed in its mission.

He was coming back to life, that horror, with a police-court ordeal before him, and a judge who would tell him a man couldn't do what he liked with his life, even if no one cared a farthing for it.

A child's cry, sharp, agonized, rang out above the laughter in the children's ward. Some little creature was coming from the spell of the anaesthetic, back to life, back to feeling, back to pain, like the man guarded by the policeman—the thin featured man with the large, dark eyes and the weak mouth, who looked as if he had been rickety since he was born and would soon be tried by an intelligent, refined, highly cultured member of Society. How full of pain the world seemed!

A sunbeam danced cruelly along the ceiling of the long room, touching the coverlet on her brother's bed. As if conscious of the bright passing thing, he opened his eyes, full of the mists of sleep, and yawned. Then he looked up, and saw his sister's face bent above him.

"Car!" he exclaimed, in the old careless way. "Why, Car, old girl. Don't cry. Nothing's worth crying for!"

The little nurse drew near again, saying she would try to see if Carrie could stay longer, for the quarter of an hour allowed was almost up.

"How smart you are, Car," he said critically. "What style! That husband of yours must be good to you."

"I've left him," answered she, brusquely, the plume of her hat waving as she moved a little restlessly.

"Drifted, old girl?" he asked a little pityingly. "It's a bright road at first, but it ends—in the gutter."

"No," said Carrie, but not proudly as she would once have done. It was so easy to drift when one was alone, unhappy, wretchedly poor, and no stoic, but a human being with a longing for comradeship. She remembered the tramp on the white road, and the invitation that had tempted whilst she laughed at it.

"No," she answered, bending down. "Charlie, you and Clara and me have come into a fortune! Not huge fortunes, old boy, but enough to give us a fighting chance, which we've never had before. Get well."

He smiled ironically.

"*I'm done,* Car," he said. "The doctor told me yesterday I shouldn't live more than a few days. That knife should have been sharper, then I should have missed the pain of thinking. I think of all manner of things as I lie here— jokes, country lanes, woods where I've slept, people I've pinched from," with a laugh as humorous as of old, and with as little remorse in it. "It's hard to die at thirty, Car. The only thing that hurts me is my having tormented you, Sis. You were my own. I seemed to have a claim on your tolerant affection. Our own! We grumble more, dare more, tyrannize more over our own than any one else—and they love us most! I've been a bad brother, Car. If I'd stayed at the furnace, I could have made things easier for you. But, no—it was impossible."

It was strange to Carrie to hear him speak in this manner. She was surprised to find that she liked him better as he was before, when he made her angry, or made her laugh, but did not fill her eyes with tears, making her remember all the times when she had been vexed with him.

His hair was curly and yellow, his eyes full of daring, reckless life, and he seemed very young.

He seemed to dream for some little time.

"Car," he cried suddenly, "I was just thinking what a rare old time I'd have had. Oh, Car, old girl, what hard lines! To think," he went on bitterly, "all this time I've knocked about in doss-houses—how much is it, Car?"

She told the amount into his ear, in choking words that she had to repeat to make clear.

He whistled, a long, clear whistle, resounding through the ward.

"Petroleum and lying," she answered his questioning look. "I've got his little biography at my lodgings. It reads fine, but it's nothing to be proud of. He started by robbing our saving-box, and the money mother had hidden, to pay his passage. Well, it's been like that ever since. He hasn't cared who sank if he swam," the tears drying with her anger. "What made him remember us at the last?" inquired Charlie, curiously, with a floating memory from the past of a father who ate mutton whilst they had treacle scraped on their bread.

"But it's a decent sum, Car. You must have my share, and help that woman I saved, on condition she leaves Bill, so that the children have a chance. He'll get time for this, and she'll miss the bit of money he was sometimes good enough to throw at her."

The little nurse came, with word from the matron that Carrie might stay—to the end. She whispered the last part of the sentence, so that the patient should not hear; but when Carrie told him she might stay the afternoon out, he seemed to understand.

"Are you afraid?" asked Carrie once, wondering that he took it so philosophically.

"Not of what's there," he made reply; "but of losing the earth, the sun, and the moon, and Cartmel, who was so jolly good, and people who stole your butter when your back was turned in the doss-house, and people who made you look after them in the street. Yes, Car, it's a big thing for the sun to go out when you're only thirty."

Then Carrie knew that her brother was a brave man. He dared to avow himself a coward, and to fear the loss of the beautiful old earth. It had not given him much, but glimpses of it, its goodness, its jolly colour, its men and women, stained, human, no angels, but weak and strong as he himself was, these he, the vagabond, had eyes to see. Then he fell asleep. All the time as he slept death crept nearer, life ebbing away before the painless mortification that crept up towards the heart.

Sometimes the little nurse came and sat by Carrie, and they talked in low voices. The little nurse talked of the lover waiting her away in California, when she had finished her time and saved enough money to go out to him.

Whenever the patient woke, she went delicately away, leaving the brother and sister together. Charlie said what a good little soul she had been, during the intense agony which was his share when first he came in. She was very pretty, too, he said, and remarked that it was pleasanter to view beauty than ugliness, even when half dead.

The hours drifted by.

Outside the sunlight faded, and the shadows crept up slow and sure, and amongst the shadows, death. The lights in the wards were lit. Charlie had written out the paper bequeathing his share of the money to Carrie, with the aid of the little nurse's hand guiding his. He was glad to lie down again.

Sometimes he spoke of the men of the doss-house. Once he tried to sing a popular song, about roses and sweet lips, but had to ask Carrie to finish it. When she did so, in a clear voice that did not tremble, the man in the next bed, still guarded by the policeman, grumbled that he could not go to sleep, as if it disturbed him.

Once Charlie opened his eyes as they thought he slept, saying, "It's awful hard dying, Car." Another time he asked the nurse to give his respects to the fellow in California, and tell him he said he was lucky. Then he began to complain of gathering darkness, and to wonder why the lights were not lit in the ward.

Carrie did not tell him that the darkness was in his own sight.

"Carrie," he said at another time, "when we were children in the House, I always ate my own bread, and then joined at yours. I've been a bad brother. But I've found things out in the doss-house. I've found out that the folk there weren't no worse than all the others— only different. But it hurts to think I ate your bread as well as my own, all those years back."

"You were hungriest," answered Carrie, glad that he could not see her tears this time.

She patted his hand, not being able to say more.

The nurse came once to ask if he would like a minister to pray with him, as a man at the other end of the ward was being visited by one of the clerical order, and it would be no trouble.

He shook his head.

"Let Car stop," he said. "I'm not afraid of heaven or hell with a good woman holding my hand. You'll hold my hand, Car, right to the last, won't you, old girl? Say, Car, do you think I'll get any more chances—over there, wherever it is? One real big chance?"

"Sure," said the voice close to his ear.

Then silence fell again, and he remarked that they usually lit the place up before this time.

Sometimes he would tell Carrie a joke, fearful that he was making her sad, and laugh, forgetting the grey shadow creeping nearer, ever nearer.

In the middle of relating a funny story a pedlar had told round the doss-house fire, he went drowsy.

The little nurse felt his pulse, and looked at Carrie, telling much in that look. Death was struggling round the heart now, like a chill tide, striving to engulf it.

"Sing something—something gay, Car," he asked. "Something simple, like children love. I can't think now. I'm too tired."

So she sang, very close to his ear, so that it should not disturb the rest of the ward, the old song their mother used to sing to keep them quiet as she sat over the pile of shirts for a shilling a day. It was about the little Tommy who would steal apples, because they were temptingly rosy and sweet, and whom the farmer caught.

"Mother always liked me best," he said, at the end of the first verse. "And I was naughtiest. I wonder if God's anything like that. Go on—Car."

Then, as if he became conscious of the chill touch upon him, he tried to rouse himself from the lethargy seizing him. Suddenly, startlingly, his laugh, rich and mellow as of old, rang out upon the silence of the ward, upon the low, suppressed murmur of pain—the sibilant snore—the slumber of those who had lately had some drug administered.

"Funniest thing in the world, Cartmel," he cried in that strong voice. "Do you remember Burns buying that bulldog and banjo with his pension money—and what a lovely liar he was! Oh, Cartmel." Then the laughter choked in his throat, and he clasped Carrie's hand so convulsively that she, with difficulty, repressed a scream. Then in a faint voice he said drowsily, "Why, Car, mother says it's bedtime. All the others are playing yet. Ask for another half-hour!"

His head fell back on the pillow. There was the sound of heavy breathing. Every breath was longer before it was drawn. Carrie counted them, those breaths drawn with pain. When the last was breathed she waited for another—but it never came.

Her face was white and still.

"Eleven," she said to herself. "Thank heaven there were no more."

"He did not die hard," said the little nurse. "Some have to be held down."

They made arrangements for his being brought to Carrie's lodgings. She was still with Julia and Fanny, whom she now paid a pound a week, so that they felt like millionaires.

A fair star or two was shining as she entered the street, whose bustle she heard as in a dream, from some removed place. Over and over she was hearing that sudden, strong laugh—then the breaths, so hard to draw: one, two, three, four, five, six, seven, eight, nine, ten—eleven.

Still blue pools were in the evening sky, and piled up fleecy clouds looked like mystical mountains. The road was aglitter with lights from shop-window and lamp. Sometimes a motor ran smoothly along, its white acetylene glare lighting up the faces of those on the flagstones.

Cabs were rolling swiftly, taking people to houses of birth, death, wedding, or the frivolous whist-drive. Young trees were budding to green life, struggling against the city smut, near the Park, and lovers wandering there saw a honey-coloured moon in a blue sky through branches. Carrie remembered that it was the night of the students' ball. The moon was getting higher. The dance would go on till it sank, and white dawn made the street-lamps ashamed, and lit up the fields in the country—in Greenmeads.

Her brother was dead. He would have outrivalled many of these students, she thought, if he had only had a chance. He was only thirty. Once he had taken her to a social, and she had been surprised to find that he was a splendid waltzer. How well he would have looked in evening dress! So young, and the sun, moon, and stars had gone out for him.

She went to an undertaker's. He received her orders with the indifference bred of habit, and she walked on once more, with the recollection of the artificial violets held as garlands in the hands of the naked female Memory in the window.

Charlie had given her the address of Bill's wife. She determined to call and see what kind of woman it was whom he had given his life for so recklessly. She felt that she must take some interest in this life that was only alive through his life laid down.

She found the street at last, after divers inquiries. It was a street full of cookshops and of chipped-potato businesses, that cast a heavy, greasy feeling on the atmosphere. An old Italian near the entrance was turning the handle of a barrel-organ, with a miserable-looking monkey sitting servilely near to catch a chance copper, and anon scratching himself feebly, looking as if he wondered why fate had cast his lot in such places rather than in a Ceylon forest full of nuts and wild, screaming birds of flaming colour.

Around the organ, the Italian, and the monkey gathered a group of children and young girls. Factory girls many of them were, still unwashed, with the fluff of the mill upon them, like a premature greyness. Their hair hung down in long, practical plaits to their waists, and they laughed and screamed alternately at the mistakes each other made in attempting to dance to the music from the barrel-organ. Their little woollen neckerchiefs fluttered to and fro with their movements, which were not ungraceful, and below their short skirts of the strong striped sateen their clogs clattered a rude music upon the pavements. They hummed the melody together as they whirled round with the music-catching ear of the North.

For a brief hour they were free.

The *bon camaradie* of the girls seemed to please the old Italian, and he watched their feet, his head wagging to the music. They criticized him and his monkey, wondering how often he washed himself, as they danced round; but one of them threw him a penny, and when he disappeared, a bent figure pushing the organ along, with the monkey hopping after, they felt a sadness and emptiness, and soon separated company, bidding good nights with ironical phrases such as "See you at the Alhambra to-morrow!"—which was a gibe at the old, grey factory. One or two of them had been to Blackpool, and come back with wonderful tales of the ballroom of that name, with its velvet-cushioned seats and ivory-smooth floor, upon which you could dance to exquisite merry music, floating round in a lad's arms, until you forgot you were only a *number* in a cotton factory, but imagined yourself some beautiful, wonderful flower, a golden lily, or something equally fair and gorgeous, floating on a pool of joy. After the grey gloom of the mill how glorious had seemed the streaming multi-coloured lights, the crowd in gay, light dresses, the music, the dance!

Carrie paused to watch them, her heart going out to them. But she did not tell them so; they would have thought her mad. After giving a sixpenny-piece to the old Italian, she walked on, and came at length to the house she sought.

A pale young woman answered her knock, with a baby upon her arm crying plaintively.

"Come in," she said, and gave the child a little shake for its "naughtiness."

Carrie explained that she was the sister of the man who had gone to the hospital, and died there, through interfering between her and her husband.

The woman put the baby in the cradle, and slapped one of the elder children who was in her opinion misbehaving himself. He was a small child, with the furtive look born of fear, and whimpered in a subdued voice lest he should get "more."

"Like his father as he can crawl!" cried the young woman, angrily, and offering to strike him again as if for that fact. Then she lit the gas.

The house had the painfully tidy look some working people's houses have—a bare, impoverished look, like a clean-washed but anaemic face, without any bloom or beauty. The children were also clean and tidy, and were being brought up "respectable"; but they seemed a trifle afraid of their mother. Poor soul, she was doing the best she knew for them. She fed, clothed, and washed them, besides doing miraculous piles of washing, that kept her hands white and shrivelled-looking. She pulled eternally up the hill, down which Bill had tried to drag her, and there were hard lines round her mouth, telling of endless struggle. She had not time to appeal to the children's reason, only time for the quick box on the ears, the readiest way of correction.

How astonished was Carrie as she told the woman of the money her brother had left provisionally—i.e. on condition that she did not go back to Bill when he came from prison—to be told she wanted none of the money. Bill was her husband, she said. He was "a bad 'un," but he was hers. She wasn't going to turn her back on him for any one or anything. "When he came out of jail he came back 'ome," she said. That was what she'd gone to ask him to do when the row started—"to come 'ome," and come 'ome he should.

Carrie left, but gave the small boy snuffling on the doorstep a purse to give his mother.

It contained several pounds.

Chapter XII

SARAH FINDS CARRIE

SUMMER had come, even to Ancoats. It was very hot there, and that was all the difference it made, excepting that the dwellers burned less coal. Julia's window, however, was aglow with geraniums, a pet rose-tree, and the dresser almost on top of the fire was likewise gleaming with the colour of hyacinths, pansies, and all the flowers that Carrie could buy.

Julia was not in bed, but walking about the narrow space of floor between the place where the bed used to be and the door leading into the damp scullery. There was a light of wonder still on her face, for it was only three weeks since she had first dared to attempt to cross the floor without help.

Carrie had spent a large portion of the money her brother left her in the operation which had borne such good fruit. It had been the best way she could think of to spend the money. It was the finest monument she could have reared to the memory of the vagabond, who had such a glorious physique, such high animal spirits, and who lived on chances.

Carrie only asked in return the old coverlet with its thousands of varied pieces, triangular, quadrangular, of all the colours in the rainbow, which Julia had lain under so long. Fanny had made that quilt years ago for "the bottom drawer," when she had had visions of marrying the picture-framer, before Julia's accident. Julia had patiently suffered under it, struggling against the irritability that comes to torture a nature that generously wishes to help and not hinder others.

It seemed like life, that vari-coloured quilt, with its many pieces, and almost every piece different, yet making an harmonious whole. Julia could not understand why Carrie should think the old coverlet, thin and almost breaking in places, a fair exchange for such magnificent kindness as she had showered upon them.

But to Carrie that old coverlet was sacred as a banner that has waved in the thick of shot and shell. It spoke of victories as proud as any won on famous battlefields, such as school reading-books told of. It had covered the limbs of one who had conquered self. Here and there was a gay little pattern, side by side with one of dark hue, and both the bright and dark pieces were wearing away.

Sometimes Carrie wondered if Fanny thought of the picture-framer yet, but gave it up, because she only laughed at it as a bit of girlish folly when the subject was mentioned. Who can paint Julia's delight at being able to walk again? This afternoon the three women were going to look at the shops, and really to have a little feast in commemoration of the miracle of Julia's walking powers.

All the street turned out to see her, from the old woman who alternately drank herself mad on gin and read tracts, to the man who was a bookmaker, and gave his wife black eyes, gibing at her because even that wouldn't drive her away.

And Julia.

How wonderful to move from a narrow room into the world again, and pass people and be passed by them. Her eyes shone like stars, her cheeks glowed with excitement, and all the steady calm of the long weary years, full of helplessness and suffering, was gone. Joy made her dizzy, so that she trembled as she went forward, and yet was steadied again by proud exaltation. She had a grey hat with mock apple-blossom in it, a vanity-bag, and her feet felt delightfully queer in shoes.

How wonderful to be able to stand and jostle at a shop-window, to see some blouse Carrie or Fanny pointed out to her. The rapture in her heart was such as the fledgling's when it first finds its new power of cutting its way through the air, higher, higher, till the sod is a dim, green thing far below.

She could scarcely speak for joy, and laughed at the smallest things. It was dusty. Hot winds blew the dust into their faces, so that they had often to shut their eyes tight when turning a corner. People grumbled at the heat, the dust, the jostling, and a thousand and one little inconveniences that make up life.

Julia did not grumble.

A gigantic joy such as she felt made little troubles unnoticed. Oh, the glory of the people in the street, the horses, the swift motor-cars that she thought must surely have a gladness in going so swiftly. Little giggles welled up in her heart through the calm endurance of those years of pain, and fluttered musically on her lips. For the time being she was drunk with joy. Carrie and Fanny discussed fashions, wished the dust would settle, elbowed people ruthlessly to get to the windows, and once Carrie had a passage of arms with a stout lady whose umbrella poked too far out. Julia did nothing but giggle. But all at once she went tired. Her spine was better, but her heart was yet diseased. Joy wears the soul as much as sorrow.

She was very glad when Carrie said they would have tea at the café across the road.

As they were crossing, Fanny collided with a tall, short-sighted man, who leaned slightly forwards as if looking into the future; many years had given him that forward tilt. The apology upon his lips was never uttered, and the two stared at each other, unconscious of the babel of the street.

"It's him!" whispered Julia to Carrie, and Carrie and she went to stare into Lyons's window at the little pink cakes, and the menu bill, waiting for Fanny to join them.

She was so long they went in at last without her.

Carrie ordered strawberries and cream, and some of the frivolous cakes. Whilst they were coming Julia and she wondered about Fanny, and if she were going to turn up to the feast.

The opening of the street door to a customer let in the cry of a newsboy, "Amazing Moorland Mystery."

"What a time they are," said Carrie, crossly, when they had waited some few minutes and the tea had not appeared. She went to the door and bought a paper, returning to read little bits of news out to Julia.

Suddenly her voice was strangled in her throat.

In great headlines she read that Robert Gibson, farmer, of Greenmeads, was arrested on suspicion of the murder of one Simon Stone, found dead on the moors.

"Oh, Julia!" she cried, and Julia, looking at the whitened face and the paper fallen from the nerveless hand, thought Carrie had had a paralytic stroke. Carrie pulled herself together, however, for the cakes arrived and the tea, but she paid the bill with a trembling hand. Julia was reading the paragraphs Carrie pointed out to her, and thinking of the disgrace to be the wife of a man up on suspicion of murder. The thought of the disgrace had never entered Carrie's mind. As she allowed her tea to go ice-cold unheeded she was thinking of a pal in trouble, and wondering what she could do to help.

She couldn't believe that Robert would kill a man, for she had seen him squirm when the trap set for rats who had stolen his hens' eggs was full with the enemies squeaking and struggling within it.

There must be some mistake.

As Carrie stared before her deep in thought, she became conscious in a dim way that she was looking at something she had often seen before. It moved nearer and nearer to her, and she shook herself wide awake to discover that it was Sarah's old, dowdy bonnet with the green ears of wheat stuck in it, quivering violently with every move of the upright figure.

What was she doing here, and did she know of her brother's plight, thought Carrie, with lightning rapidity.

Sarah had not seen her, but felt a hand on her shoulder as she put her own on the door-handle.

She gasped as she faced her sister-in-law.

A hard look came into her eyes. It is easy to forgive and be forgiven in theory. But Carrie's face was a soft, friendly, broken-spirited look that made Sarah's own eyes soften.

She thought life must have used her young sister-in-law roughly to bring that look there. How could she guess that it was sorrow for herself, sorrow for Robert and the madness of life in general that haunted the woman's face as it met her own?

"Well, it is a fine afternoon," she began scornfully. "You were a fine body to go off like you did."

Carrie put an arm through hers, and bade her come back and sit down a moment, with pity in her voice. How she broke the news she never knew, but Sarah bore up better than she had expected. With flaming eyes she refused to believe that Robert Gibson had lifted a hand against Simon Stone. She termed the police a set of blind bats who couldn't see for looking, and announced her intention to spend every penny piece she had to get him released. Poor lady! The bitter thought that she had but few penny pieces came to her as she was riding in a taxi-cab with Carrie and Julia, and pulling out her Paisley-edged handkerchief she wept, with a bitter, beaten feeling, for almost the first time in her life.

"Never mind," said Carrie, softly, "I've heaps of money, Sarah."

Sarah dabbed her eyes, listening in bewilderment to Carrie's tale of her good fortune.

"And you'll spend every penny," she echoed, "to free our Robert?"

Carrie nodded.

"I always thought that you'd married our Robert for the farm," she said bluntly. "I did you a wrong. Forgive me."

Carrie's face flushed, for it was difficult to accept such an apology.

"I believe I did," she answered. "But folk change, I suppose."

And then the taxi-cab stopped at Julia's door.

CHAPTER XIII

SIMON STONE

THE haymaking season was in full swing at Hilltop Farm. Sarah, in a print frock, passed up and down the scorching fields in the full glare of the noonday sun, pouring out cider for the men. To look at her strong, quiet face no beholder would have guessed that a heavy trouble—the most awful trouble than can haunt a human being—was upon her. The suspicion of bloodshed held against Robert was such a blow as she had never dreamed of.

Simon Stone had got the title-deeds of the farm in exchange for sums of money lent to Robert, and had been continually browbeating him. He had been a bully from his childhood upwards. He had been confident in avoiding punishments for faults and sneaking tricks because he had heart-disease, and his mother always said to the village schoolmaster, "Don't you dare to whip that boy, sir, no matter what he does. His lips are blue as bilberry, and he may drop dead any minute. My boy has been punished enough in this way without anything adding."

Poor mother! How she would have grieved had she lived to know that her darling had been found dead on the moors, the rain-pool near him tinged with his blood, which streamed from a great hole in his head. To her he was no bully or sneak. She never believed the tales brought to her by his schoolfellows, who, not daring to punch his head in orthodox fashion, yet burning against their wrongs, tried to appeal to his parent. To her he was one who had been hardly dealt with, and must be shielded from the storms of life. To the village he was the most despicable cur who ever went on two legs and wore the name of man.

The complaints Martha Lane, his young wife, breathed at last to his mother, Mrs. Stone said were wicked fabrications of the brain. Even when Martha, rolling up the sleeve from her comely, round arm, showed the rainbow-coloured marks of pinches he had inflicted, the fanatical mother would not believe her own eyes. It was hard to her to think Simon had so many malicious enemies. It would have been harder still to believe her boy to be what they said he was. To her he was a martyr of patient suffering, unfit for this polluted world. Her blind affection was such that she lost all her friends. If there is anything higher than reason it must be a mother's love. The criminal, the outcast, the coward, the unrecognized are crowned here. They cannot wander away from this kingdom as from others; it is boundless, and without frontiers. It sees only the good, and refuses to believe the bad. Perhaps it sees best, after all.

But Simon's mother had died with prayers for his welfare on her lips, her only pang that she was leaving him alone in the world, with no one to wait late for him when he came from the Red Cow, and to make him eat when his drinking bouts were on. After her death he was a little more cruel, irritable, bullying, and drank more deeply—that was all the change it made. The only person who believed in him was gone. His heart kept him awake often through the long nights, beating furiously, or almost stopping, and his lips were bluer than ever. Martha Lane had refused to return to him, having got a place in service, leaving the boy (with the same heritage of blue lips and fits of rage) in the care of her mother.

A dark night, and Simon Stone, rising from the warm, snug kitchen of the village inn, his legs almost like jelly beneath him, had avowed his intention of having a walk across the moors to steady himself before returning to his lodgings. There was a laugh as he went out into the darkness, for the company realized that it would take more than a walk to steady him. Still, he gained the object for which he set out. He stumbled for the last time, and that night was the last on which the terrier under the inn settle shrunk under at the crunch of his heel on the sanded floor.

Children having a picnic party the next day found him near a reddened pool, staring wildly at the blue sky, with contorted features.

A day later Farmer Gibson was arrested on suspicion, excited by the fact that angry words had been exchanged between the two men prior to the mystery. How the fact leaked out no one knew, but the police got hold of it, and, like hounds after the fox, tried to trace it to its hole. The innkeeper, a good-hearted, somewhat timorous man, when interrogated as to what had really taken place in the kitchen that night, made matters worse by his well-intentioned diplomacy, and his convictions that Gibson was innocent of the least evil towards Stone. The police got it into their heads that when Michael Winter contradicted himself—saying once that a few words had passed between Simon and Robert, and then that it was nothing out of ordinary—that he had something to hide. Between the two constables Winter was plucked as bare as a pigeon of all he knew. They tossed him from one to the other until he scarcely knew where he was, and what he was saying. He only came with a start to his self-possession when he realized that he had admitted to Robert Gibson's saying darkly in answer to a taunt of Stone's regarding the farm, "The game is not played out yet. I shall smoke my pipe by yonder hearth when you are cold as a clod." Michael hurried to say that there might have been only an innocent allusion in this sentence to the fact of Stone's heart-disease, and the way he was hurrying himself to the grave with spirits, and his violent outbursts of wrath provoked almost by nothing. He went on to state that Gibson was a harmless man, who went about the village with paper dolls and ships in his pocket for the children, and they smiled (being from the town) at the good-heartedness and thick-headedness of this country innkeeper. Weren't all men harmless till the test came? They had got a clue, they thought, and meant to run it to bay.

They possessed themselves of the fact that Stone had dashed a pot of ale in the farmer's face half an hour before he left the place, insulting him by saying that he would jolly soon turn that old dragon of a sister of his out to grass. A scuffle had ensued, and the two men were parted with no more damage to each other and the place than an upturned table and pools of ale on the floor. Both men, who were almost drunk, had seemed to get friendly before they parted, and harmony had been restored. The police, however, thought this more incriminating than if things had been otherwise. They suspected that Robert had hidden his wrath, and leaving soon after Stone, had followed him, and taken his revenge for innumerable insults, with only the quiet sky looking down on them.

Gibson himself could render no account of the hours between his leaving the inn and the morning, when he had awakened to find himself stiff with the cold, his head resting on the floor of the pigsty, with Peter's successor grunting about for his morning meal, the chill daylight over all. Only the pig could have given evidence about his time of arriving there, and when Sarah went to feed him each day, wishing that he were gifted with the powers of speech that he might clear things up a little, his only response was a philosophical "Grumph!"

Jane Wilkins said she had heard nothing at all. She had gone to bed on that eventful night tired out with a hard day's work, having waited for Robert until she couldn't keep her eyes open, and knowing he had his latch-key. Jane, however, was a heavy sleeper any time, and a dozen men could have stumbled up the hillside roaring a hundred songs, and she would never have heard them, having once got into her first sleep.

Carrie had great faith that everything would come out right. She was young, and youth cannot think that innocence will suffer long.

Sarah, without being a cynic, was not so hopeful. Besides, she thought this was a punishment on Robert for his weakness in giving way to strong drink because his wife had left him.

Carrie drew money from the bank, and engaged a local solicitor. He told her that it would be useless to try for bail. Robert's inability to tell where he passed his time after leaving the Red Cow was greatly against him, and he was accordingly committed for trial at the next Assizes on the charge of wilful murder.

Carrie only smiled scornfully as they left the court. Under the smile her heart was sore. How pale and thin Robert looked, and as bewildered at all the jargon of the lawyers as if he was almost bound to believe that he had killed Simon Stone. The fact that his wife did not live with him had even been used against him; but the lawyer Carrie had engaged (deeming that Robert would be discharged immediately on this trial) had corrected that by saying the defendant's wife was present in court, and ready to spend every penny she had in her husband's defence. Then Robert looked up, meeting her eyes across the heads of the curious crowd, with a light in his own.

Through the confused haze of these mad events, like those of some horrible nightmare, he realized that Carrie had come back to him. He read in the glance of her eyes that she believed in him; against all the circumstances that had been so staggering, no one could but be shaken by them—scarcely himself.

Carrie remembered a hundred things to contradict the idea that her husband, even in a fit of rage, would strike down a man on the lonely moors, stealing behind him like an assassin. She remembered that he was slow to stir to anger. He had too keen a sense of the ridiculous to harbour revenge. Even the theory that Gibson had killed Stone in a fit of sudden rage did not convince her, for the fact that he was "a straight-up man," as he had said on his visit to the oyster-shop, was against his striking a man down from behind on a pitch-dark night on the lonely moors. He was a man who believed that things would straighten themselves out when crooked, not one to commit murder and think he could make bad better by such an act. It was this very quality of easy-goingness, inherited from his father, which had made him unwilling to interfere between the two women, even when he had got an inkling that they were not on the best of terms.

In the end Carrie decided (when a disease is complicated, folk generally find fault with the doctor) that she would go to her beloved Manchester, and get a city lawyer to diagnose the case. She avowed her intention to Sarah that morning at the breakfast-table, where neither of them had eaten more than a mouse would, and each had expostulated with each about the fact.

Sarah, in her trouble, began to feel a luxurious pleasure in being expostulated with and looked after.

Carrie continually revealed new, rich sides to her character. It is not strange that the best withers within us at the cold look of distrust, and blooms with tropical luxuriance at the eyes of love and faith turned upon us.

Perhaps, too, the fact of Carrie having money gave her a new importance in Sarah's eyes. Perhaps, too, this fact, lending Carrie a sense of independence, and of freedom, made her more generous towards the little eccentricities of her sister-in-law.

Sometimes Sarah showed Carrie a glimpse of gold running through the hardness of her nature. They drank strong tea together many times a day; the old teapot was never off the hob during this awful time.

Sarah once questioned Carrie if she didn't think that Robert, his control gone for a moment, might have struck Simon Stone, not intending to kill him, of course. She remembered that Robert had talked of emigration, in the case of their having to quit the farm, only a few days before the murder. When Robert talked of emigration, he must have been rather desperate, for he had all the narrow conservatism inborn in a family who had lived in one house generation after generation.

"Bob," answered Carrie quickly, "hadn't got the necessary courage to kill a man, or even strike him; he'd let him alone and hope for the best."

During this terrible time Sarah was as hard upon a lazy haymaker as if Robert was there to superintend, and came to eat his meals and throw morsels to Jack, the Airedale.

She made a huge raisin loaf and sent it for Robert, sighing hard as she mixed it up, and hoping that the officials would not eat it before it reached him.

All the outward difference in Sarah was a little thinness showing in her face, and dark circles round her eyes, that told of sleepless nights. She was bothered lest Robert get rheumatism through not having sufficient bedclothes, and wondered if they'd allow of a hot bottle. Carrie thought not.

When Sarah did lose heart, it was in the quietude of the farm kitchen, with only Carrie there to witness it. Carrie became consoler, reprimander, and tonic to the strong woman.

In a burst of confidence Sarah told her of old Jonas, and of the daffodils she had taken to the new cemetery; and those far-back days when she had thought Jonas Bleasdale a fine young fellow any one might be proud of, bless you! It tickled and touched Carrie, both at once, because she had only known Jonas when he was as rough and as grumpy as the proverbial bear with the sore back.

Carrie sometimes felt a wild desire to laugh at the gravest things. This was the result of tears repressed for the sake of Sarah. Sarah seemed to have broken up, and needed caring for, in these evenings by the hearth. Carrie would have liked best to sit and weep about everything and anything.

The long, hot fortnight wore away, taking some of their hope and courage with it. The hay was got safely stowed within the barn. Hearts may break, but the cattle must have their food against the winter. The milk must be churned, sold, and the usual hum-drum go on as if nothing is at stake.

Carrie took the trip to Manchester, having asked Jane Wilkins to come up to keep Sarah company, lest she should think too much. Sarah found her old friend less tactful and sympathetic than her sister-in-law, and the time long until her return.

First of all Carrie went to see Julia and Fanny, for Fanny had an address of a lawyer who had once won a case for one of the flax-mill girls, and whom they consequently regarded as the greatest man on earth.

She came to the street where he resided at last, and

read upon the brass plate on the gate the mystic words, "O'Neill, Solicitor."

It was a house with brown Venetian blinds, a huge aspidistra-plant in the window filling the space between the lace curtains, as if to skilfully keep out the gaze of passers-by. It wore a look of antique reserve and respectable conventionality. It impressed Carrie.

Pressing the button, she heard the bell tinkle; then silence reigned.

The silence was broken by the dull echo of a pair of feet running up and down, in and out of rooms, and of doors slamming. This went on for some time, during which Carrie's patience was worn out, and forgetting the antique reserve of the place she pressed with such vigour on the button that it gave a long and startling peal.

The door was opened suddenly. Carrie saw a woman in a brown dress, evidently put on in a hurry, and with the artificial look of naturalness that fits so badly on some people's countenances. Her hair was twisted up unevenly, her face flushed; and Carrie guessed that she had been engaged in domestic work when first she rang and had had to change to open the door.

In spite of her trouble Carrie could not help reflecting in the back of her mind how curiously like a red herring the woman was, particularly when she smiled and asked her to step inside the "sitting-room."

There she left her, going to another room, on whose door she knocked, saying in a very loud voice, "Mr. O'Neill, sir. A lady to see you." "Thank you, Mrs. Proudlove," answered a man's voice, and then there was the sound of the woman's steps coming back, and she was telling Carrie that the model of the Eiffel Tower on the mantelpiece was made by her son "out of his own head." It was an interesting spectacle, as such, but not otherwise.

Carrie thought the room very dingy for a solicitor's room. When the woman went out and left her again she even made the discovery that one of the chairs had had its broken leg mended. Ghastly-looking photographs stood on the mantelshelf on each side of the model, and there were books that looked much battered piled on the baize-covered table, in the centre of which stood another aspidistra-plant.

"Good morning! Sorry to have kept you waiting," said a man's voice; and O'Neill, a handsome, dreamy-eyed youngster of thirty, a large red rose stuck in his buttonhole, came forward and immediately restored Carrie's fading faith that the owner of this dingy room was not the best-fitted person to save Robert.

How Carrie would have stared in astonishment had she known that this prosperous-looking young man had never really fought an important case before! He had once defended a boy charged with pouring a bucket of water on an old eccentric whose land had a well which the country people needed, and had got him off. He had fought a sordid case for a flax-mill girl who brought her old lover up to prove him the father of her puny child. He had got the girl her rights. His eyes had grown stern almost to cruelty as he fought for the pale, draggled creature; seeing in imagination by her side another girl, dainty, blooming, happy, and realizing that only a shuffle of Fate's hand had changed their places.

He had won.

But these were such small victories that he was not put upon the roll of honour, excepting by the people he saved. He had what people so mysteriously term "prospects," but they had become so remote that it was sometimes difficult for him to see them, even with an Irish eye. The money his changeable aunt had given him to back himself up was almost gone. He thought ruefully, sometimes, that he was the wrong man in the wrong place. Everything he touched seemed to fail—except the little case. Everything seemed all right, however, as he took his evening strolls through Withington, lingering always midway in a proper, privet-hedged street until he saw a light appear in an upper window.

Rose Eldon and he had met at St. Patrick's ball. It was difficult to think that Rose really was anything akin to her father, the dealer in pig-iron, the man who thought everything out in figures, and who possessed an amazing bump of reverence for property with a capital P. He said the Irish plays were nonsense, and the people who loved them insane. In his youth he had worked in a rubber factory, and was what the world calls a "self-made man." In making himself his jaws had developed to an alarming extent, and his head had become almost as hard as the iron he dealt in. Trade was his goddess, but after her he loved his daughter, and determined that she must marry well. Rose was a girl.

She read poetry, and went into raptures over a bowl of roses, and haunted the Mosley Street Art Gallery. She was a girl. That explained such nonsense to Geoffrey Eldon. But a man—a man should make money, and understand things. He did not like O'Neill, and told Rose that if ever she married him he would disown her; and Rose had answered, putting a wisp of dark hair into her comb, "Oh, papa, how can you think me in love with Mr. O'Neill! I never cared for large, lazy men." The merchant, more familiar with pig-iron and Russian ore than the feminine heart, was easily thrown off the scent. The young Irishman had been allowed to attend Rose's tennis-parties and the doll tea-parties on the lawn, and her father had troubled no more about him.

How O'Neill's heart leaped as Carrie told him the case she wished him to fight was a murder case. Dear little Rose! He was taking notes as Carrie told him the circumstances of the affair. She told him that Robert

Gibson was committed to the Assizes on a charge of murder, and that the chief evidence against him was that a button from his coat had been found lying on the path near the dead man; that he could give no account of many hours that night, and that he had been prevented from fighting Simon Stone in the alehouse prior to leaving it.

He promised Carrie to come to Greenmeads soon to do all that lay in his power.

Taking a linen bag from her neck, she poured a little heap of sovereigns upon the table. He spat on the first yellow coin when she had gone.

Dear little Rose!

He took her gilt-edged note from his desk. It smelled of cherry-blossom, and was reminiscent of her sweet, dainty ways. He sniffed it as if it would give him inspiration, and a laugh came into his eyes as if he was too happy.

Then he laid it down again, settling to the consideration of the case in hand. He was sure that he should win this case and make his mark, for was he not fighting for one man's life and to make his own worth living?

Chapter XIV

THE IRISH HAYMAKER

THE next morning an Irish haymaker hired himself to one of the Greenmeads farmers, Toby Smith, who was in a hurry to get his hay in, having unwisely delayed to begin until the glass was coming down.

Jenny Jones, Toby's servant-girl, gave him a glass of milk as he sat waiting outside the farm on the little wooden bench, the dust of the hot roads upon him.

Toby came stumping out. He was a sullen-looking man with a wooden leg.

He looked at the glass of milk, and he looked at Jenny.

She ran up to him.

"I'll pay for it, Mr. Smith—I'll pay for it," she said.

"Oh, yo' will, will yo'?" he gruntled. "Well, don't be fa'ing in love, Jenny; an' yo' needn't pay for the milk! I'll warrant he have a wife and five children in a mud cabin away over yonder."

"Six," chipped the stranger. "Like steps—Kathleen, an' Bridget, an' Moira, an'—"

Jenny went away, saying that it didn't matter to her if he'd a hundred.

"Well, what do you want?" asked Toby, eyeing the dusty figure and the stick with the red-bundled handkerchief at the end of it.

"W—urk !" said the man.

"Where are yo' fro'?"

"Connemara—God love its skies!—an' may I soon see it again!" said the stranger, piously.

"Happen yo' will," said Toby, stumping about with his leg. "Are yo' sure yo' want work? 'Cause I shall give yo' what yo're asking for."

Down in a corner of the hot hayfield the men discussed Robert Gibson's chances of getting off.

"Do you think Mr. Toby did it?"asked the Irishman, a twinkle in his eye. "Couldn't he have screwed his wooden leg off and used it as a truncheon?"

There was a roar of laughter.

The Irishman learned the names and characteristics of half the hamlet. He told weird tales of murders over in Oireland, mysteries cleared up, unexpected people who had done crimes. Toby said if he liked to live at the farm whilst he worked there, he could. Patrick O'Flannagan refused. He went down to the village inn at sundown, and sat in the clean, pleasant parlour.

One by one the men began to file in, with slow, country greetings, taking their places on form and settle.

"Good ave'ing to ye," said Patrick. He was watching their faces as he sat there. Was it possible, he thought, that amongst these quiet country men, talking of the weather, ferrets, and farm topics, that the murderer of Simon Stone was to be found? Who knew?

He could sing "Kathleen Mavourneen" and "The Irish Emigrant" so well that Willy Mare, who had never been known to cry—no, not even when his old mother died—blew his nose fiercely. If there was one thing he couldn't stand, he said, it was an Irish song. Give him an English one, about flowing seas and rollicking hearts, an' none o' these baby things about sitting on stiles and having nobody to love you! At which expression of his sentiments the company laughed uproariously, which further increased his ire.

He bet Joseph Latimer a crown, which he would give if it could be proved, that the water in his eyes was not due to an inflammation. But he treated the Irish haymaker to a pint of Wheatley's best all the same, and said he had a rare voice. That same rare voice could recite, too, and in the course of the evening made their blood run cold with "Eugene Aram's Dream." The clean, cheery parlour, its grate filled with flowers and heather, and a picture of a giant salmon proudly exhibited over the fireplace—the jolly company sitting over glasses in various stages of fullness—all these things were forgotten. Each man saw a ghastly murder; the dark cave, the ragged stick, the jagged stone became actualities. They heard with quickened pulses the gurgling groan of a dying man. And from under his sleepy lids the haymaker was watching—watching.

What was more natural after this than that the conversation should turn upon the murder of Simon Stone on their own moors? The Irish haymaker, fresh from Connemara, had to be told all details, and hear every one's theory by turn. The conversation waxed long and fierce; throats got dry and glasses were filled. The lamp was lit, and still they sat on. Several times a difference of opinion was on the verge of being settled with fists. The haymaker poured oil upon the troubled waters.

In the corner sat a little man, with large head and staring eyes. He never spoke, nor was spoken to, but anon went the round of the tables to drink the dregs of the glasses pushed aside by their owners.

"Who is he?"asked the stranger.

"Silly Peter Moss," and Will tapped his forehead.

"Is he safe?"

"Safe!" exclaimed the villager, bristling. "I should think he is. He once sent a stone at Snuffy Sally's house-winder and hit a chimney-pot; and once he ran up Moll O'Sandy's stairs 'cause he saw a goose in t' lane an' it stared at him. But safe—he's as safe as any here," looking round on the assembly with a challenge.

"Did anybody ever hear the story of the lunytic?" inquired the Irishman. "No! Well, I'll tell ye. A friend o' mine was going past a lunytic asylum the other day, an' he sees a lunytic looking at him 'through the railings. Says he, 'Old man, what's the difference between thee and me?' The lunytic he thinks a bit, then he says, 'None,' says he; 'only the railing is between us, an' I'm on this side of it.'" It was not a new story, but they had not heard it before, and they laughed.

The stranger was laughing his way into their hearts. "Have a drink?"invited his new friend.

Peter Moss was lingering near them, waiting for their empty glasses.

"Bring three," called the stranger to bonny, cherry-cheeked Mary Winter, whose entrance in the room always caused a lowering of the noise and a cessation of the oaths.

Peter Moss, for the first time in his life, drank a glass full to the brim.

"Bring him another," shouted the Irishman, and Peter's head began to sway, and his great eyes to light up.

Then Joe Baines would play his concertina, though the company pleaded with him not to, and every one at last awoke to the fact that it was time to go home.

"I've got no lodgings," said the stranger, suddenly; "where could I lodge cheap?"

Will Mare said his wife would be glad to take a respectable lodger provided that he wasn't a vegetarian, for which there was no argument, he said, except that monkeys ate nuts. They mostly ate bacon, eggs, potatoes, and such-like fare at their house. If a pal could get along on that, he might come and welcome. As for fatty cakes, he said, well, he could back Milly against any woman in the three kingdoms for her cakes. Her muffins were so good to look at that a pedlar selling buttons and thread, looking in at the open door and seeing a brown batch cooling on the dresser, had burst into tears, because it reminded him so strongly of his mother.

So Patrick Flannagan became a member of the Mares' cottage.

Mrs. Mare did not greet them very kindly that evening. She came downstairs, candle in hand, to speak very loudly and rapidly whilst she made their supper.

But at last all was still.

In the middle of the night the lodger was aroused by heavy groaning sounds from the other side of his bedroom wall.

"Don't be scared," cried Will's voice from the other room. "It's only Peter Moss. He's always like that at the full of the moon."

The Irish haymaker drowsily answered that he was not at all scared.

Stepping softly out of bed, he put his ear to the wall, thanking the stars that the houses were jerry-built, and were only one brick thick between.

"Don't touch me! Don't touch me!" he heard continually, and a jumble of wild words besides. Then the noise grew less, and he crept back into bed. If a lamp had been placed close to his eyes, they would have been seen to be not closed in slumber, but wide open, full of thoughts—eager, active thoughts that knew no rest.

In the morning when he came down to breakfast his back was so stiff he felt he could have done with hinges to it. Once, twisting suddenly in his chair, he gave a cry of pain.

"Folk that makes themselves ill with what they like can't grumble," said Mrs. Mare's sharp voice.

The Irish haymaker smiled to himself. His back ached with the toil of one day, and he had never liked work in his life.

He ate the crisp bacon in silence, and was so civil that Mrs. Mare relented, telling him what a pity it was when a nice young fellow like he came to his lodgings in such a drunken state.

"Was I dhrunk?" he asked innocently, getting another piece of toast.

"Drunk wasn't no word for it," said the young woman. "You took the cat for a cob of coal, and I had to stop you from putting it on the fire. I've seen Mare drunk time and time, and him standing against the yard gate whistling for us to come and open the door. Ha-ha!" and her laughter rang out. "And his father—*he* had a funny way when he was drunk. Sent his cap in afore him to see if he was welcome. If we picked it up, he came in; if we didn't, he went back and had another. But I've never seen any one so drunk as you were last night, mister. Not even Mare playin' on his trombone, and the neighbours knocking on both sides for silence, and him callin' me unsociable because I wouldn't sing to him. The only man I've ever seen quite so drunk as you were last night, was once when we went to Bringford playhouse."

Patrick suppressed a smile, and was suitably penitent.

"That young man's decent," Mrs. Mare took the first opportunity to tell her husband.

"Certainly he is, or I wouldn't ha' brought him," as proudly as if he had known their lodger all his life.

Patrick retired early to rest several nights, winning golden opinions from the housewife. Will, said, however, as they discussed him one evening during his absence, that many a lazy haymaker he'd seen in his time, but never one quite so much so as Patrick.

"Perhaps he wasn't cut out for it," pleaded Mrs. Mare, who was beginning to be impressed by her lodger, and even to point out to Will little things that he might learn from him.

"He'll get the sack if he doesn't speed up," responded her husband. "He's too slow to catch cold, but he's a quick enough temper, for all that! Once when the old man was hurryin' him up he says, 'Go to blazes! Do you want me to kill meself?'"

"What did Toby say?" inquired Mrs. Mare, testing the heat of the hot iron a distance away from her rosy cheek.

"He says, 'If I didn't think it would rain before I got this in I'd kick you out of the field, yo' Irish lazybones.'"

"And what did he say to that?"

"Says he, 'The docthor said I'd heart-disease, and I'd got to be careful,' and the old man walked away laughing, and shaking as if he was a jelly."

"I was raking one day, and hears him talking such gibberish, and when I told him of it he only says, 'Oh, that's French. I learnt it from a French polisher I once met in Connemara. It's devilish convenient to swear in. I'm surprised more working folk don't study French, if only for that reason, though begorra, if they did, and everybody knew it, 'twould be no good.'"

"Perhaps 'tis French he studies of nights, burning my gas," said Mrs. Mare. "I looked through the keyhole once, and there he sat on the bed, heaps of papers spread out before him, and his brows knitted—and he looked so different. I almost thought—Will, for a moment I thought that he couldn't be a haymaker."

"Workin' folk are getting intelligent these days," said Will, puffing at his pipe, and then there was silence in the kitchen, and Mrs. Mare tried to get her ironing done, for she and Will were thinking of going to Bringford market. Patrick came in early, pulled off his shoes, and went to bed.

Mrs. Mare told him not to be alarmed if he heard them come in late, and hoped he didn't mind their going.

How surprised they would have been if they could have seen their lodger knocking down a portion of the wall behind his bed-head, and cunningly stuffing it with paper, that he might at his convenience look into the room of the next house. Just before coming in he had seen Peter Moss setting off for a long ramble, and the man had told him that his sister had gone to the vicarage to take the washing. The sky grew darker, then the moon rose, and Patrick lay full length on his bed, looking into the room on the other side the wall. Will Mare and his wife had long been back from Bringford. He saw the idiot come into the room, undress, then dive into a box in the corner of the room, and take out some papers.

Patrick had good eyesight.

Some queer red spots on the edge of the papers attracted his attention. They might be spots of red ink—or blood! Peter turned them over and over, and all the time he was murmuring to himself. Patrick listened until the whispers had died into silence, then he, too, slumbered, with the consciousness of having partly accomplished what he set out to do.

On the next day he announced his intention of leaving Greenmeads, and straightened things up with Mrs. Mare. Afterwards Will saw him talking over the old farm gate, very earnestly, with Carrie Gibson, as they called her now. Mrs. Mare said, with a toss of her head, that it would be more seemly for Carrie to be thinking of her husband, when Will told her. Will was not altogether displeased that their lodger had gone. He felt a poor, plain, everyday sort of fellow beside Patrick Flannagan, and was inclined to be a little jealous of him.

People were surprised to see Patrick Flannagan set out with Carrie and Sarah for a walk on the moorland path, and not only Carrie, but the elder woman, came in for a share of their indignation at this. To encourage her sister-in-law to carry on flirtations whilst her husband was in prison, awaiting trial for murder, was the height of human folly and wickedness.

They even began to make excuses for Carrie, on the grounds of her youth. But Sarah! Well, they could not have thought it of a Greenmeads native unless they had seen it with their own eyes. It was dark when the three people came back from their walk. Silently they walked up the hillside. There was a great joy in the hearts of all the three.

In a tangle of purple heather they had found a clue.

Chapter XV

A WEDDING AND TWO HONEYMOONS

THE trial came off at last. The court was crowded. Robert Gibson looked a shadow of his former ruddy strength as he appeared in the witness-box. He had very little to say, but what he said was palpably true, so far as he knew. He had had a quarrel with Simon Stone, and Simon had bullied him a good deal, and always been taunting him, waving the mortgage papers in his face, etc. That night they had both been drunk, and after leaving the inn he could recall climbing the hill, seeing the lights of the farm-house, but could remember no more.

Cross-examination could not shake any more out of him. And the cross-examination was very rough.

Carrie asked if she might hand a note to her husband, and the lawyer told her she might if the judge could read it first. She tossed her head and gave consent.

The note read:

"Keep your heart up. You will come home, and we'll all be happy together.

"CARRIE"

Robert felt sure from this note, brief and to the point as it was, that his wife had some security for her hope.

It told him too that if he came out they would begin a new lease of life together. Their real marriage would begin.

O'Neill, the young solicitor, gave evidence. He told of his masquerading in Greenmeads as an Irish haymaker, and Will Mare, who had got half a day off work to hear the trial, almost swore to think how they had been deceived. Strangest of all was the tale he told of Peter Moss, who lived next door, and from whose wandering talk at night he had got his first clue. Peter had talked of a woman, and search had since revealed the fact that a woman had been in the case, for he held up a sham emerald brooch which he had found in a bush near the pool red with Simon Stone's blood. Possibly, he said, it was not a murder case at all, but an accident. Could not the drunken man have received a push from behind, which, causing him to stumble, threw him to the ground, where, catching his head on a sharp stone, it might cause a wound similar to that in the head of the deceased?

A murmur, quickly suppressed, ran through the court as a sharp jagged stone was handed to the judge. Even that stoical individual could not suppress a start of surprise. And well he might start, for there was blood, dark crimson blood, on that stone, and, dried upon it, a few human hairs, short and coarse, as Simon Stone's hair had been. In spite of the awfulness surrounding the trial, the court was convulsed when Peter Moss gave his evidence. His ideas were so unique, and the milking-machine mania was introduced pretty frequently with his story of the moor where he had his temporary abode on the night of the supposed murder. He had heard voices, and listened, thinking the villagers had at last discovered his retreat, and had become interested. It was a man, evidently drunk, insulting a young woman. She had screamed, but he dared not go to her aid.

Suddenly a flash of lightning lit up the whole scene, and by its intense light he saw the woman as plainly as by day. She was dark, handsome, and strongly built, as if she had been amongst milking machines all her life, he added.

He saw her suddenly push Simon. Then it was dark. He was frightened, and kept inside his hut. In the morning he went to look, saw that the man was dead, and came home. But he kept the little jagged stone, stained red, and some papers that had tumbled out of the man's pocket. Cross-examined, Peter said the young woman did not strike Simon. She only pushed him.

"Is there any one in this court like the young woman?" asked the counsel for the defence.

Peter scanned the many faces, and shook his head.

O'Neill pointed towards the back of the court, where a young woman on the arm of her sweetheart shrank back before his glance. He had been watching her face for some time. It was a speaking face, which told more than its owner was aware of.

Peter stared.

Then the great light came into his eyes.

"That's her," he said shortly. "That's her who pushed him."

The girl, almost fainting, came forward into the witness-box at the request of the judge, and told her story. She had come to tell all, she said.

Her name was Rose Heltonzig, and she was of English birth, though of foreign descent. They were show-people, and she was a shooting-gallery girl. They had been to Bringford, and whilst there a young farmer, coming to shoot at the target, had fallen in love with her. They had a few hot words one night, and he had left her to go back to the town alone. She was not afraid. When Simon Stone said "Good night" in his drunken tone, she answered him politely and passed on, but he overtook and tried to make her kiss him. When she could not get away from him she pushed him, then ran, and the day afterwards her father ordered the gallery on to another fair. The young farmer had not written, though he knew all the places they would touch for the next six months; but at last, as their quarrel was only about a trifle, he had come to see her, and in the course of their conversation told her of the body found on the moorland path.

She told him of her pushing Simon Stone, and was afraid. At last he persuaded her to come along with him, assuring her that if he believed her story others would, and telling her that a man's life hung in the balance.

The jury retired, and after some little delay, more formal than anything else, acquitted Robert Gibson of the charge brought against him. There was the evidence of the button, but the only conclusion they could come to regarding that was that Simon Stone in his scuffle in the alehouse with Robert, must have clutched a button, dragging it from his coat. Unconsciously he must have kept it in his hand, and in trying to kiss Rose Heltonzig had dropped it, where it became a bit of damning evidence against the man to whom he had been such an incubus. The papers Peter had kept were the mortgage deeds, which, being missing, had further incriminated the farmer, Robert Gibson, for the counsel had said he must have destroyed them, and thus have had a motive for murder. Peter had thought there might be pictures in them.

The judge commended the skill and zeal with which O'Neill had carried out his work. The farmer might have got off, he said, in any case, but public opinion would always have been against him, and he would have been a shadowed man.

O'Neill took his leave, after shaking hands with his clients! He had received a few words of praise from counsel which augured well for his future success. Will Mare stammered as the solicitor spoke to him in passing out. Peter Moss accompanied the Gibsons from court. They felt they could not make him welcome enough. Even his poor crazy brain seemed to comprehend that he had done something, and between the talk of milking-machines he was very good company.

But in spite of the fun he was troubled also.

When they put him into a cab, and went through endless streets, he became very quiet. Shortly afterwards they were surprised to find him in tears. When asked for the reason, he replied that he would be glad to get back to Old England again, and said he set no store by those foreigners, pointing out of the cab-window at the harmless women sweeping their flags.

Carrie left Sarah to rest at Julia's. She was conscious that Julia seemed in a flurry as she opened the door and pushed Sarah in, and noticed also that Fanny was dressed in her best. But she had not time to stay and inquire into the cause. Robert was waiting on the kerb with Peter, whom they had decided to take to the station and send home on the first train back to Greenmeads.

He thanked them with tears in his eyes as they assured him he would go right through to his own country.

Carrie and Robert had a very serious talk after the train moved out, sitting close together on a bench on the chill platform. Porters came officiously up now and then to inform them that such-and-such a train was going out, but got used to them after a while.

"Sarah will wonder where we ha' got to," said Carrie, blushingly, at last, and they went away, out into the streets and on to the little house.

As soon as Carrie opened the door she knew that there was a wedding. Working people never have such a collection of guests except for birth, death, and the culmination of love. Such a clatter of teacups, hub-bub of voices, sly jokes, and jolly confusion could only mean a wedding. And it was a wedding—Fanny's wedding.

There was the picture-framer jammed in between his father-in-law who wore a very high collar, and the old woman over the way who showed her corsets whenever she lifted her arm up to help herself to anything on the table. Anon she pulled out a bottle, tippling something into her tea, and telling Mr. Winklesworth that she had a beautiful tract in her pocket which every man and woman in the land should read.

Fanny was seated at table doing honours, and Julia and the woman who used to run in and attend to Julia sometimes were serving at table in new white aprons. Julia found two more chairs, and put Robert and Carrie together.

They had known for some time, said Fanny, that they were going to have half a day's stoppage at the flax-mill and so had fixed the date of the wedding for that day. It saved expense and trouble. They apologized for having it on Robert's trial day, but as it had turned out so well thought it lucky too—a double celebration, in fact.

"Aren't you having a honeymoon?" joked Carrie.

"Can't afford," answered Fanny. "Besides, you never had one, Carrie."

"No, but she can have one. It's never too late to mend," chimed Sarah, and then everybody began to air their views of honeymoons. One or two people had felt a little afraid of Sarah until she spoke so pleasantly.

Sarah was seated next to stout Ben Thomas, who had brought his concertina. If report spoke true, Ben had other accomplishments besides being a first-rate concertina player. He had got his nickname, Herring-bone Ben from the rumour going about that when his old mother's hands (long since crossed on her breast, with almost the first flowers she had had in life) were crippled with rheumatism, Ben himself had undertaken the making of her winter's woollen petticoat, and not having pulled the blind down to the bottom had been seen by some joker at his task. The old lady was very particular about the hem at the bottom being "herring-boned," and the spectacle of Ben fumbling at that work under her instructions had fixed upon him the laughter and the nickname.

Ben had been laughed at so much he did not mind it now.

All the girls he had been smitten with had laughed whenever he attempted to make up to them.

As he ate seed-cake until he could hold no more, he told stories of those love-affairs, and did not mind in the least the bursts of laughter greeting his naïve accounts of them. He told of standing under the parlour window where Nancy Jane, his first love, was practising her lessons on the piano. Sometimes it was raining and the rain got down the back of his collar, but so long as he could see the back of her head and a bit of the music-book he didn't care, he said. He had never told any one about it. He loved in silence. (Another burst of merry laughter.) One day he plucked up courage to buy a valentine, a lovely silk handkerchief with forget-me-not border. She returned it the day after to him at the mill where he worked across the alley, and as he unfolded it a red herring tied up with blue ribbon fell out.

Poor Ben! No one could look at him without laughter, particularly when he wore a pathetic look—no one, excepting his mother. She took him seriously, and wondered why others laughed at him. Perhaps only her eye could penetrate beneath the curious overstrata to the soul within, seeing it beautiful, earnest, even grand in some ways.

People laughed again, when, on her decease, he placed on her grave a wreath of flowers, in the midst of which stuck a card with these words in his pot-hook-and-hanger writing,

"With loving sympathy,
"From her son,
"BEN"

It was the mistake of an uneducated man. If there were angels who read human hearts, they did not laugh.

There was Fanny's husband's apprentice, a pale youth who knocked his teacup over, and told Fanny not to mind, thinking she was mindful of his clothes, when all the time it was of her white linen cloth, almost the only one she had. He afterwards redeemed himself by singing comic songs to Ben's concertina, under the eye of Sarah, who was on the look-out for anything objectionable in them. Finding that they were all right, she even got affable with the youth, and advised him to get into the country all he could, and expand his chest, or he wouldn't be here long. The old washerwoman on the other side of the street, with her creased hands, asthmatic wheeze, and her funny way of saying "Lord, help us" when anything took her by surprise, had brought her little grandson with her, a knock-kneed child with rebellious mouth and beautiful eyes. There was Julia's aunt from Hulme, gifted with second sight, but who had not done too well in life for all that. There were the woman of the gin and tracts, Herring-bone Ben, the youth of the comic songs and troublesome cough, Sarah, Robert, and Carrie, and the woman who had once waited on Julia. Besides these were the main players in that day's drama, and several nondescript and uninvited guests who had put Fanny out by coming at first, but whom she was glad had come on second and kindlier thoughts.

She sent cake and tea in to the woman at the top house, who had scalded her foot. When all was cleared away, six people filled the scullery to overflowing, treading upon each other's toes in order to help clear the pots away. Fanny would have to go to work in the morning—be tired at night on her return—so they wished to wash up.

They made a circle round the hearth, and Sarah broke the ice by singing a country song. Herring-bone Ben "vamped" it over with her first, both of them standing behind a door near the stairs to get it off. Folding her arms, she struck up in a not unharmonious voice the queer old song.

The company took up the chorus (and the chorus was twice as long as the verses) with a "Hi, Falary, my canary, When you get married you're sure to rue!"

Then they had riddles, and Mr. Winklesworth told stories. They pushed back the table, and the washerwoman gave them an Irish jig, in which her tattered skirt-bottom played a prominent part, though it is true that the white cat played one scarcely less in importance.

Mr. Winklesworth began to laugh and could not stop, and drew his breath the wrong way so that he began to cough, until the whole company had to help unloosen his collar. Julia tried to persuade him to put his silk muffler on, but he determined that at Fanny's wedding he would wear that collar, or die in the attempt. Whilst the mirth was in full swing, Fanny took Carrie upstairs to look at the presents. They were stored in what had been Carrie's bed-room.

Didn't the copper kettle bought by the entire flax-mill hands fairly flash? Wasn't the honeycomb quilt her husband's brother's wife had given white and thick? The sixpenny china ornament bought by the little girl she had lately learned to be a flax hand looked worth three times the money at least, and had surely been got by mistake. Those crochet-mats, too, worked by the grass widow when she should have been eating her dinner at the mill, weren't *they* lovely?

At everything she touched, Fanny's face shone more and more, until it fairly beamed.

"I didn't know; so I couldn't bring a present," said Carrie. "So I'd just like you to buy one for yourself, Fanny, with this."

She put a little bag into Fanny's hand. Opening it, a little heap of sovereigns showed to view.

"Why?" gasped Fanny.

"I brought it to pay Bob's lawyer," said Carrie, "and I don't feel I can take it back. I don't want it," putting her hands behind her and backing. "Don't you go back to the factory to-morrow, Fanny, nor the day after, nor the day after that. You needn't work to extend the business now. You can do it right off, and make him his breakfast in the morning, like a lady. Now, go on."

"You aren't going to have any left—" began Fanny, tearfully.

"I've got two thousand clean left," assured Carrie.

Fanny sat on the bed and wept to think that never again would she run to the call of the whistle.

When they went downstairs, Sarah was dressing Ben in her cape and bonnet, in which he looked so positively ridiculous that the whole company was convulsed.

Carrie stole a look at Fanny's tear-stained face, thinking of all those dead years behind.

Fanny was thirty-eight, and looked it. Her life had been a life of eternal struggle. Her shoulders were bent, her hair rapidly going grey, and she was pitiably sallow. It was a long time since she had linked arms with the young picture-framer (who was going to do great things!) on the Ashton New Road. How warm and fresh had been the hues of those early dreams, and they were gone for ever. The sweetness of this belated wedding was like the faint, sad aroma stealing from autumn leaves. There was a touch of frost in the air, and something ineffable had vanished.

Marriage in those early days had had nothing to do with scraping and saving, but had seemed a glory falling from the stars. Now it was a comradeship—perhaps not even so much, but a working partnership. Fanny was now troubled with rheumatism, and her picture-framer had to be careful, as his chest was weak. The best had gone by. Youth, with starry eyes, and Hope, brighter than the colours of the butterfly's wings, had vanished. What was left was the temple of the past.

Their desire now was to build up a business, so that before the light of life faded entirely they might rest a moment before entering on the great silence. The emotions of life had had to become blunted, and their outlook was practical and a little hard. It was late to begin to guide little steps, for the sun was waning. Children would "pull them down."

Such was Fanny's wedding—the sensible wedding of the thrifty poor.

The love that walks the ugly roads and streets on a Sunday evening, opening infinite windows, flooding glory into lives otherwise dark and narrow—that was gone for ever. It belonged to the days of sweet, foolish youth. Toilers soon grow old.

A touch of its transient glory came back as Fanny and her husband set out for London the next morning, for Sarah had insisted on their going, and on herself paying the expenses. Robert and Carrie refused to accompany them, saying they would prefer to return home.

Whilst the city couple were speeding to London and its wonders (they talked of it to the end of their lives) through the dim, morning fields, Robert and Carrie were returning from their honeymoon through a wild, little wood, knee-deep in golden bracken. The night before they had arrived home late.

The night was clear and frosty, the sky athrob with big, white stars as they came up the hillside. Sarah made supper, and then went to bed, leaving them to talk to their hearts' content. Looking from the window they saw the hillside aglow in the moonlight and starlight, white, glorious, dazzling. Hand in hand they went out into it, without speaking a word, seeing the streams like molten silver under the beams—on and on, hearing anon the chirp of a cricket in the wet, tangled grass, fast beginning to sparkle with hoar-frost. The beauty of the night bathed them in a baptism of joy and filled them with a sense of the wonder of the universe, each other, and life. Jack the Airedale followed them silently, excepting when a cat on the white road startled his antipathies into activity, and then the echoes from the hills answered his vendetta.

Through the little wood, into the deep, purple shadows of the trees, and away again. The world was like a huge silver flower, opening petal after petal, fuller and fuller, as the night wore on. There was a mystery in the spectacle of the little houses perched here and there on the hills. Robert had brought the thick horse-rug with him, and when the light of day waged war with the stars, and they paled their trembling fires in the mystical blue that is only seen at dawn, they slept wrapped in it, cheek to cheek.

It was Carrie's honeymoon.

Chapter XVI

FROM BLACKSTONE CRAG AND A HANDFUL OF MEMORIES

PETER MOSS had been missing longer than he had ever been known to be before in the history of the village.

Since the trial of the farmer, and Peter's evidence, curious strangers had come from near and far to see his dwelling on the moors. Even schoolboys came, sending stones with deadly accuracy, and running away hooting as he strode after them. Peter had been crazier than ever before his disappearance, and some of the villagers had expressed an opinion that he was hardly safe to have round. Their children, not of stone-throwing age, were afraid of him, as they saw him coming along, mumbling to himself and sometimes even running after them.

He had grown more moody, and could not be prevailed upon to tell the story of the sixpence he once found in an old wall, and showed to his neighbour, Thomas Walden, who delighted to make fun of him. Thomas was a weaver by profession, and a niggard by nature, making a lot of money out of curing sheepskins in his spare time. The villagers said he was so fond of money that he could eat it with a knife and fork. Still, he had a love of a joke, too. To make fun of Peter, whom he knew to be hiding his sixpence in the old wall, fearful lest his sister should claim it, he exchanged it for a shilling, telling him if he would leave it there it would breed more. Peter left the shilling there. Walden then put a half-sovereign in place of the sixpence, meaning, of course, to change it back again afterwards, but the idiot got the better of him by keeping the half-sovereign, saying that his sixpence had now got the jaundice and must be kept warm.

So the laugh was against Thomas, the weaver of webs, and for quite a fortnight any one would have thought he had had a severe domestic loss, as he went about lamenting that half-sovereign.

Peter even brooded over some idea which he would not communicate to any one. He had even ceased his old crazy talk about his pet theme, the milking-machine. In spite of watching, he wandered away, as now he had no cottage on the moors, which he termed his hall, and his solitude was rudely broken in upon whenever he went there. His sister was afraid that he had fallen into water and got drowned. The ponds were dragged, but all to no purpose.

One night Will Mare came up to the farm to see if Robert would join a search party which was going out on the hills to try to find him. The fire was warm, and Robert was very happy where he was, watching Carrie's needle as she sat by his side. But he put on his great-coat, got the lantern from the barn (the lantern that had discovered the ring he now wore, whose story was told to him by Carrie), and agreed to meet them in five minutes beside the Red Cow.

Carrie put on her cloak and hood, and said she was going too. Sarah thought women should stay at home by the hearth, but was now wise enough not to say so, and even to tell herself that an old woman could not be a fair judge for the rising generation.

Through the winter night, accompanied by the shivering knot of men, they climbed in the teeth of an icy wind. Sometimes the yellow lantern rays fell on black ling, ragged heather, glittering with hoar frost. Sometimes the light fell on Robert's face, brown-red with the wind, which seemed very good to Carrie. The stubby strength of him, suggestive of hardihood, pleased her, and the clasp of his rough hand, helping her from crag to crag.

He had not liked her paying off the mortgage to the cousin of Simon Stone, because he had old-fashioned notions that it belittled a man to accept help from a woman. But what could he do with a softened voice threatening to run away again, with another man, if he didn't give in? Since then Sarah had begun to boast of her sister-in-law, and the villagers said she was getting changeable in her later days.

These were happy days for Carrie and Robert.

Sarah had become a not inharmonious third, and instead of she and Carrie differing as to who should make Robert's "whistler," they often joined at the task now. Carrie bought Sarah so grand a bonnet that no amount of persuasion could induce her to wear it; she said it was too good, but got the money's worth out of it by showing every caller at the farm her treasure. "Sarah'll ha' some hot coffee for us, if it's stayin' up all night," said Robert as they climbed.

Over the barren darkness of the hills they went.

It was Carrie who first spied, near the top of Blackstone Crag, a man's figure. The morning sunrise was at his back, the valley of pale mists below. A shudder ran through her heart as she looked. She had the memory of Peter's wild words, on the occasion that she visited his moorland dwelling, in her mind.

Will Mare said it was naught but a piece of rock, but after some little period of waiting, to an accompaniment of chattering teeth and impatient oaths, they saw it move. Then they climbed nearer and nearer, and came within sight of Peter, wilder-looking than ever he had been seen. Even in the morning light, not yet sufficiently strong to show objects in sharp focus, they could see a new, ferocious attitude of mingled fear and cunning.

When they got within earshot they hastened to reassure him, and to tell him they only wanted to take him home. In the back of his poor, muddled brain he remembered hearing the boys shout that he was going to be taken to the asylum.

These creeping figures, coming nearer and nearer, with the lanterns dimly burning, were after him, to take him away, shut him up, where he could not see the light of sun, moon, or stars.

"Robert," whispered Carrie, hiding her face in his coat, "something is going to happen."

"Nonsense!" he answered, giving her hand a squeeze. "See, Big George is gaining on him fast, is almost up to him. In another minute he will have gripped him."

That minute passed slowly.

Then Big George put out his brawny arm to clutch the idiot. Suddenly Peter Moss snatched himself free. He rose to his fullest stature, a dark figure against the growing light of the sky, with outstretched arms making him look like a huge, black cross against the sky. A paling star or two yet lingered in the heavens.

Suddenly, before any one could move a muscle, with a shrill, wild shout of terrible joy he leaped, disappeared over the verge, and fell down, down, down, the shout growing into a shriek.

They carried him to the little house where he had been so unhappy, back through the silent, sunny valleys. He was quite dead, must have been so almost as soon as he touched the earth. In his pocket was the little book with the coloured pictures.

He had said that some day he would climb the Crag and never come back to the village again. So it was.

They buried him in the new cemetery, next to old Jonas Bleasdale, and Carrie took flowers there every summer, from the farm-house rose-bush.

The years went on. Carrie had two children, of whom Robert could not be fond enough. They loved to roll down the green hill, and Sarah allowed them to put her to unbelievable indignities. The boy was short and ruddy, and a trifle slow, with a country calm about him; but young Sarah was slight and fanciful, with light hair that flew behind her like a golden cloud as she raced down the hillside. She was unhappy under any sort of bondage.

They grew bigger.

Sarah the elder began to ail. Carrie took her to a Manchester specialist. It was that terrible scourge, cancer—and so she crept to rest slowly, painfully, through a valley of terrible suffering. During the year that she spent in bed she could not bear Carrie out of her sight. Even Robert took a secondary place. His step, however careful he tried to be, shook the bedroom floor. No one could make her pillow soft like Carrie.

During the years prior to her death, they had not pulled together without difficulty. It was a sore trouble to Sarah when Carrie took a fancy for spring-mattresses, and even joined a literary club in Bringford. She didn't like to hear Carrie discussing subjects with Robert that were above her own grey head. But Carrie was strong and warm-hearted as the sun, and so these little failings were but as spots upon that generous planet.

Bit by bit they had grown together, until they joined in usefulness and love. In that last illness, when she felt like a dragging traveller in a desert, it was Carrie's voice at whose sound her face grew less weary. Robert could not bear to see the agony of the end, and stood outside the room listening on the stairs. Carrie held the pitiably thin hands in hers, looking deep into the filming eyes staring into hers for comfort, and thought, "I must not be afraid, she will know."

When Sarah was gone, the old farm seemed empty. True, there were the children and Robert, but the children were often out, and Robert at work. To have had Sarah back she would have eaten the nettle-stew she detested, and have gone back to sleep in the old four-poster.

The pear-tree blossomed year after year. But the same thrush did not sing there year after year!

The younger Robert began to help his father on the land. He was all for modern ideas, and took in scientific papers, but it is doubtful if he felt the same keen joy as he stood with his feet on the sods, his outline against the sky, and a fresh wind blowing. Sarah went to Victoria University to train for teaching in the Bringford National School.

Whilst there, she met Moira O'Neill, who invited her to tea. She was introduced to the famous lawyer, whose name was dreaded by any opponent.

"Gibson!" he murmured, rising to his feet. "Gibson of—"

"Greenmeads," answered Sarah, carelessly, throwing her gloves upon a chair.

He pulled out his pipe and sucked it long, looking into the fire, hearing the chatter of the two girls as one in a dream.

Over the waveless flow of the years gone by floated a whiff of cherry-blossom, the scent that had mixed in with his first big case.

Rose had died without even kissing the baby once, passed out into the silence without a word, whilst he walked the house praying he might not go mad.

"You will excuse my going out, children," he said, and was leaving the room when Moira said fondly, "Oh, papa, and the rain coming down and you going out without a coat."

"I forgot," he said.

"Such a forgetful old father," she said, and helped him on with it.

He smiled and passed out into the grey, moist evening. It was spring!

Just before him, on the flagstones, a little sparrow was picking up the crumbs. She looked funny, with the feathers gone from her head through the young ones pecking at her. It was spring! There was the eternal sweetness and sadness of the season in the air.

His pipe had gone out.

He walked on, and found himself sitting at last under the trees clad in bright, crisp green, on the way to Fallowfield.

A pair of lovers were seated on a companion bench two yards away. They were whispering together.

He rose from his seat and passed them, and as he did so he lifted his hat.

"I don't know him, do you?" said the maiden.

"No," said the youth.

But he knew them.

He was lifting his hat to the happy love and life of the world.

What matter if some old nest were empty? It was all in the great game.

The night closed in mistily.

The two girls knelt on the rug in the firelight, talking of all they meant to do, try, and be. A satyr on tip-toe on a little bracket seemed to laugh.

But up and down the lamplit roads Youth wandered, and Hope, and Love, arm held close in arm, full of faith, dreaming star-hued dreams.

Are not our dreams the lamps on a rainy road?

Printed in January 2022
by Rotomail Italia S.p.A., Vignate (MI) - Italy